DEMCO

Rolling Thunder
A STOCK CAR RACING NOVEL

WHITE LIGHTNING

Kent Wright
& Don Keith

TOR®

A TOM DOHERTY ASSOCIATES BOOK
NEW YORK

ROLLING THUNDER #1: WHITE LIGHTNING

Copyright © 1999 by Kent Wright & Don Keith

A Tor Book
Published by Tom Doherty Associates, Inc.
175 Fifth Avenue
New York, NY 10010

Tor Books on the World Wide Web:
http://www.tor.com

Tor® is a registered trademark of Tom Doherty Associates, Inc.

ISBN: 0-812-57506-7

First edition: March 1999

Printed in the United States of America

10 9 8 7 6 5 4 3 2 1

You know how it feels when you see and smell and feel that herd of gaudy monsters, roaring out of the last turn, heading for the green flag, shaking the ground like the stomping of Godzilla, sounding for all the world like the end of time is coming straight at you at nearly a hundred miles an hour? You know how it feels, the power of the motors vibrating in your chest, stunning your ears, your heart pumping in your throat, your arms high in the air as you wave them past, and then you taste the grit of their spent tire rubber in your mouth and their exhaust smells like hot dragon's breath? You know how it looks and feels and smells from up there in the grandstand? Then just imagine how it looks and feels and smells to the old boy behind the wheel of one of those monsters. Just imagine!

—*Jodell Bob Lee*

PARADE LAP

Earliest memory: the hot day he rode in the old rusty truck's tattered seat, straddling the floor gearshift, wedged between his daddy and momma.

"Why we goin' back to church, Daddy?"

"Aw, we ain't goin' back to church, Jodell. I'm gonna take you and your momma up to Goodner Mountain. They're gonna be runnin' the jalopies today."

"Jalopers?"

He was only three or four then, and the word felt strange on his tongue. He pictured bizarre animals, like the dragons and unicorns in his picture-story books his momma read to him at night. Peculiar, bright-colored animals, running wild among the pines and cedars that grew on the mountain.

And he sat up straighter, stared ahead through the

oily windshield of the truck, and waited to catch his first glimpse of such an odd, exciting thing. And when he saw the dust cloud in the air ahead, rising from the ridgeline, he was sure he was about to. Then he noticed there were others, in their cars and trucks, heading the same way in a long, meandering line. He stood up in the seat and pointed emphatically ahead of them, up the rutted road leading to the dust cloud.

"Hurry, Daddy! Hurry! We gotta be first ones there!"

The unusually sticky warmth of the early summer afternoon has already become plain and simple hot. The heat is all the harder to bear because it is usually so cool there in the dry mountain air that blankets the Tennessee brushy hills, only a crow caw's echo from the Great Smoky Mountains. But this day the weather is close, humid, more like that of the Carolina low country on the far side of the mountains, or down yonder in the broad valley that has been carved out by the Tennessee River as it rises and spills out of the hidden coves and hollows of the Smokies.

"Ain't it hot!"

"Lord if it ain't!"

Those words have been swapped at the breakup of more than one church service this Sunday morning.

"Ain't a breath of a breeze to be found, is they?"

"Nary a breath."

Hazy hot or not, the view in any direction from the knob-tops of the mountains would be considered spectacular by even the most disinterested observer. The nearby hills and distantly layered mountains pile up on top of one another like waves on an ocean, for as far as the eye can see, until they are finally smudged out by the fine blue mist.

And that same observer might notice a narrow dirt road that traces the middle of one of the deeper hollows like a strand of ribbon someone has purposely laid there, then it seems to disappear over the top of a tree-lined ridge, maybe heading for the hills that run beyond it. And he would surely see the long, steady string of well-worn cars and of rusted, dented farm trucks, their beds piled full of laughing, singing people, as they snake their way up the rutted road. They climb higher, toward a growing cloud of dust that hangs in the air at the top of the ridge like a tan canopy. As the parade of vehicles bounces and twists its way slowly up the hollow, the rumbling and complaining of the engines drowns out even the incessant dry rattle of the cicadas in the high grass alongside the road and the songs of the birds that hide among the pines from all the trespassers.

The road comes to a sharp turn at the top of the hollow, then seems to play out completely. It ends there at a wide-open field, fenced for cattle and nestled on two sides by round-topped green hills. The back edge of the field rises in a sweep to yet another ridgeline and a sharp outcropping of upturned rock and towering cedars. The effect is to form a neat bowl, a natural, perfect, three-sided amphitheater.

The field itself is a couple of hundred yards wide and several hundred yards long. Circling the flat center part of the pasture is a makeshift dirt track, scribed more by use than by construction machinery. In the near side of the field at the end of the road is a car park where the train of vehicles is pulling to an orderly stop, each one of them arranging itself neatly next to the others, as if in some logical, predetermined order.

The people pile from their cars and walk directly up the side of the hill, away from the road. Some hold hands or walk arm in arm, some pick at each other, chicken-fighting, while others hold the hands and help the older ones to climb the grade. Some carry picnic baskets, many have blankets, quite a few lead children, others tote gallon jugs of mysterious, clear liquid. But they all end up sitting in clumps, scattered all across the sides of the hills among the bitter weed and dog fennel. The thick green grass is already trampled short, leaving a perfect place for the crowd to sit and look down on the dirt track below them.

The cars are there already, well before the onlookers arrive. About fifteen or so old coupes and sedans rest there, nose to tail, lined up on the raceway like overfed greyhounds but clearly ready to run. The track itself is probably only forty feet wide at its broadest and cuts a third-of-a-mile circumference out of the pasture.

On a cue from a tall, skinny man in faded bib overalls, a simple wave of the furled flag he holds, the engines of the assembled cars suddenly growl to life with the throaty rumble of unmuffled tailpipes. Pigeons and doves flutter away in terror. Rabbits hop madly for better cover.

The sound is near deafening, captured and held as it is in the bowl-shaped valley, and even those perched on the very top lip can feel the ground vibrate and almost instantly smell the oil smoke and gasoline the motors are belching.

The couple of hundred or so people gathered there can no longer tolerate sitting on the ground. They rise to their feet as one, as if someone has announced the doxology, then they are cheering, screaming, hollering. Even so, they are hardly able to hear their own voices over the bellow of the engines.

Down on the track, the brave soul in the bib overalls unleashes the tattered white flag, then jumps out of the way as the echelon of cars lurches past, headed off into the first left-leaning turn. All but one car, anyway. That one still sits there, unmoving, its engine obviously dead. A couple of men jump from among a clump of others who have been standing there in the center of the track. They put their shoulders to the car's turtle shell and begin to push, straining hard against its dead weight. Then, with the boom of a loud backfire and a puff of black smoke, the engine finally awakens. The other cars are already entering the third turn, only a quarter of the track away from passing the straggler as the stalled car finally moves off its mark.

The late starter spins its rear tires in the dirt impatiently, raising powdery rooster tails, as it races off to catch up with the end of the rest of the field. Working hard, it slides through the first and second turns, losing traction, spewing dust, dirt, and gravel, clearly on the verge of a three-sixty spin, or of skidding off the track into the cow grass.

There is another pair of thunderous backfires as the car's driver eases off the throttle at the end of the straight stretch and lines up the nose for the groove of the next corner. He deliberately places the car in the center of the turn as he jumps hard again on the gas, steering deeply as the car beneath him powerslides off the corner and finally catches up to its mates, who are by now making their way out of the fourth turn and on to the final straight stretch.

While the covey of cars makes a second lap, the fellow with the dirty white flag stands timidly beside one of the two fence posts that mark the starting line, watching the assembled jalopies. Those spectators scattered along the hillside now stand in unison, waving, still screaming as if the drivers could actually hear them, as if they could take their eyes off the track ahead long enough to actually see them.

Finally, another lap around the circuit done, the cars come slowly out of the fourth turn, so close to each other that the billowing dust can hardly find enough room to work its way up and between them. As they reach the straightaway and point as one toward the first turn, the flag man flutters his ragged banner just long enough for the lead cars to see, then turns and hightails it like one of the scared rabbits. He is only twenty feet from the outside cars when the pack roars past, already gaining speed. The dirt their tires fling dusts his backside as he dives into the crowd of spectators.

The noise level, deafening before, is now almost unbearable as the racers circle. The air is thick with dust, the crowd straining to try to see what's going on through the haze, most of them sneezing and hacking when they remember to breathe.

Through the dust they may be able to see that three cars at the front of the line have begun to noticeably break away from the others. They are steadily pulling out front by four, then five car lengths, then extending their lead even more each time past the fence-post start line.

Suddenly there is a crunch and a thump as two of the cars bump together hard on the far straightaway. Once, twice, then a third time the cars kiss, rub fenders, then bounce apart. But the final smack sends both spinning, out of control, off the edge of the track, across a small ditch, and into the tall, axle-high grass.

The outside car spins, hood following trunk, skewing, bounding wildly. Its driver never lifts his foot from the accelerator, shoe leather glued to gas pedal, throttle stomped to firewall. Finally, when he senses that the tires have once again found some semblance of bite in the dirt and rock, he eases up on the pedal. Once the wheels have traction and the car is back under control and pointed roughly in the right direction, it roars off, giving chase once more to the rest of the field.

The second car, though, slides to a shuddering, smoky stop, its motor dead. The driver, so busy trying to get the spinning car under control, has made an elemental mistake. He has forgotten to push in the clutch when he jammed on the brakes, stalling the engine. He cranks frantically on the starter, pounds the steering wheel, begs, cusses, prays, trying to get the engine to turn over again. He talks to the car as if it is a stubborn horse that refuses to climb out of a ditch. And the field roars past him at least three more times before he finally surrenders and crawls through the open window on the driver's side of his dead mount. He can't get out the conventional way because the door is tied shut with a length of hemp rope. Kicking cow pies, head down, he walks to the shade of a skinny sycamore halfway up the hill and sits there to watch the rest of the race.

After twenty-five or so more circuits around the oval and a couple more fender-swaps and spinouts, the fearful flag man tiptoes down the side of the hill, hides behind the fence post until the lead cars come out of the fourth turn, then waves his white flag just enough times so they can maybe see. Last lap.

The crowd has not yet sat down again since the start. Nor have they stopped their constant cheering.

But now they scream even louder for the rusty old black coupe that leads the entire final orbit and passes the fence-post finish line first. The rest of the cars, the ones that had not won, chug off the track, making for a stand of oaks and some blessed shade. There they will find a drink of something cold and wet, let the engines and tires cool a bit, then pop the hoods, jack up the rear ends, and look for another mile per hour any place they can find it.

The winning car makes a slow victory lap, then eases up in front of the bulk of the crowd, shuts off the engine, and coasts to a stop in a clump of saw briars. Now it is the silence that is deafening until it is finally broken by the renewed cheers of the people. The driver leans out the window, takes a swig of something liquid someone has kindly handed him, gives a wave of the bottle at those who salute him, then recranks the engine and roars off to where his brothers have gathered.

He slides the vehicle in among the assembled toolboxes and helpers and openmouthed cars. Several men help him out the side window. Someone fetches him something cold from a cooler and he presses it to the back of his neck as he joins an assembly of red-faced, sweating drivers. They are all talking loudly due to their roar-numbed ears, their arms waving as they relive twists and turns and knocks and bumps in the just-completed race.

Then, in the middle of another swarm of cars and drivers under the shade of one of the tall oaks, a noisy scuffle suddenly breaks out and spills out into the hot sun. There is an eruption of pushing, shoving, and shouting, and then, as quickly as it flared up, the scuffle is put out. Someone has taken issue with a particularly enthusiastic bump or rub they had taken, but quickly, before someone has to actually back up big words, hands are shaken, backs slapped, and everyone is friends once more. Heads again disappear under hoods, beneath rear axles, into beer coolers, getting ready for the next start.

The interlude between races allows the spectators to flush the dust out of their craws, retell their favorite move by their favorite driver in the last race, and say grace over their picnic baskets. They mostly know each other and tend to socialize the way country folk do everywhere while the cars and drivers are readied for the next run. And the half dozen more dogfights that would be repeated over the balance of the afternoon.

These are the northeast Tennessee mountains, but other impromptu rituals are taking place in amazingly similar detail all across the Carolinas, southern Virginia, Alabama, and north Georgia, like far-flung religions that somehow end up with comparable beliefs. There is something satisfyingly primal about it all. It is clearly something that's inbred, this genetic obligation to drive fast, run hard, and, most important, finish first.

Get together an assemblage of automotive machinery, young men crazy enough to pilot them or mechanical enough to coddle them, put them all in a reasonably flat place, and they are likely to try to outduel one another, each of them viciously pushing for first place. And it is all for nothing more than bragging rights, for "mine's faster than yours," or a chance to impress some yellow-haired girl from up the other side of the mountain.

If the opportunity is there, they are going to race, surely as they are going to eat, mate, or breathe. It is all that simple.

They are bound to race. One way or another, they are bound to race.

"Are they gonna run around again, Daddy?"

"I expect they will. They's a few of 'em still got tires left on 'em."

The boy stood there, leaning against his father's broad shoulders as he and his momma sat down together again in the fragrant grass. The youngster couldn't take his eyes off the assemblage of cars down there below them, the men who excitedly talked and waved and danced among the vehicles as if they were being jerked around by invisible wires.

And he especially watched the one who had finished first. The one who had been saluted by the crowd.

Especially him.

GREEN FLAG

ON THE MIDNIGHT RUN

Damn, he really *is* fast! Jodell Lee thought as he maneuvered through the last curve that dumped him out level at the foot of the mountains. Ahead of him, out there past the hood ornament, the road ran straight as a bullet's path for a good ten miles or so. Shoot, I've gotta get a move on and some kind of quick. Come on, baby, let's see what that old boy back there can really do.

The car trailing him had closed to within a couple of hundred yards at the most. Jodell kept a close eye on his rearview mirror. He imagined that he could almost catch a glimpse of the luminescent glow on the man's face from the dashboard lights. And he was beginning to wonder what in the world was under the hood of that car back there. Man, it had closed in on him so quick and had hung so close the car almost seemed to be chained to his own rear bumper, in tow.

Suddenly the front grill of the trailing car erupted in an explosion of flashing red lights. The law! No surprise at all.

"Hmmm, this makes things real interesting," Jodell whispered out loud, through a big grin. "This could be some fun."

But it was a furrowed look of concern that crossed his face next as the trailing car eased a bit closer. He gripped the wheel a little tighter as he concentrated on the familiar roadway that spun out ahead of him, looking, thinking, trying to plan a way out of this fix.

As soon as he was on the longest, straightest stretch of highway, Jodell dared to take one hand off the wheel and reached beneath the dash, fumbling until he found the lever for the exhaust bypass. The voice of the engine changed noticeably, from a throaty roar to a deep, resonant rumble. And there was the distinctive crackle and pop from the set of straight pipes, allowing the exhaust to now come directly off the headers beneath the car's hood. It sounded for all the world like a large swarm of very angry bees.

He kicked down hard on the throttle and the car leapt ahead like a freed deer. It cleared the next small rise as if it might actually take flight and then sailed down the strip of narrow, unlined blacktop highway into the night.

This was the best time, the almost mystical time. Sometimes it felt as if he were not merely driving the car, but that the car had become a part of him. His hands were the steering box, willing the wheels which way to turn. His arms were an extension of the gearshift lever, linked straight to the transmission, determining which set of gears would mesh best. His feet on the gas and brake pedals were no longer simply a part of his body, but were now welded to the car itself, doing his will.

Sometimes he felt the car might take off like an airplane and soar over the valleys and mountains. He wouldn't have minded if it had. Grounded or flying, he was always certain that no one, not even the Feds, could any more catch him than they could capture a hurricane in a croaker sack.

Jodell knew that in the still, cool night air, the howl of his engine could probably be heard for miles up and down the hollers and coves.

A young boy sitting on his front porch halfway to Chandler Mountain could certainly hear the deepening of its bellow, in sequence, as each of the three deuces sitting on top of the manifold kicked in, and the boy might long for the day when he, too, could make such a machine sing such a powerful song.

Or a grandpa somewhere, long since gone to bed for the night in his cabin at the top of a deep holler, might be awakened by the din, maybe roll over and smile, and wish that he still had a smidgen of his own youth left, and that he could once again feel such tingling, throbbing power working beneath his loins.

Jodell's flathead V-8 surged with power like a caged cat. She clearly wanted to prowl, begged to be set loose. And when he did set her free, the old Ford raced off down the straight open stretch of road as if shot from a cannon, immediately putting serious distance between herself and the following sedan.

Jodell smiled. The motor work he and his cousin, Joe, had done on the engine had already paid off in the last few seconds, just as it had so many times before.

He fiddled through the gears expertly. Behind him, the sedan was now struggling to keep up, fighting to stay between the ditches on each side of the narrow blacktop, in real danger of being long since left.

Jodell found the switch under the dash that disconnected all the tail and brake lights. The lead on the sedan had grown to a good half mile, but he knew that might not be enough. The Feds could be maddeningly tenacious, hanging on like an old snapping turtle. This was their job. They had no other priorities.

Jodell ran over in his head the significant features of the countryside from memory, looking, searching in his mental picture for a good place to pull off that would have thick enough vegetation to cover a chance glint of starlight off a chrome bumper, or maybe a building he could dart behind and hide like a fox in its lair. He knew the law could simply radio ahead and have a roadblock waiting for him if they wanted him bad enough, so it was best to go to ground.

And by this time, he figured, the law wanted him powerful bad.

It looked now as if he had put a little more distance yet on the cop car, but he was never able to get completely out of sight of the sedan. Without his rear lights to gauge, the cop would have a hard time judging the distance between the two of them. But without the curves in the road that he would have had if he had been jumped back up there in the mountains, he would have a hard time hiding his headlights, shaking the chaser long enough to turn off the road somewhere.

His best shot was to make the next series of hills and dips that lay ahead, at the end of this stretch of straight roadway. And he had to do it before they could steer him right into the inevitable roadblock. If he could get to the dips and curves near Caney Creek

Church, there would be a series of dirt roads and fields that would allow him to cut through and get away, disappearing like last week's paycheck in the moonless darkness.

Then there suddenly appeared on the horizon one more thing to worry about.

Ahead of him only a couple of miles, the next stand of mountains would take the road on a twisting, bucking climb. Jodell began to sweat at the very thought of it. Outrunning the cops down here in the valley wouldn't be easy, but he had a better than even chance. However, if the law ran him all the way to the mountains, it might be a different story. The sedan would have a much better chance of outmaneuvering him in the sharp switchbacks that ran up the sides of the bluffs, and there were too many places where a single lawman's car could block the road, leaving him the choices of climbing a rock bluff straight for the sky, diving off a sheer cliff, or surrendering.

None would appeal to him.

Now Jodell was feeling every bump and sway in the road. The Ford was running high and tight because of the set of truck springs he and Joe had installed on the rear wheels. With the heavy load of white lightning already delivered, though, the stiff rear springs had already served their purpose and were no longer needed. Instead, they now kept the car from handling as well in the turns, caused the rear end to seem to have a mind of its own sometimes. Every bump and dip threatened to bounce the back of the Ford all the way around to swap places with the front end.

"Jesus, Joseph, and Mary! What I wouldn't give for a plain old set of passenger springs back yonder right about now," he said out loud to himself, his voice raspy, parched. "And a cold soda pop about the size of a fifty-five-gallon drum, too!"

Then something else disturbing caught his eye high on the mountainside ahead. It was another car, winding back and forth, heading downward, coming to meet him and the law enforcement officer still on his tail. And though the oncoming car was still several miles away, Jodell could easily see the flashing red light on its roof.

More company. Damn!

"Lord, it's sure nice to be so popular," he said, but he didn't bother to laugh. The strong, cool wind through the windows would have only whipped it away anyhow.

He shot a glance in the rearview mirror. At least he was beginning to lose sight of the sedan's headlights and red flashers for several seconds at a time now. It was getting to be time, one way or the other. Decision time.

He scanned what he could see of both sides of the road as they swirled past, looking for something familiar in the inky darkness beyond the headlights. He needed to spot somewhere to whip off the roadway while still speeding along at over a hundred miles an hour.

The distance between Jodell and the sedan behind had stabilized, but the cop car coming to meet him was closing much too quickly for comfort. If Jodell was going a hundred and the cop was oncoming at sixty, that was a hundred fifty miles per hour, closing speed. It wouldn't take long to kiss.

Then Jodell knew what he had to do. Off to his right, he knew, there were the ramshackle remains of an old farm, long since abandoned when someone had finally given up harvesting more rocks and Johnson grass than they did corn or tobacco. The highway dropped sharply directly ahead, dipping down to a small, bamboo-choked creek bed. Just beyond the stream, he remembered, there was an old gravel road running nowhere in particular. Probably once leading to an old house place or a fallow field, it was mostly used now as a lovers' lane. Then, a couple of hundred yards past that, on the opposite side of the road, was an old barn that sat in the middle of a five-acre, freshly mown, open hayfield.

The chasing sedan was still a good three quarters of a mile behind him. The approaching police car was not in sight for the moment. That was not good. Clearly the government man had reached the bottom of the mountain already and would soon hit the straight, coming his way.

Beneath him, Jodell felt the black Ford drop heavily down into the dip of the creek, ready to take on the narrow bridge. He jumped on the brakes hard to ease the car from well over one hundred miles an hour to something close to slow enough to take a hard turn. The front end dipped sharply as the brakes immediately took hold with a squeal of metal against metal. He pumped the pedal quickly, up and down, trying to keep the brakes from locking, to keep the car from sliding out of control into the cold little creek, or off the road into a water oak tree or a muddy ditch. Then all the law would have to do would be to fish his carcass out and haul him, or what was left of him, off to jail.

Brakes or not, the car flashed across the one-lane bridge and was immediately at the gravel road that veered off to the left. Jodell was still moving so fast he slid right on past, the wheels now locked hard, trying to stop. He did a perfect one-hundred-eighty-degree spin in the road and was headed the opposite direction when the car finally came to a stop. The tires had squalled as if in agony, leaving a heavy cloud of blue smoke and swirling dust hanging over the roadway.

Jodell swallowed hard, caught his breath, killed his headlights, and goosed the gas again as he turned in to the side road. He steered behind the first wall of honeysuckle bushes he came to, thankful there were no kids parked there tonight.

"Please, Lord. If you could just send me a little breeze to blow away that tire smoke . . ." he prayed out loud.

Then he grinned in the deep darkness. Grown man, talking to himself all the time. But he spent so much time alone, there behind the wheel of the Ford, driving along through the night. After all, who else was he going to talk to?

He looked up then just as the Federal man in the sedan flashed by on the highway, not thirty feet away through the brush, never slowing. Jodell held his breath as if the guy might could actually hear him. He watched the rearview mirror, listening, still afraid the cop would see or smell the tire smoke and know his prey had turned off here to hide in the bushes.

Jodell didn't breathe again until the dark sedan had roared on down the highway a half mile at full throttle, engine growing quieter with distance, his grill lights still strobing.

When he could once again hear the crickets and the hooting of an owl, Jodell threw the Ford into reverse, popped the clutch, and backed out onto the highway. He followed the sedan, his headlights still off, searching the pitch dark night again for the nearly hidden offshoot that led to the field.

"Gotta be here somewhere, Hortense," he said to the dark dashboard in front of him. He called the Ford a different name each night. Tonight she was Hortense. "Gotta be within the next couple of hundred yards or we've missed her already somehow."

He had to find the turn before the two police cars met up ahead. Even a jackleg rookie revenuer wouldn't take long to figure out that Jodell had somehow snookered them, and then they would backtrack, looking for some sign of him. There would be some, of course. A tire track, a stretch of bent grass, a snapped limb beside the road . . . That was all it would take to betray him.

Fast as those old boys were moving, he figured he only had a couple of minutes to find a better place to hide the car and his own butt.

Then there it was. The long field he'd been looking for.

He tried to look ahead, to see if he could spot the cop cars' headlights coming back, but there was nothing yet. Didn't mean they weren't coming, though, because there was another series of dips and bridges in the next few miles, and the highway ahead was lined with big water oaks and banks of honeysuckle. Then he saw the cut in the tree line where the hardly visible farm road crossed the ditch and entered the field. And there was the rusty old gate guarding the field and the long-abandoned barn from God-knew-what.

Jodell stood hard on the brakes again, slowing the car in the darkness, looking for rocks or stumps in the turnoff, anything that might puncture an oil pan or slice a tire. He closed the straight pipes to drop the engine rumble to a minimum. No use waking up some old sleeping farmer who might come out shooting, or

risk getting somebody's coon dogs riled up. Any kind
of ruckus could lead the government men right to
him. He swung the wheel sharply and pointed the car
through the narrow gate, thankful it was left open.
Otherwise, he would have had to plow right through,
hoping the Feds didn't notice it had been busted.

"Somebody's watching out for us, Hortense," he
told the car, and lovingly patted her dashboard.

She bounced and bumped like a boat on rough
water as she left the smoother pavement, rumbled
over a half-fallen-in cattle guard, and entered through
the overgrown hedgerows into the rutted field.

Thankfully, the night was dark and the field relatively level. Even so, Jodell moved slowly, straining to
see through the darkness so he wouldn't drive right
up a sapling tree or straddle a terrace he couldn't get
off of. He had just rolled around behind the side of
the barn farthest from the road when he saw the lights
of the first cop sedan bouncing up and down as it hit
one of the dips. He was headed back and Jodell could
only imagine the fury and frustration the guy must
have been feeling. The red lights on the car's snout
seemed to flash more frantically, as if in rage.

There was a second set of headlights, too. The
squad car with its own angrily flashing red light,
bouncing along right behind the sedan. And they were
both zooming, flying. Jodell could hear the big police
special engines straining, pulling in tandem, almost
like airplanes revving for takeoff. He could even make
out the sound of their radios, squawking madly at
each other. Then they were past him, apparently
without ever suspecting where he had gone.

As he sat waiting for the two cars to pass, he
scanned his surroundings, looking for another way
out. There appeared to be another gate in the middle

of another fence that cut through a break in the tree line behind him.

But then he noticed again the sound of an engine, quickly coming back along the road. The sedan, this time without the squad car, sailed by on the highway, passing the entrance to the pasture for a third time, still searching desperately for its prey.

But once more it flew by, missing the rough road Jodell had taken. A sliver of a moon had just smiled at him from behind a bank of clouds, finally giving off enough light for Jodell to cross the field to the back gate without wandering into a gully or a random stretch of barbed wire. The Ford bounced roughly across the deep grass and furrows to the gate, even though he eased it along carefully.

"Sorry, girl. I'll make it up to you. You've been a real friend tonight."

The gate was closed but, fortunately, not locked. Jodell had to climb from under the wheel to pull it open and prop it back with a big rock someone had obviously left there for that purpose.

The cool night air felt good on his wet skin. He was surprised how stiff and sweat-soaked he was. He stretched to try to unknot his kinked muscles, then crawled back into the Ford and cautiously pulled out onto an old gravel road that ran along the fence line at the back of the field.

He took the roundabout route the rest of the way home, minimizing the chance he would accidentally meet either of the cars again. Jodell was still pumped, the adrenaline surging, knowing he had once again successfully outrun and outmaneuvered the law.

He had done his job well. He always did. Another load of 'shine, safely delivered, was now in the possession of some distant nameless bootlegger, ready to be divvied up to a thirsty bunch of parched customers.

Next week, and the week after that, and on and on, there would always be another batch to be run off, a load to be delivered somewhere in the shadow of some dark mountain. And Jodell knew he could get the job done, just as his daddy had done before him and his grandfather before him. Close as it had been tonight, he knew he still had what it took to outrun those who would deny him his heritage. Not only the car but the skill to drive it, too. Man and machine, working together.

Sure, he took pride in getting the moonshine where it was supposed to go. And sure, he was more than happy to deny the tax men their pound of flesh.

But lately, he had realized more than ever that it was the actual chase that he lived for. He had caught himself taking foolish chances sometimes, only so he could maneuver, drive like the wind, make a cunning move or two, and then manage a clean getaway.

"We had ourselves another good night, Hortense," he said, as he glided the purring Ford into its spot inside the old barn at home. "We finished ahead. That's always a good night."

That, Jodell knew, was what drove him to do what he did. To be ahead, always being chased by everybody else. Not to be back there in the dust, sniffing exhaust fumes, doing the chasing.

Ahead. That's exactly where he planned to stay.

COMPETITION

The trip into Chandler Cove was twelve miles of twisting, bucking road, running past red cutbanks, rocky farm plots, and simple, white clapboard houses. Jodell Lee took the turns slowly, in no particular hurry to get back to town and then back to the farm and to work. And on this trip he was driving his grandfather's pickup truck with the two bald tires on the front and the same brake shoes Jodell himself had put on eight years before, when he had been a fourteen-year-old eighth-grader at Andrew Jackson Junior High.

He took his time loading up at the Farmers' Co-op, then started back up Main Street and toward the highway home. It seemed, though, that the old truck wanted to have its own head, and before he knew it, Jodell had made a left and a right, crossed the railroad tracks, and was pulling to a squeaking stop in front of the ramshackle old building that housed the town's pool hall.

A few games with the boys? What would it hurt? Grandpa wouldn't mind. Besides, he had worked hard already this day, clearing some new ground up the side of the mountain, helping mend some snagged fence, nailing together some feeding troughs for the new calf pen, then loading all the feed sacks on the truck at the Co-op. Jodell ordered a soda pop and visited a minute with Bessie, who manned the greasy grill behind the counter at the snack bar, then made his way through the swinging doors that led to the long room where six well-worn pool tables waited.

Jodell knew most everybody in the room by name and waved his pop bottle at them as he passed. It looked as if a fair share of the first shift from the textile mill below town was taking lunch at the Corner Pocket. Several hot and heavy games were under way and voices were already being raised good-naturedly as minor disputes broke out.

There, bent over the table at the far end of the room, was Jodell's first cousin and best friend, Joe Banker. Joe's father and Jodell's mother had been brother and sister, and anyone who took time to notice could see the family resemblance. Both young men were tall, slim, and dark-haired, with flashing blue eyes and a muscular build. Being practically the same age and growing up a couple of houses down the road from each other, they felt more like brothers. Joe, too, worked a farm. In his case, it was for his father. But he spent most of his spare time at one of three places, here at the pool hall, at the Dairy Dip Drive-in just down the street in Chandler Cove, or in

Jodell's barn, helping him work on his cars and the farm equipment.

Joe had managed to keep his distance from the moonshine business. His mother had pointedly told Jodell's grandpa early on that no son of hers was getting within a country mile of whiskey distilling and running. Grandpa Lee, already familiar with how hardheaded the females in his family could be, simply and readily acceded to her wishes. He had Jodell, after all, and as long as Joe kept the 'shine car's engine in top shape and its suspension finely tuned for late-night runs on corkscrewing country roads, it really did not matter to him anyway.

Joe Banker had a real talent with internal combustion engines of any kind. He could make even the sickest one go from wheezing, coughing fits and smoky spasms to running like a healthy, purring cat.

"Hey, Joe! What's up?" Jodell called as soon as Joe had neatly pocketed the billiard ball he had been aiming for on the table's worn green-felt top.

"Joe Bob! Where you been hiding all day? I stopped by the barn this morning, but you were already gone."

"Some of us gotta work, you know. I was helping Grandpa out in the back pasture before good daylight this morning. He was fixing the fence. Some of the cows got out the other day and he was none too happy. He cussed so hard all the trees within earshot just withered up and died."

"Well, I reckon so. He loves them cattle more than he does his grandkids, I think sometimes."

"You should have seen it, Joe. Grandpa and that old yellow dog of his spent the better part of the afternoon chasing them cows trying to get 'em back in the pasture. They'd run 'em right up to the gate and the critters would do an about-face and take off right back up the hill. Grandpa would have to high-step it on back up there, hem 'em up again, and start all over. They must have run halfway across that mountain and back a half dozen times."

"I bet that was a sight," Joe said, already sighting his next shot down the length of his cue stick. "Durn cows probably run off all the fat he had put on 'em already this spring."

"I don't know who looked funnier when I finally got out there to help, him or that dumb old coon dog. Grandpa was running around waving his old hat like a bullfighter, and that yellow dog was sitting there in one spot, barking like he had a big old coon treed, not moving a whit. They had the cows so mixed up, they didn't know whether to uphill or downhill!"

"I bet. I'm surprised he didn't have those crazy old mules of his right up there in the middle of everything. He loves them things as much or more than that old coon dog."

Joe gave the cue a quick shove and two balls clacked together hard in the center of the table. One skittered to the pocket on the opposite side and dropped in neatly.

"That would have been a sight," Jodell chuckled. "I'm laughing now, but I thought the old feller was gonna have a stroke yesterday. I swear, he would have made hamburger out of the whole lot of 'em if he could have."

"Glad I missed that little adventure, Cuz," Joe said, and whacked the cue ball again.

"Who's got the winner?" Jodell asked as he selected a cue stick from the rack on the side wall.

"You do if you want. Bubba and me have just been

screwing around. We ain't even been keeping score, have we, Bubba?"

An impossibly big man was propped heavily against the back wall, almost like a big-trunked tree that the wind had blown over and left leaning there. He might easily have been mistaken for a chifforobe or an icebox. Bubba Baxter was definitely a bear of a man, a farm-raised and obviously farm-fed country boy. He could only nod a reply to Joe's question. His huge hands were busy, shoving most of the remaining half of one of Bessie's grease-dripping cheeseburgers into his mouth.

To the casual observer, Bubba didn't seem to be the sharpest knife in the drawer, but those who knew him also knew he was far brighter than he appeared. He was also strong as day-old coffee and stubborn as one of Grandpa's beloved mules. Food and cars were about all that ever seemed to occupy his mind. Girls didn't appear to be a consideration. Couldn't anyone remember if he'd ever even had a date.

"You want to play Bubba?" Jodell asked as he began to rack up the balls on the table.

Bubba managed another grunt as he chewed away on the burger and waved at Jodell to go on first. Jodell lined up the cue and took the opening shot. One ball dropped in and he took the solid balls.

"You're stripes, Bubba."

He got another grunt in reply, then went ahead and surveyed the angles for the next shot.

Then something caught Jodell's eye, distracting him from the table. It was a yellow page of paper, thumbtacked to the back wall of the pool hall. While he chalked the point of his cue, he casually moved closer and quickly read the words printed on it.

It was an announcement for an automobile race to

be held the next Sunday afternoon. A race to be held
at a track that had been scraped out of a pasture last
year at the Meyer farm, off the state highway halfway
to Morristown. But the main thing that had caught
Jodell's eye was the posted prize money: fifty dollars
to the winner.

The race was to be fifty laps around the one-third-
mile track, and the top finisher was to receive "a nice
trophy and fifty dollars first prize money." Second
prize was to be twenty-five dollars and a tank of gas
from Roy's Texaco. And even third place paid "ten
dollars and a case of soda pop."

Jodell played on, jawing with Bubba and Joe all the
time, but his eyes kept straying to the flyer on the
back wall, his mind to the race and the prize money.

Fifty! Man!

When no one was looking, he snatched the paper
from the wall, folded it, and slid it into his back
pocket.

Jodell was so intent on the game, he hardly noticed
a pair of men who had been playing quietly on one
of the other tables nearby. They had apparently finished their own game and had wandered over to
where Jodell and Bubba played while Joe watched.
Neither of them looked familiar.

"How about a friendly game?" one of them asked.

"Sure," Jodell answered with a quick grin. He was
always looking for someone new to play. Jodell Lee
had a certain thing about competition. He thrived on
it. But Joe and Bubba were about the only ones left
in Chandler's Cove who would take him on, be it
billiards, marbles, mumblety-peg or any other competition. "I'll rack 'em up and you break. How about
that?"

"Sounds good. You play much?"

"Naw. Barely enough to keep the rust off," Jodell answered, setting the balls in the rack.

The first game went quickly. Jodell handily beat his opponent with mostly simple shots while the other man missed everything he tried, sometimes amazingly badly. His buddy ragged him constantly, chiding him for how bad he was playing.

"Damn, Steve, you look like you ain't never picked up a cue stick before this very day."

"I'll get my stroke directly, Ray. I need to get used to the lay of this table. The felt, you know."

But he never did. Not for the entire game. Jodell almost felt bad, thumping so badly someone he didn't even know. It took most of the fun out of the game.

"What they call you? Jodell?" the one named Steve asked. "You look like you're pretty good with that cue. You been playing long?"

Jodell appreciated the compliment, but he also knew when he was being set up. Still, the competitive juices were flowing already.

"Well, Steve . . . It is Steve, isn't it? I've played a little bit of pool, but I reckon luck has more to do with my game than anything else. What about you?"

"You saw how good I am. But I kinda like to play the game. Say, you want to make this a little more interesting? Sometimes I can play better if there's a little bit riding on it. What do you say we play for a couple of dollars? Just for the fun of it, of course."

Jodell knew for certain now that he was being baited, but he went right ahead and allowed himself to be reeled in. He leaned back against the table and pretended to be thinking over the offer. Joe and Bubba stood behind the two men, huge grins breaking out on their faces. He hoped the two strangers wouldn't see them or they might realize all three of them were on to their clumsy hustle.

"Boy, I don't know. I work so hard for that money, I hate to lose it to somebody so easy."

Jodell was having a hard time keeping a straight face himself now. He knew if he looked at Joe or Bubba again, he would burst out laughing.

"Shoot, Jodell. Way I'm playing today, you'll take me for all I'm worth. It's gonna be the easiest money you ever made. But it'll be worth it for me to get some tips from watching you play."

"You surely ain't brought your stroke today, Steve," the other stranger offered, doing his part to further set the hook. "Maybe you better not play for no money this time, Steve. Maybe another time."

Jodell felt the hot blood rising inside, his pulse quickening. Competition. God, he loved it! He knew he was being hustled. And he knew he only had a single quarter left in his jeans pocket after paying for the soda. But by God, he had to take this stranger on.

"Okay," he finally said, as if it had been a terrible decision to have to make. "How about we play for a dollar a game, three games. That sound fair, Steve?"

The stranger didn't hesitate. He was almost too eager now to take this rube's butter-and-egg money.

"Well, sure it's fair. We're just playing a few friendly games, right?" Steve said, tossing an obvious wink at his partner but smiling all the while at Jodell.

"That's right, a few friendly games."

"Here, let me rack 'em up. You wanna break, Jodell? Since you won the last game and all?"

"Okay, if you insist. Just a friendly game now. Right?"

"That's right," Steve assured him one more time. Then he gave Jodell a sideways look, still smiling.

"Now, friend, you do have the three dollars on you, don't you?"

"Right here," Jodell lied, tapping his rear pocket, where the only thing inside was the racing announcement he had taken from the wall. "And pardon me for asking, but you do too, don't you?"

"Course I do. Quit stalling now and break 'em," Steve spat, his smile instantly gone. And he suddenly didn't sound like such a friendly stranger.

Jodell promptly stepped up to the table and lined up his break shot. With a loud crack, he broke the rack, dropping a solid.

"Solids are mine. You're stripes."

With that, Jodell proceeded to quickly run the table with little lost motion or even a pause for effect. Steve and his partner stood there, staring dumbfounded at the empty green felt table. After only another ten minutes, Jodell had won all three games, missing only two shots in the entire process. When the last ball fell, he calmly laid his cue across the table and looked over at the two wide-eyed, openmouthed men.

"Enjoyed the game, Steve. I think you owe me three dollars."

Jodell stretched to his full six-foot-four height, grinned at the man, and held out his palm.

"Wait just a minute here," Steve said. His eyes narrowed and shifted nervously, and his feet danced as if he were looking for an opening through which to flee.

"You owe me three dollars, friend. Fair and square."

"I don't know about that. I think you done hustled me. I don't think I owe you any money a'tall."

The grin promptly left Jodell's face and he took a step toward Steve, his right hand still outstretched for the money. He noticed that Bubba had calmly made his way between the strangers and the pool-room door as stealthily as somebody his size possibly could.

"Look. Why don't you just pay me what you owe me and then y'all get the heck on out of here and run your little hustle someplace else?"

Steve apparently took the offered hand as the best opportunity to take a swing at Jodell's jaw. But Jodell had anticipated the move. He caught the punch in midair with a quick left hand, easily deflecting it to one side. In almost the same motion, he planted a hard right fist deep in Steve's exposed gut. The man lost all the air in his lungs and doubled over in pain. That left him open for a sharp upper cut, and he tumbled hard like a toppled tower.

The other man lifted a handy pool cue with the idea of taking a swing at Jodell's head. The cue whistled through the air but was stopped a foot short of its target. It had been cleanly snatched by Bubba Baxter's huge mitt of a hand. He had caught the cue stick in midswing and, with a single twist of his wrist, the cue was yanked out of the stranger's hand.

Wild-eyed and terrified, the man bolted for the door, leaving his friend still crumpled, breathless, on the pool-room floor. For good measure, Bubba gave the fleeing stranger a swift kick in the rear as he passed, almost sending him sprawling.

The other players cheered and clapped. They would have a good story to tell when they got back to the mill.

Jodell pulled Steve to his feet by the collar of his shirt and dragged him to the front of the room. Joe held open the door, ready to help usher him out.

But first Jodell carefully and deliberately removed three one-dollar bills from the fellow's pocket, then tossed him out the door like so much refuse. He collapsed into a pile on the sidewalk. Steve's friend eventually sidled over and dragged him off while Bubba stood watch, swinging the cue above his head like a sword.

Jodell knew it wasn't simply winning the games that now had him feeling so elated. It wasn't the short, successful fight. And it certainly wasn't the money, although three dollars was most of a day's pay for work on Grandpa's farm.

It was coming out on top, winning the competition, whatever it happened to be. God, he loved being the best!

And right now, being the best had made him powerfully hungry.

LET'S RACE

What say we get some lunch at the Dairy Dip?" Jodell Lee asked. He waved in the air the dollar bills he had just won from the pair of pool hustlers. "I'm buyin'."

"Sounds good to me," Joe said immediately. "Watching you two do your Joe Louis imitations has made me powerful hungry."

"How about you, Bubba?" Jodell asked.

"Reckon so," the big man said. Bubba was always game for anything edible.

As they walked to the truck, Jodell thought again about the flyer in his rear jeans pocket. Racing. He'd done a little paint-swapping with some of his friends, mostly just raising a dust cloud in some of the fields and pastures around the county, a few drag races on backcountry roads. Even then, he usually only ran the beat-up old farm truck. A dent here or there in that old buggy didn't matter one way or the other.

He'd heard about the more serious races, events like the one to be run out at the Meyer farm. Friends who had gone to them had reported that they usually attracted fast, slick machines from many miles around, some from as far away as the other flank of the Smoky Mountains in North Carolina or from up the Blue Ridge into Virginia. And some of the whiskey runners usually showed up to do some serious race car driving, too.

Jodell would have loved to get out there and run in circles with the rest of them. He didn't fear going up against the other drivers or even the other more experienced whiskey runners. He was confident he could hold his own, that he could give as much as he had to take. But he was realistic enough to know that Grandpa's old truck, held together with baling twine and best wishes, would be no match for any of those cars.

"Jodell, what do you think about this race next Sunday?" Joe asked as they all three climbed into the truck. He must have been reading Jodell's mind. He seemed able to do that sometimes. "You wanna go?"

"Yeah, I was sorta thinking about it. That ought to be fun. What about you? You wanna go?"

"Sure, I wouldn't miss it. They say there will be some really fast cars down there. And you know what else? I hear some whiskey runners are coming from over yonder the other side of the Carolina line. You gotta figure their cars are going to be something special."

Jodell ground the truck's starter until it caught and backed it into the street. He heard something growling and at first thought it might be the truck's differential going out again. Then he realized it was only Bubba Baxter's stomach making all the noise.

"Chili dawg. I'm wantin' a chili dawg," the big man offered. Jodell ignored him. His mind was on the race.

"Yeah, Joe, but I can't believe they would bring their good whiskey cars to run 'em round and round in some old rutted cornfield."

"They don't care. They'll be running for bragging rights as much as they will for the money. All them old boys care about is outrunning anybody they can. And it don't matter to them who or where. 'Sides, I hear they got a pretty good track built down there."

"I suppose you're right, but who cares if all you do is beat the fastest local flash? Most of them boys around here are nothing more than high school kids whose daddies are rich enough so they can buy themselves a fast car."

"From what I hear, the whiskey runners don't give a damn. Them guys from Carolina are pretty tough characters, or so the rumors go. I'd say if you could beat them, you'd have done a day's work and really have something to brag about."

"I've heard they do a bunch of racing over in the Carolinas. Specially out east and down toward the south. There's that big old track down south at Darlington." Jodell shook his head and grinned. "Man oh man, could you imagine running on something that big and smooth?"

Jodell had heard about the South Carolina track over the radio. He could only imagine what it must actually look like with its banked turns and thousands of bleacher seats for the spectators.

"Yeah, I've heard talk of it myself," Joe said reverently. He might have been talking of the Empire

State Building or that big orange bridge in San Francisco. He'd seen pictures of both but couldn't imagine how they would look for real.

"Maybe I'll get me some French fries, too, and a shake. Chocolate."

Bubba was thinking of things equally awe-inspiring to him.

"It's hard to even picture something that big and that fast. Joe, what do you imagine the Ford could do, wide open, if we could run her around that thing? That would be tops. The absolute tops."

"Well, if you're so danged curious, why don't you take her out to Meyer's place and let's see what she can do," Joe said. And again, he was reading Jodell's mind.

"I know you ain't scared nor nothing," Bubba piped in, suddenly aware of the conversation on either side of him, and thinking for once of something besides his gut and getting it filled. "Hell, Jodell, your car is fast enough to whip them all in second gear. They wouldn't stand a chance up against you."

"Aw, Bubba, that car is fast enough, all right, but I have to drive it to make the 'shine runs. You know that. Grandpa would skin me and make a throw rug outta my hide if I tore it up racing and failed to make even one of the weekly runs. We all depend on that money."

"Hell. Maybe you *are* scared to run against them Carolina boys after all," Bubba stated, as if it were proven fact. "You're afraid they'll kick your butt and have you choking on their dust all day. That's all it is."

Jodell bit his tongue to keep from pulling Bubba up short, and he gripped the steering wheel so hard he threatened to squeeze it in half.

"Now, Bubba, I don't know so much about that. I believe I can drive a car good as anybody. I sure as hell left them two Federal boys the other night like they were driving soapbox derbies. Man, when those three deuces kicked in, I was gone like a shooting star. I bet they're still out there somewhere along that stretch of road wondering if the ground opened up and swallowed me whole."

"Well, Jodell, if you think you're such a damn good car driver, then why don't you just climb in and run Sunday? You know me and Joe here will help you with the car. Won't we, Joe?"

"For most likely the first time in his life, old Bubba's right, Jodell. Me and him, we could help you get the car ready. As fast as that Ford is when we got her tuned up and the suspension all dialed in, you oughta win that old race before some of 'em get up to speed." Jodell glanced over at the two other men. Their eyes were on him, shining. "Come on. Whatta you say? It ought to be the easiest money we ever make and a passel of fun to boot."

"I don't know, boys," Jodell replied. He still wasn't as sure as the other two were. But he would have loved to find out if what they said was close to true. And the old competitive fire was already getting re-kindled in his gut. "It doesn't look quite so easy to me as it does to y'all. These guys coming in just to race are going to be tough birds. And I don't mean just racing-wise on the track. I hear they like to pick a fight, win or lose, and I sure don't want to get any feuds started."

"Well, we sure as hell took care of them two back at the Corner Pocket, didn't we?"

"Those two weren't anything like some of them hillbilly racers from across the state line. I hear some of them are crazy and don't even know it."

"If you're worried about gettin' into a fight, well, hell, that's what old Bubba is here for, Jodell. That and jackin' up cars without a jack. You got Bubba at your back and me under the hood. We'll win the damn race, then we'll win the damn fight!"

"I still don't know about any of this." Jodell couldn't believe he was being so hard to talk into going racing. He desperately wanted to do it. Every fiber of his being wanted to climb into that Ford and smoke the rest of the field, leaving those Carolina whiskey runners in his wake. But something didn't feel right about it. "Besides, Grandma will kill me. You know how protective she always is of me."

"Aw, don't worry. Grandma Lee won't ever find out. What do you say, Jodell? Let's do it. One race won't hurt nothing. If you don't like it, if it's a bust, we don't ever have to run again."

"Jesus, Joe! Give me a break! I'll think about it."

With that said, Jodell slid the truck into the drive-in, next to one of the speakers on a post. Their food showed up quickly and they ate in virtual silence, Joe and Jodell obviously deep in thought, Bubba engrossed in his three chili dogs and double order of fries.

After he had chewed and swallowed the last bite, Jodell finally, quietly, spoke the words the other two had been waiting to hear.

"Okay. We'll run."

Joe Banker and Bubba Baxter cheered and clapped as if Jodell Lee had just scored the winning touchdown.

THE OTHER SIDE OF THE MOUNTAINS

Jodell dropped Joe and Bubba off back at the pool hall, then headed toward home. Grandpa was expecting him back with the supplies from the Co-op, and there would certainly be hell to pay if he wasn't home in time to get the truck unloaded before it was time to feed the cattle.

Work always came second in the Lee family, just after church. Everything else was on down the list somewhere. If Grandpa found out he'd been hanging out in the pool hall instead of coming straight home with the supplies, he'd probably pop a fuse. And when Grandpa Lee blew a fuse, sparks always flew.

Even at twenty-two years old, Jodell Lee knew to play by Grandpa's rules. Or at least make certain the old man thought his grandson was toeing the line.

And if he were to start racing, he wasn't exactly

sure how such a thing would actually be covered in Grandpa's unwritten rule book. The old man had never specifically said Jodell couldn't climb behind the wheel of a race car and risk life and limb. No sir. Never specifically forbade him to do such a thing.

But that was simply a technicality. Grandpa had also never specifically said Jodell couldn't set fire to the barn for a wiener roast or bring home an elephant to keep for a pet, either. Some things you instinctively knew wouldn't set well with Grandpa Lee.

And no matter what Grandpa's opinion might be on the matter, Jodell knew precisely where Grandma would stand. If she found out, she would first cry and pray to Jesus, then she would take a broom handle to him, twenty-two years old or not. Since what had happened to his father, she was smotheringly protective of Jodell.

"You may get too big for your britches," she would say. "But you ain't never too big for me to whoop with a switch."

Jodell knew he would have to be careful to keep his little Meyer farm adventure a secret from her, too. And so would Joe. She was his grandmother, too, and she'd just as soon take a hickory-limb switch to him as she would to Jodell.

During the drive back to the farm, Jodell mulled over the race in his head. He had no doubts about his driving. He knew he could run with the best of them, anywhere, anytime. He had proved that every single time he drove off into the night on another whiskey run.

He'd grown up driving on dirt and gravel roads, first sliding behind the wheel of a vehicle when he was ten years old. The track in the cornfield at the Meyer place shouldn't be a problem for him either.

Staying alive if he tore up Grandpa's whiskey car would be a much tougher challenge. They had an especially big load set to be run the next Wednesday after the race. No run, no bootlegger money for anybody. And that would be disastrous to the Lee family.

But the closer he got to home and the more he thought about it, the better he felt. The car was plenty fast. He had proved that. And Joe could doubtless crank out even a few more horsepower if he tried. It already had a roll bar installed, too. They'd have to add some seat belts of some kind, and he'd have to dig up a hard hat or something he could use for a helmet.

As Jodell downshifted and pulled into the barnyard, he smiled. What the hell? The decision had been made. There was no reason why he shouldn't race the Ford next Sunday.

Smiling, shaking his head at the wildness of it all, he hopped out onto the truck's rickety wooden running board, then down onto the dust of the barnyard, and walked to the back of the truck to start pulling off the big sacks of feed.

"Boy, what took you so long?" Grandpa's raspy voice brought him back to reality in one big hurry. "I must've been mistook. I thought you told me you'd be back hours ago."

"Hi, Grandpa. I ran into Joe and Bubba in town and we got ourselves a hamburger."

"You knew your grandma was going to fix you lunch. Why did you figure you had to stop and eat in town?"

"I was just in the mood for a Dairy Dip hamburger, I guess."

"Wasted money, I say. Y'all was at that blessed old pool hall, wasn't ya?"

"Well, we did meet up there, but then we went on to the drive-in to get our burgers."

Jodell wasn't exactly lying to his grandpa.

"I told you to be back before lunch. Your grandma is going to be real mad. She done fixed you a great big lunch in there. You had better go on in there and act like you're hungry enough to barbecue one of them cows and eat it. Soon's we get done unloading this truck, that is."

"I am still hungry. Loading the truck helped me work up a pretty good appetite. Then I ran into Joe. I tried to get back as soon as I could, but you know Joe. He kept wanting to play one more game."

"Well, ole Joe is just like his daddy. Neither of them was much of a pool player," Grandpa said with a laugh, already apparently getting over his mad spell. "Nor was he much of a worker either. Now, let's get this truck unloaded and everything put up in the barn 'fore Ma has to call us. She'll be hot as a hornet."

Jodell didn't really mind working for his grandfather. His own father had done the same when he had been a teenager, working the farm during the day and making the Wednesday night 'shine run every week. Jodell had heard many times about how his father could drive the 'shine cars like no man in the county. How it came so natural to him folks said he was born with a gearshift in his hand and an itchy accelerator foot.

It had been Papa Lee's intention to pass the farm, the still, and the 'shine contacts on to his son when the time came that he could no longer do it all. The war, though, had twisted all those plans around. Bob Lee Jr. had rushed down to the recruiting station the day after the radio had described the horror of the sneak attack on Pearl Harbor. He had proudly signed up for the Navy and even drove down to Knoxville and got himself a tattoo before he shipped out. Grandma had threatened to whip him good for that.

When the navy said they needed volunteers for the submarines, Bob Jr. had raised his hand first. After all, he had been a Tennessean, a natural born volunteer, so it had been the only thing to do. He had spent six months in submarine school and then had been assigned to a sub in the Pacific. The end of his first patrol had brought a stack of excited letters, one almost every day, jointly addressed to Jodell's mother and grandmother, describing his experiences on board the cramped submersible ship, his voyage across the equator, the strange lands he had seen, and the friends lost in the fighting.

Grandma still had those letters, tied together with a length of ribbon and tucked away in her sewing basket in the parlor. She still brought them out sometimes and read them out loud to Grandpa and Jodell, as if she had only received them that very day and the scratched words were fresh and new.

Three patrols after he had been assigned to the sub, it had been reported missing and never returned to port.

Grandma seemed to accept the tragic news. "It's God's will," she would say, and then would go to the Bible for comfort.

Jodell's mother, though, continued to hold out deep but futile hope throughout the dark months of 1943. Finally, mostly drowning in her own grief, she climbed into the only life raft she could see. She left the eight-year-old boy, Jodell, with Grandma and Grandpa Lee, caught a ride down to Knoxville, and took the train cross-country to California to look for work and peace, as far from the lonely foothills as she could get without jumping into the ocean.

They had received a few short, precise letters and colorful picture postcards from her after she had first gotten settled way out there. After a year, the letters had grown shorter, less frequent, and finally had quit coming. They had not heard a word from her since, not in fourteen years.

Grandma had not bothered to save those letters.

Later that evening, still stuffed from the extra meal he had been forced to eat, and stiff from all the day's work, Jodell took a walk down to the barn. He swung open the heavy doors on the front of the building. From outside, the old weather-beaten structure looked ramshackle, like a good summer thunderstorm wind could easily lay it down. But from inside, it was clear the barn was more sturdy than it looked, was surprisingly spacious and well sealed and insulated from the cold winter winds.

The barn no longer served the farm and its needs. Grandpa had long ago taken to parking his ancient tractor underneath a shed at the back of the building. The implements had their own storage shed up the hill behind the house. Now the barn's interior and stalls had been cleared away to make room for a large, well-equipped shop. In the corner sat a gleaming black 1950 Ford. Off to the other side, an old pickup truck and an engineless '38 Ford sat side by side as if waiting for someone to pay them some attention again. The motor from the '38 sedan hung swinging from a hoist strapped to one of the overhead joists. The car's hood leaned against the back wall of the shop.

It was still a warm evening even though the sun had already fallen low in the sky. There was barely the hint of a breeze. Jodell had left the barn's big doors open to catch what little air might stir. Even then, it was still hot in the barn, a leftover from earlier in the day when the sun had drilled down on the barn's steep tin roof.

Sweat dripped off Jodell's face as he worked away, screwdriver in hand, on a chunk of machinery he had detached from the engine. It was the car's carburetors. He would occasionally pause to pull a rag from his back pocket and wipe his face dry. But mostly he worked.

A careful eye could see some unusual features about the Ford Jodell was working on. First was its deep black paint job. Most people nowadays preferred some color in the car they drove. This one, though, needed to be black as night for quite practical reasons.

There was no spare tire in the trunk. It had been left out purposely, to make more room for the boxes that contained the car's normal cargo. A heavy set of truck springs sat on top of the rear axle, helped along with heavy-duty shock absorbers. It would be unfortunate if the car should ride low in the rear end and betray the weight of the liquid freight it was usually carrying.

And welded securely to the car's frame, running up the sides and along the top of the roof behind where the driver sat, was a heavy steel roll bar. From the outside, the roll bar was all but invisible. It was well hidden behind the door post and the cloth fabric that lined the roof. The sixteen-inch tires on the vehicle carried plenty of good rubber, at least enough tread to grab a sure grip on the roadway as it cornered.

The outward appearance was strictly that of a stock car, just as it came off a dealer's lot when new. Except for maybe riding a bit high in the rear when empty

of its occasional cargo, the black car looked like any
other Ford of its year and model on the street.

Jodell had recently noticed something wrong with
it, though. He'd picked up a slight hesitation in the
motor a couple of days before when he had punched
hard on the accelerator, forcing the second and third
of the three deuces to kick in. He'd adjusted the throttle linkage the day before, but that did not seem to
cure the problem. He'd finally narrowed the problem
down to the carburetors. Either one of the floats was
sticking or the jets were off. It was a knotty problem
and he was proud of himself for having narrowed it
down.

He would never be as good a mechanic as Joe, but
he was learning. Jodell's primary talent was noticing
such a seemingly minor anomaly before it got worse.
Joe said he had rabbit ears and could hear a robin
feather land on a sheep's back. Such sensitivity to the
slightest change in pitch in the engine or the most
minute rumble from the front end could avoid something major later. Something fatally major.

Most drivers would have never noticed the instant
of balkiness in the way the engine worked. Jodell certainly had. Such a blip could have grown into a much
more serious problem that might leave him stalled in
the middle of a dark highway some night, surrounded
by less-than-friendly folks who wanted desperately to
put an end to his deliveries.

While he had been in town that day, he'd stopped
at the auto parts store and picked up a new float and
a rebuild kit for the jets. He replaced one of the floats
and went to work on the second set of jets. Jodell took
the carburetor over to the work bench and laid it
down on a shop towel. He picked up a screwdriver
and quickly began to disassemble it. As each part was

removed, he carefully inspected it with a practiced eye. First his dad and then Grandpa had taught Jodell the intricacies of various engines and how their parts worked from the time he had been old enough to pick up a wrench.

Next, he reached for the body of the carburetor, carefully removed the float, flipped it over, and inspected it. Even though it looked fine to his eye, he replaced it with a new one anyway. Better safe than sorry.

Then, as he picked up the base of the unit, he immediately saw something. There was a minute lump of carbon buildup on the head of one of the jets, just enough to partially block it. Jodell smiled to himself, satisfied he'd actually found the source of the problem.

He set about replacing the jets and was almost finished when he heard an especially noisy car pull into the turnaround of the driveway between the barn and the house. From the ragged sound of the engine, he knew right away it was Bubba Baxter's old clunker. The hole in the tailpipe was the dead giveaway.

Bubba steered the beat-up '38 Chevy right up through the open doors of the barn and pulled in behind the black Ford. He let the engine revs drop down to an idle. The car gave a final backfire, belched some blue smoke, shimmied vigorously like a wet dog shaking out its coat, and then quit. Jodell could only laugh. He always wondered if the poor old Chevy had finally died for good or if Bubba had actually turned off the ignition key.

"Hey, Jodell! What's the best dad-goned race car driver in east Tennessee doing acting like a common, ordinary grease monkey?"

It was Joe Banker, talking much too loudly as he

popped open the passenger side and climbed out.

"Shhhhh!" Jodell waved wildly for him to hush his trap. It was past seven o'clock already, so Grandpa had gone to bed and might be able to hear such carryings-on.

"Sorry," Joe whispered, grimacing. "I don't want you trying to steal my job is all."

"You got nothing to worry about. All I'm doing is rebuilding the jets on these carburetors. What are you two birds up to tonight?"

"We decided to catch the movie at the picture show. You wanna go?"

"Naw, I'm almost done, but I want to take the car out for a spin after I'm finished to make sure I have it fixed. Before I have to use it, you know."

"I thought you fixed it yesterday when you adjusted the throttle linkage," Joe said.

Bubba had joined them now, standing there over Jodell, intently watching him work. He had a bottle of soda in one hand and a candy bar in the other, and took a hit of one or the other every few seconds.

"I thought that would solve the miss, but it's still bogging down on me just a little bit whenever I really get into the gas."

"So did you find the problem?"

"Yeah, I had some buildup on one of the jets in this one."

He showed Joe the clogged jet.

"Yep. That little bit of gunk can mess up a good engine, all right." Joe held it to the light so he could see the gummy buildup on the nozzle ends. "You need any help? We can pass on the movie. Bubba here has already seen it three times, haven't you, Bubba? He's just going for the popcorn and Milk Duds."

Bubba offered a grunt through the mouthful of candy bar and took another noisy swig of his soda.

"I could use a little help adjusting the settings when I get it put back on. But I can manage by myself. Y'all go ahead and go if you want."

"We heard the Thompson twins might be going to be at the movies. That's the other reason we were going. They will probably be at the Dairy Dip after the show, too. And you know what? I actually think one of them might have an eye out for ol' Bubba here."

Joe grinned as he pointed a thumb over toward Bubba. Bubba swallowed hard and fought back.

"She does not, Joe. I'm gettin' tired of you picking on me about her all the time. It ain't funny. Y'all leave me alone!"

"What do you mean? Her sister says all she does is ask about you. I think she's sweet on you, Big Bub!"

"She does not."

"Okay, okay," Jodell intervened. "You two kids cut it out. Tell you what. Y'all help me finish this job and we'll ride it over to the drive-in to test her out. And I'll be the judge about Miss Thompson. Fair enough, Bubba?"

"I reckon, but you two had better not start picking on me once we get there. I've had enough of it already from this one."

Bubba pointed at Joe and gave him a mean scowl. Anyone who didn't know the huge man might have been frightened by such an expression, but Joe Banker merely made a face right back and then laughed out loud.

It took another hour to get the car bolted back together. Once both carbs were back on and the linkage reset, Bubba climbed in and fired the car up. The engine turned over on the first crank. Joe manipulated the throttle through the linkage on the side of the carbs' body while Joe worked with the screwdriver to adjust the screws controlling the carburetor settings.

It took about twenty more minutes for them to get the carbs adjusted to the point where they were satisfied. Bubba sat and ran the engine up through the different RPM levels. Jodell and Joe stood and listened to the sweet sound emanating from under the hood. Finally, Jodell signaled Bubba to let the engine drop back to idle.

"Let's get cleaned up and we can head down to the drive-in and get a bite to eat. We can try her out on the way and see if we've got her close."

"Sounds good to me," Joe said.

"Eat?" was all Bubba said.

"What time is it anyway, Jodell?"

"Eight-thirty or thereabouts. Why?"

"The movie ought to be over by the time we get there and the twins may be there. I like working on the car, but I'd just as soon spend the rest of the evening working on a little romance."

"You spend too much time thinking about girls," Jodell said.

"You're just jealous. You need to find a girlfriend for yourself. Then you'd understand why them sweet little things are so important to Bubba and me."

Bubba merely grunted, not sure whether to agree or not.

"All right, I'll take your word for it. I know I've had enough of this for right now. Let's load up and see how she'll run on the way over."

Jodell reached in through the open driver's window and pulled on the door handle. The other two climbed in on the right side, Joe up front, Bubba in the back. Jodell shifted up into reverse and backed the car past Bubba's junk Chevy and out of the barn. He swung around in the driveway and pointed toward the road, coasting down the long drive that led to the main road so as to keep from waking the old folks if he could.

He pushed the column shifter up into first gear and gunned the engine, then released the clutch. The tires completely lost their grip in the loose gravel of the driveway and kicked up a small cloud of dust as they spun their way toward the highway.

"Hang on!" Jodell cried over the roar of the flat-head as he kicked down hard on the gas pedal. "Here we go!"

The rebuilt carbs kicked in, changing the sound of the engine to a high-pitched whine. The force of the acceleration slammed the three of them back in their seats. In a flash, the farmhouse and barn had disappeared from Jodell's rearview mirror.

"Looks like that fixed her," Jodell yelled over the roar of the engine and the cooling wind rushing in through the open windows.

"I'd say so," Joe hollered back. "This thing is really flying."

"Yeah. I wanted to make sure I had it fixed before we go and race it next Sunday. I certainly don't need it hesitating every time I want to give it some gas."

They drove along the rest of the way without talking, just enjoying the breeze they made, the smooth ride of the big car. The ten-mile trip took only a few minutes.

The Dairy Dip Drive-in was the hangout for everyone in Chandler Cove from sixteen to thirty. They came from as far away as twenty miles in any direction, not so much for the food but for the gathering that was inevitable there most evenings.

Jodell claimed the last spot under the canopy. He cut the engine as soon as they left the blacktop and coasted in. Joe adjusted the station playing on the radio so everyone parked around them could tell they were listening to a cool station. It was a signal out of Knoxville and they were playing a song by that new guy, Elvis Presley. The cars on each side of them had the same song cranked up loud.

Carol, the pretty blond carhop, came skating up to the window to take their order.

"Hi, Jodell, Joe, Bubba. How are y'all tonight?"

"Fine, Carol. Y'all been real busy, it looks like," Jodell answered. Joe waved at her from the passenger seat. Bubba was already studying the plastic menu on the pole outside his window with great interest.

"Yeah, things have been really busy. When the picture show let out a little while ago we got the usual rush. What will y'all have anyway?"

They ordered, but Jodell had one more request before she skated away.

"Have you seen the Thompson twins? These two Romeos here are looking for them."

"Really? Well, I saw them pull in a little while ago. I think they have Catherine Holt with them, too. They're probably parked over the other side next to the Rexall. I'll tell them you're looking for them the next time I run an order over that way."

"Thanks, but don't bother," Joe said as he started to get out of the car. "I want to walk over and surprise them myself. Come on, Bubba. Time to work your romantic magic, big 'un!"

Bubba reluctantly crawled out of the backseat, grumbling all the way, but he followed Joe. The pair of them made quite a spectacle as they slowly made their way around to the other side of the drive-in's parking lot through the maze of cars and flock of people. They reminded Jodell of a couple of characters out of the cartoons that were shown before the features at the town theater.

He turned the radio's volume down a bit after they had left and slid down lower in the bench seat, breathing in the warm evening and the aroma of hamburgers on the grill from inside the drive-in. He laid his head back in the seat and closed his eyes, listening to the music that drifted out of the radio's speaker. Despite the hisses and static, the song the deejay was playing caused his mind to wander.

More than ever before, Jodell Lee had become acutely aware that there was a wondrously big world beyond the brushy ridgetops that had fenced him in all his life. A whole wide world out there on the other side of those mountains. Often, lately, he had considered the fact that he was twenty-two years old already, still living with his grandparents, still running moonshine, with no more plans for the future than old Bubba had.

He was bright enough to know that no matter how good a whiskey runner he was, he would forever be pushing his luck. One dark night the odds would catch up with him, and so would the Feds, whether through error, breakdown, or simple bad luck. The money was good, and could be even better if he branched out and hooked up with some of the more serious moonshiners. But even then, it would not, could not, last forever.

Jodell had used his earnings over the last couple of years buying up patches of land that bounded the forty acres he had inherited from his father. He always paid cash for the land. Someday there might be enough of it to actually be called a farm. And he supposed he would eventually be willed a portion of Grandpa's place, but that would be split so many ways it wouldn't much count. And he still wasn't necessarily sold on the idea of scratching a living out of the rocky ground for the rest of his life, pulling moldy tobacco leaves or wormy corn out of the soil for some semblance of a living.

As the love songs on the radio drifted lazily from one to another, Jodell watched the starry sky out his windshield and thought again about how desperately his life needed a change. He had never seen any of those stars up there from any angle other than the one he had right there in Chandler Cove, Tennessee. Shoot, he had never been more than a hundred and fifty miles from this very spot in his life.

All Jodell knew or cared about were his friends and family, fast cars, whiskey running, and farming, and in that exact order. And as much as they all meant to him, he felt empty somehow, as if he were missing his spot in a big parade that would soon pass him by. He might never have a chance to join it again.

Carol tapped him on the arm and brought him out of his deep thoughts.

"Got y'all's order, Jodell."

He rolled the window up a couple of inches so she could hook the tray. The other two were still nowhere to be seen, so Jodell reached deep into his jeans pocket and paid for the entire order. No girls were going to come between Bubba Baxter and a platter of food for long. He and Joe would be back soon enough.

He watched Carol's attractive backside as she skated off, then reached for his own shake and burger.

Two lunches or not, he was suddenly, ravenously hungry.

The crowd had begun to spill out of the lot, the younger kids already hustling off to beat their curfews, the movies over for the night at the theater next door. As he chewed, he watched the mini traffic jam in front of the drive-in as the exodus home began. Or at least, the closest there ever was to a traffic jam in Chandler Cove.

That was when he saw two people coming his way. Joe Banker. And someone else. It certainly was not Bubba Baxter. As they passed under the neon sign at the front of the drive-in, he could see it was Catherine Holt that Joe had in tow. She stopped fifteen feet away and shyly leaned against one of the canopy supports, pretending to watch the stars, while Joe came on and leaned in the passenger window. He gave Jodell a sly smile and a knowing wink.

Jodell Lee felt exactly as he had at the pool room that afternoon when he had first realized that he was being hustled by the two strangers.

"All right, Joe. Save me the con job. What's going on?"

Bubba had not come back for his food either, and that was even more unsettling.

"Oh, not much, Cuz."

"What do you mean, not much? Bubba's food's getting cold, he's missing in action, and you show up with Catherine Holt tagging along like a sheepdog. I'd say something's most assuredly up."

"Actually, Bubba's doing just fine, thank you very much. I think Susan Thompson actually is sweet on him. They're over there right now, sharing a double malted in the backseat of the car. No kidding."

Jodell tried to imagine such a thing but was having

a hard time dialing in that picture. The Thompson twins weren't identical. Betty was drop-dead beautiful. Susan was, to put it politely, a full-figured woman. But even then, it was a stretch to imagine Bubba Baxter in a romantic encounter.

"Well, I don't believe it. But if it's so, what's in it for you?" Jodell inquired, still suspicious about what Joe was trying to pull.

"Susan and Betty want me and Bubba to ride up on the mountain with them, but there is one little problem."

"Oh, no!" Jodell spurted. Now he knew where this arrangement was leading. "No way. Absolutely no way."

"You don't even know what I'm asking yet," Joe said, his face split in a big grin. He turned from the window just enough to gave Catherine a thumbs-up, then a "wait a minute" sign. "Look, all you have to do is give her a ride home. Catherine's a real sweet girl, just a little bit on the shy side. You don't want to hurt her feelings."

"Damn, Joe! If anybody saw me, at my age, with a high school senior, I'd never be able to live it down."

"Cuz, you're just giving her a ride home as a favor to me, your favorite cousin, and for your very best friend, old Bubba, who may not ever in his lifetime have such a chance present itself again. You ain't marryin' the girl, for God sakes! Besides, it's practically on your way home."

And that was that.

Catherine Holt lived fifteen miles up the county road toward Green Mountain. That was not on Jodell's way home by any stretch. But Joe didn't give him a chance to argue against his faultless logic. He jerked his head out of the window and waved vigorously for Catherine to come on over to Jodell's car.

Joe opened the front passenger door and waved her in with a grand sweep of his arm, like a prince offering her a seat in his coach. She demurely slid in, pretending not to notice that Jodell had his head down on the steering wheel, his eyes closed.

"Catherine Holt, you know Jodell Lee. Jodell, you remember Catherine. Y'all had the same English teacher at Consolidated, didn't you? Old Jodell did real good in English, didn't you? You already speaking the language and all?" Joe babbled as he leaned on the door, not caring whether he made any sense or not.

"Hi, Catherine," Jodell mumbled, mostly to the steering wheel.

"Hello," she said quietly to the glove box.

"Now, you young folks have a real good time," Joe said, then slammed shut the car door, slapped the right fender as he scrambled around the front of the car, took two steps toward the far side of the drive-in, and then stopped, turned around, came back, and grabbed his and Bubba's food off the tray. He disappeared into the tangle of cars in the drive-in lot.

The silence was painfully awkward inside the car. Jodell had had a few dates over the years. No guy as naturally good-looking as he was could have ever avoided it. But what with school, chores on the farm, working on the cars, and the weekly whiskey runs, he had never had the time to get serious about anyone. And, he had to admit, he still felt a bit uncomfortable around girls.

"Look, I'm sorry about the setup," he finally said.

"Don't apologize. It's not your fault. Why don't

you just take me on home and you can go on about your business?"

"I know you don't want to be here, stuck with—"

"Jodell Lee, if you don't want to take me home, just say so and I can walk to that pay phone right over yonder and call my daddy to come get me."

Her eyes flashed in the light from the neon outside. She looked him straight in the eye and he could see the concern in her face. She was, he immediately noticed, beautiful. Her hair was sandy blond, long and wavy, and her eyes were deep and blue. They could cut right through a man.

"Whoa! I didn't mean—"

"That is, if you don't mind . . ." She was rummaging through the purse on her lap, but then quickly stopped and dropped her head. "If you don't mind loaning me a dime. I gave Susan Thompson the last penny I had to buy that milk shake for Bubba."

Then they could hold it back no longer. In unison, they erupted into deep, natural laughter. She finally turned on the seat to face him and touched his arm.

"Jodell, I do really appreciate you agreeing to give me a ride home, even if Joe Banker forced you into it. I didn't want to be in the way back there. Susan and Betty really like Joe and Bubba a lot. Joe said you wouldn't mind giving me a ride home and I actually believed him."

"Aw, you know I don't mind. I was just afraid you would think I had put those two up to something."

"You mean you didn't?" she asked. She was smiling at him now, teasing.

"And what if I did?"

They laughed again and Jodell was feeling better about the situation already. So what if somebody saw them? She was surely eighteen. And in the mountains, an unmarried eighteen-year-old girl was already an "old maid" in the eyes of the old-timers.

"Can I confess something, Jodell? I have wanted to talk with you for a long time, to get to know you, but I just didn't know how to go about it without looking like some silly high school girl."

"Well, if you don't have to get home right this red-hot minute, then let's talk."

They shared the rest of his fries and he ordered both of them fresh cherry colas. The radio still played mostly romantic songs, perfect for a date night. They talked easily now, their shyness fading, getting to know each other, and Jodell soon felt as natural with her as he might have with any of his old friends from high school.

By the time they headed the car out of the lot and up the highway toward her house, she had slid over on the seat near him and his arm was around her shoulders when he didn't have to shift gears. Jodell drove as slowly as he ever had, in no particular hurry at all to drop her off.

The moon overhead was full and the warm breeze through the windows of the car brought the scent of honeysuckle and sweet shrub and fresh-turned earth. Jodell couldn't tell if it was the moon, the fragrant air, or the soft feel of her body next to him, but something was making him strangely weak and dizzy.

She must have felt it, too. When he walked her slowly up the front steps to the porch of her house, she still wanted to talk, and seemed reluctant to leave him to go inside. But then, when she finally told him she had to go, she suddenly turned, gave him a long, natural hug, and then a quick kiss on the lips when they parted.

"Thank you again, Jodell."

"Don't mention it. Uh, Catherine? They change shows at the theater Friday night. You want to go with me?"

"Absolutely!"

And it was done.

When Jodell pulled the Ford out of her driveway, he was feeling something he had never felt before. He waited until he was a good mile from her house, then he kicked down hard on the gas pedal and yelled at the top of his lungs as the engine growled immediately in response to his touch. He pushed the car hard through the turns, over the rises, down the straight chutes, loving the coordinated throb and pulse of the machine as it worked beneath him.

The exhilaration of the evening's events had not worn off by the time he got home. He parked the car back inside its room in the barn shop. But he knew there was no point in his going up to bed yet. He didn't think he would ever sleep again. It might break the spell Catherine had cast over him.

He settled down in the swing on the front porch and rocked gently in the cool, damp night air. A couple of doves were cooing at each other across the valley, and he smiled at their flirting. A lonely dog was howling at the moon, its echo eerie and haunting against the mountains.

And somewhere, far off, Jodell could hear the deep-throated grumble of a souped-up car, its driver power-shifting, working his way quickly through the gears as it gained momentum on some dark, deserted straight-away. Some whiskey runner, leaving the Feds in his wake? Or merely another car lover, letting his baby stretch and breathe on an empty mountain road?

It didn't matter. Jodell Lee realized then that things were about to change for him. He still had the race flyer in his pocket. And he could still smell Catherine's perfume on his shirt.

Right then, he didn't know which he looked forward to more.

Catherine on Friday?

The race on Sunday?

GETTING READY TO GO RACING

Friday night had been a blur for Jodell Lee, and then his Saturday had finished completely wearing him out. He had so much to do to get ready for the race the next day and no time to get it done, considering all his grandfather had planned for him to do. It was almost as if the old man suspected what Jodell was up to and was making sure he wouldn't have the time or the strength to pull off his mischief.

But there was no way.

The night before, at the last minute, he and Catherine had decided to leave Chandler Cove and drive over to Kingsport for dinner at a place a little nicer than the Dairy Dip. They could actually park and go inside and sit at a table to eat, and use real forks and spoons.

Then they had seen a picture show in a theater

there that was much different from the old movie house in Chandler Cove. This one had real live air conditioning instead of big, noisy box fans rumbling away down front so loud you could hardly hear the sound of the picture. There was also a nice, new screen there, one without holes that you could see the moon and stars through. Even then, when it was over, Jodell hardly knew what the movie had been about or who its stars were.

The evening was perfect. Catherine didn't seem to notice the stubborn grease and dirt he had not been able to dig from under his fingernails, nor to mind his palms, rough and callused from handling the twine-tied hay bales. She held his hand throughout the picture anyway, and she had her head on his shoulder most of the last half.

He let her shift gears for him on the way back and laughed with her when she couldn't find third. Then he took her on a quick drive along one of the mountain roads he negotiated when he delivered whiskey. But, of course, he never mentioned to her how it was that he knew how to take the curves and cutbacks so well.

Finally, they sat and talked in her driveway for a good hour, until her daddy finally flipped the yellow porch light on and off to let her know it was past time to come inside. This time her good-night kiss and their parting embrace lasted much longer, and the feel of her lips on his, her body against him, followed him all the way home.

When Jodell finally got back to the farmhouse, he was so keyed up he couldn't find sleep for at least another hour or so. Next morning, Grandma had to stomp upstairs, bang on his door, and threaten him with no breakfast to finally get him out of bed.

"It's near about six-thirty, Jodell Bob Lee. Your granddaddy's already out and gone, and I'm fixin' to throw these biscuits to the dogs if you don't come get 'em!"

Jodell groaned, stretched, shook his head, and finally rolled sluggishly from the bed, still tired from the late night, still dreamy from the date with Catherine. He doubted if she would actually throw out his breakfast, but he knew he was in serious trouble when Grandma used his entire name when she fussed at him. Nobody else ever called him Jodell Bob.

Then he'd remembered that he had another reason for living this day. He couldn't wait until he could finish his day's work and start to get the car ready for the race tomorrow. But he'd known he would have to postpone that for a while, although he was certainly in no mood to string fence or cut hay alongside his granddad.

Especially if Grandpa stayed in such a foul mood all day long.

"You up there gettin' your beauty sleep and these old heifers will be out this fence and halfway to Bristol 'fore I can get it fixed by my lonesome," Grandpa growled.

"Sorry. Guess I overslept."

"Little wonder. Out burnin' up gas and usin' up tire rubber till daybreak. You don't want to draw attention from the Feds. They see you out late and they might think you're doing a run. You know that."

Oh, Grandpa, if you only knew, Jodell thought.

Then he pitched to and grabbed one end of the strand of new barbed wire his grandfather was stretching between two rickety, termite-eaten fence posts.

With only a short stop for some beans and cornbread at lunch, the two men finished the fence job, hauled in a load of fresh-cut hay for the mules, mended some bad wood on the back side of the barn, and sawed up a tree that had come down in a storm a few weeks back. The firewood would come in handy in a few months and they had to clear the tractor road out to the back forty that the tree had blocked.

Even Grandpa was ready for quitting time when the sun had finally dropped too low for them to see to work anymore. He and Jodell retired to the back porch with glasses of iced tea while Grandma put a big supper on the table for them.

Jodell had drawn a bucket of water from the well, poured it into one of Grandma's big porcelain basins, and they washed up in the cold water, not even bothering to heat it first. The lye soap cleaned just fine anyway and the scratchy suds actually felt good.

The day's work and the meager lunch had left both men famished, and they did serious damage to the wonderful down-home spread that had been laid out before them. Grandma Lee knew how to cook and she loved to do it for her family. There were no quick meals for her, nothing from a box or a can. Everything was whipped up from scratch and with fresh ingredients from their garden or the farmers' market in town. Tonight there were green beans, greens, potato salad, sliced tomatoes, cornbread, and fried pork chops.

As they ate, Jodell and Grandpa talked about the day's accomplishments and made plans for Monday's chores. Of course, there would be no work on Sunday except for feeding the animals.

"I think I'm going to do some more work on the Ford tonight," Jodell slipped in. They never called it "the whiskey-running car" in front of Grandma. She knew exactly what it was used for, but it was still best not to say the words where she could hear them.

"What's wrong with 'er? You got the carburetor fixed, didn't you?"

"Yes, sir. She's running fine. I'm just not happy with the suspension. She didn't ride like I like her to with the load the other night."

Grandma gave him a sharp look but didn't say anything.

"You need any help?"

"No, sir. Joe's coming by directly. Probably Bubba, too."

"Well, good. It's near about my bedtime anyhow. I may listen to a little of the Grand Ole Opry on the radio, then I'll turn in."

Jodell couldn't help feeling guilty. He had half lied to his grandfather and certainly had not told him the full story. And sneaking the car out to the race tomorrow would be a major transgression.

Jodell excused himself as soon as he had finished off a huge slice of cinnamon apple pie. He was stiff from the day's work, drowsy from the late night the night before, and sluggish from the huge meal he had just finished. But he knew he had a lot of work to do to get the car ready and he was still anxious to get started.

The sun had disappeared for sure now, lightning bugs were winking at him from the woods, and the crickets were already singing like a choir when he finally swung back the creaking barn doors.

Jodell flipped on the switch to the lights and walked into the barn shop. The Ford sat in the middle of the shop on the hard-packed dirt floor, as if she had been waiting there patiently for him to finish all the other things he had had to do first. He grabbed some tools off the big workbench and dragged the floor jack over next to the car. Then he set to work.

First, he pulled out the backseat and took off anything else he decided was not absolutely necessary, all in an effort to lighten up the heavy car as much as he could. He removed everything from the trunk and put in a couple of spare tires. Next, he took his gauge and carefully checked the air pressure in each tire. He would need the pressure to be slightly lower than normal so he would get as much traction as possible in what would certainly be powdery dirt in the field. But it should not be so low as to allow the tire to roll over onto its sidewall. Then he might pinch the inner tube and the tire would go flat. No way could he win a race on a flat tire!

He also fashioned a crude seat belt out of a couple of old army web belts Grandpa had been saving for some possible use. Thank goodness Grandpa never threw anything away. These would work perfectly. Jodell ran the makeshift belts between the seat bottom and back and bolted them to the seat mounting bracket on the floorboard. That connected directly to the car's frame and wasn't going anywhere. Unless the whole rest of the car did, too, of course. He left the length of the belts just long enough to fit snugly around his waist when clipped together. Hopefully the extrawide belts would give him plenty of support without cutting him in half.

Once he finished, he sat in the car and fastened them in front of him. The fit seemed perfect. He figured the belts would be comfortable, yet secure enough to keep him in place as the car slid around the tight corners time and time again, with the centrifugal force trying to yank him right out of the seat. And if he should happen to hit something solid, it would keep him from flying right through the windshield and across the hood.

In case of such a thing happening, the fine set of seat belts would still leave him healthy enough for Grandpa to strangle!

With that job finished, Jodell checked the old railroad clock on the barn wall. Where the heck was Joe?

His cousin was supposed to be rounding up a riding helmet he could use. But there were two things you could always count on: if it thunders, it usually rains; and Joe Banker would be late for his own funeral. But tonight, more than ever, Jodell needed Joe to be there. He needed the help. And if the truth be known, he needed even more to have Joe's mouth, his confidence, to push him to go ahead with this crazy racing idea.

Jodell still wasn't afraid. And he was stone confident that he could outdrive anybody else he might come up against. But he was still skittish about taking his grandfather's car without permission and risking something so important to both of them.

It was already an hour past the time when Joe had said he would be there.

Next on the list, Jodell wanted to change out a couple of the car's shock absorbers, but he would need Joe's help to do that job. At Joe's suggestion, a few days before he had picked up a pair of used shocks that had come off an old army truck. They had cost all of a dollar apiece at the military surplus store in Johnson City, but they felt good and stiff. That was exactly what they needed.

But it was that necessary stiffness that would make them so very hard to install. And besides that, this racing setup thing was all new to Jodell. He was counting on Joe to make sure he was seeing to everything he needed to.

It was already past nine o'clock when Joe Banker finally pulled down the driveway in his old Plymouth. And for once, he was all by himself. Jodell could not believe he didn't have Bubba with him. The two of them were usually joined at the hip.

"Hey there, Jodell! What's up?"

He acted as if it were just past suppertime, when he said he'd be there. No apology for being late. No explanation offered.

"Where on earth have you been? I need some help with these shocks and it's gettin' pretty damn late to be trying to get this thing ready for tomorrow."

"No problem, Cuz. We'll get 'er done in no time and still have time for one of them cold beers you promised. I had to run over to Kingsport and eat supper with Mother and Dad. I couldn't get out of it. Specially since I couldn't tell 'em me and you had to work on Grandpa's car so we could race a bunch of Carolina whiskey runners in it tomorrow."

"Well, I guess you were stuck at that. Where's Bubba? I don't think I've ever seen you on a Saturday night without him . . . unless you were on a date."

"You ready for this? Bubba is the one out on a date this time!"

"Uh-uh! Next thing, you're gonna tell me hell just froze over!"

"I kid you not. That Susan Thompson has done latched on to old Bubba like an old snapping turtle, and I don't think she'll let go, even if it does thunder."

Bubba Baxter on a date! Things *were* changing!

"By the way, Joe. Where's your Thompson twin?"

"Uh-oh. You caught me. She did go to dinner with me and the folks tonight. They really like her. I think

Mother is already composing the wedding invitations." There was something in his tone that said Joe was not totally joking. "I did tell her I had to help you with the car for tomorrow. She won't tell anybody. That was the only way I could get her home early enough so I could get over here and help you out."

"Speaking of which, did you plan on working on the car in your good clothes?"

"Naw, I meant to change, but I didn't have time. You got something I can borrow?"

"There's a pair of Grandpa's overalls on the hook over yonder. Let's get this thing up on the jack or they'll be through racing before we can even get out there."

Once at it, the two men dived into the job and worked laboriously for the next hour and a half, crawling under and over the Ford. Getting the old shocks off had been easy, just a matter of jacking the car up and unbolting them. Putting the truck shocks on turned into a whole lot more work than they had first thought. Try as they might, the springs just wouldn't allow them to fit into their mounting brackets. They finally wound up and stretched the springs a quarter of an inch with a spacer to allow the shocks to attach. They then drove a couple of small wedges between the springs. The two of them were soaked with sweat by the time they had finished the job.

"Whew, that was more work than I signed up for," Jodell grunted, wiping his grimy face with a rag from his back pocket. "This race car driving ain't near as glamorous as I had it pictured."

"And the pay ain't nothing to write home about neither!" Joe agreed, with huge drops of sweat rolling down his dirt-streaked cheeks.

Jodell rummaged around in an ice chest that was sitting on the workbench. He had bought something else the other day in Johnson City besides the shock absorbers.

"You ready for a cold beer, Joe?"

"Yessir. Reckon you could come over here and pour it right down my gullet while I just lay here and swaller?"

"Just make sure you take the bottles with you and dump 'em somewhere. Grandpa and them find out we had beer out here in his barn and they'd take a switch to me like I was eight years old and stealing old man Clinton's crab apples again."

It had always seemed odd to Jodell that his grandfather, who made decent money distilling and selling hard corn liquor, would not hear of any other alcohol being brought onto his place. It was a fact, though, that the old man never even drank his own brew, beyond tasting it for quality and bite.

Joe downed most of a bottle in one gulp. It almost took his breath.

"Ahhhhh! Man, that's good and cold!"

"I told you they would be."

The two of them sat quietly, drinking their beers, resting, cooling themselves in what little cross breeze found its way through the barn. Jodell finally spoke.

"Joe, you still think we've got any chance at all tomorrow?"

"You think I'd be spending my Saturday night out here in this dusty old barn, crawling around under some old car, sweatin' and gruntin' with the likes of you when I could just as well be up on the mountain, doing some heavy-duty smooching with my girl, all if I didn't think we could win the damned race?"

Jodell laughed. That was exactly what he needed

to hear. He took another swig of the cold beer, but then something caught his eye. He looked again and there was no doubt about it. The angle at which the car was sitting seemed odd somehow.

"Look at the car, Joe. Have I got looped on half a bottle of beer or is it leaning to one side?"

"Well, I'll be. The damn thing is cocked over to one side. Grab that tape measure and let's take a look at it."

A quick measure on each side from the ground to the bottom of the door confirmed what was obvious. The car was cocked over toward the driver's side by a little over two inches. Jodell pushed and shoved on the car's top from the driver's side and it felt extra stiff and unyielding. It was usually top-heavy, the suspension mushy, and it would feel as if the car could easily roll over.

Both men knew that the top roll of the car was a characteristic of '50-model Fords. They came from the factory with soft shocks because most buyers wanted a smooth ride on the highway. Of course, that cost a considerable amount of stability when it came to the handling. The body would tend to roll over on the frame in tight corners at high speed, and that caused it to push away from the direction of the turn. And that was a definite disadvantage if the driver was trying to navigate a tight turn on a narrow dirt race track.

"We done good, Jodell," Joe finally said, and he was smiling broadly.

"What do you mean?"

Joe pointed to the hiked-up right side of the car and explained that the recycled truck shocks and the unintended tilt they gave to the car's body should help stabilize it significantly in a race. And that one way or another, they would know for certain tomorrow whether it helped enough or not.

"Looks like we done lucked into the perfect setup for this old buggy," Joe said, and took another satisfied gurgle of his beer. " 'Less they run this old race the wrong way around that track, we done got ourselves a running machine."

"Well, maybe so. I just hope it don't drive as cockeyed as it looks, though. We might get ourselves laughed right off the track."

"Hell, it's gonna drive better than 'all right.' I just hope it's got enough motor. Them Carolina boys will have some hot buggies. They spend every dime they got on their cars. And you know them 'shine runners are about as crazy as a bessie bug when they climb in behind that steering wheel."

" 'Preciate you building up my confidence, Joe. We built this engine plenty fast, though. You know I've done tested it lots of times in 'races' a damn sight more important than the one tomorrow. But the one that wins tomorrow will do it by outdriving and outhandling the others. It won't necessarily be the fastest car."

Joe had leaned back against the side of the Ford. He wiped more sweat from his face with the bib of the overalls and held the cool bottle to his forehead. Then he gave Jodell his most serious look.

"You silly son of a bitch. Everybody knows you can outdrive anybody in the state. We can beat anybody they can bring in tomorrow."

"Beat anybody, huh? I like the sound of that." Jodell made his voice go deep like some imagined public address announcer. " 'And the winner is Jodell Lee! Come on up and get your nice trophy and your fifty dollars, Jodell.' Yes, sir. I like the sound of that!"

Joe stood up then and used his beer bottle for a pretend microphone.

" 'And let's not forget Jodell's fine mechanic, who is, as we all know, totally responsible for all his success out there today, the brilliant and handsome Mr. Joseph Luke Banker! Joseph, stand up and take a bow!' "

Then another thought occurred to Jodell.

"You know what, Joe? I believe I know somebody that can beat you and me both, and ol' Bubba thrown in for good measure."

Joe looked at him sideways. "Who's that, Cuz?"

"Grandpa Lee. He'll whip all our butts, then start all over again at the beginning and whip some more if he finds out what we're doing with his whiskey car."

"Aw, quit saying that. He ain't gonna find out. Shoot, look at that old clock. It's done about midnight. Let's get these tools stowed and let me get going. I promised Betty I'd call her up later, and the only phone I can use is the pay phone down next to the Dairy Dip."

"Lordy mercy! Henpecked already and you ain't even hitched yet. I'm really ashamed of you, Joe Banker, lettin' all us free and single men down like you doin'!"

Joe grabbed up a crescent wrench and tossed it at his cousin, just missing his head. Then he chased Jodell all around the barn with a nasty paw full of dirty axle grease.

GOING FAST, TURNING LEFT

Sunday morning showed up bright and balmy, a clear Appalachian summer morning, but threatening to become a stifling, hot mountain afternoon before it was over with. There was only enough dawning breeze to tickle the curtains on Jodell's upstairs bedroom window.

He had been awake early, since just after daylight. No matter that he tried to roll back over and doze some more. He was wired, ready. But he knew if he climbed out of bed too early, his grandparents would be suspicious. Grandma would sulk because Jodell would be missing both Sunday school and church and wouldn't be around for Sunday dinner. That was when she usually outdid herself for any and all the relatives who would show up to eat the overloaded table full of food she would prepare for them.

He was right. Grandma did sulk. But Jodell came up with a vague excuse over breakfast, something about having work to do on the car and him and Bubba having to run up to Kingsport to help a friend with something. Grandma must have thought the "friend" could possibly be female, and Jodell didn't try to dissuade her. She was convinced he was going to end up a miserable old bachelor and never give her any great-grandbabies to rock and spoil and spoon-feed pure, thick cream off the top of fresh cow's milk. All those things she had done for Jodell, of course.

Time was wasting for her grandson. After all, he was already twenty-two, had a little plot of land assembled, yet was no closer to getting married than he had been when he had first graduated from Consolidated. The only thing he lacked was a potential wife.

"I wish you'd wait till after preaching to go off, Jodell Bob."

"We need to get an early start, Granny. Maybe I can go to Training Union tonight."

"You work so hard, darlin'. Eat you an extra helping of that sorghum syrup and biscuit. You need the energy."

A twinge of guilt shot right through him like an arrow. Lying to his own poor old grandma! Lord, he thought, I hope that doesn't jinx the whole thing.

Grandpa was not so easy a sale.

"Thought y'all finished up on that car last night."

"Not quite. We're not entirely satisfied with the handling yet."

"Pick at a sore and it'll never get well," he observed gruffly.

Jodell forced himself to eat a big breakfast. There would probably not be time for lunch, and he wasn't sure there would be room in his stomach for any food anyway. The butterflies had it filled up already.

He hoped his grandparents would be gone to church before Bubba got there. They had not exactly gotten together on their stories, and old Bubba was just as likely to pipe right up and tell them they were all going fender-crumpling racing as not, even if they had managed to work it all out ahead of time.

Jodell pulled open the big barn doors and gave the car a long, loving look. Somehow, she seemed poised, ready to take off all by herself, to start circling at some breakneck speed, clinging to the track as if she were on runners. He grinned to himself as he reached through the open driver's window and pulled on the lever to open the door. It swung open easily, inviting him to slide in behind the wheel.

He stuck the key in the ignition and gave it a turn to the "on" position. Then he gave a firm, quick push on the starter button and the engine roared to life immediately. Hardly a day went by that he didn't check the battery and add electrolyte if it was even a notch low. He shoved in the clutch, pulled down the gearshift lever, and felt the gears mesh smoothly. Carefully he eased off on the clutch while giving the engine just a sip of gasoline. The heavy, powerful car moved slowly out the doorway, into the drive that led up to the front of the barn.

Jodell smiled at the way the bright sunlight seemed to be absorbed by the deep, shiny, black surface of the car's skin. He had waxed and shined her until she mirrored the trees and sky overhead. It stood to reason to him that a clean car might slip through the wind a fraction faster than a dirty one.

He shut off the motor, climbed out, and used the bright morning sun to light the way as he inspected everything he could see under the hood. Then he stretched out on an old horse blanket from the barn as he checked beneath the car. Jodell ran through the exact mental checklist he always ticked off, one item at a time, before he started out on each and every moonshine run. Each critical system on the car was eyeballed, shaken, twisted, gauged, felt, and thumped, from the engine and drive train to the suspension and steering, oil and water, belts and hoses, grease seals and tire pressure.

Jodell knew he could help manufacture some of his own luck if he simply took the right precautions. It worked in whiskey running. It stood to reason it would be the same way in racing.

Jodell was back underneath the car again, checking for oil or grease-seal leaks for the third time, when he heard Bubba's old junker coming, even though he was still a good half mile away. He seemed to be in an unusual hurry. It normally took the promise of barbecue or homemade ice cream to get Bubba Baxter to hustle the old car along that much. As the Chevy wheeled recklessly into the narrow drive, the tires screeched dangerously at the sharp turn, then flung rock and dust behind as the car hurried up the driveway, coming much too fast for the rutted dirt road.

Bubba slid the car to a smoky, sideways stop underneath a shade tree next to the barn. There was the slam of a door and the hurried crunch of feet in the gravel of the drive, heading for the Ford.

"You going to fill in them trenches you dug all the way up the road?" Jodell asked as he slid from under the car and climbed to his feet. He was thankful his grandparents had left for church already.

"Sorry," Bubba said sheepishly, watching his feet shift nervously. "Shoot, Jodell, I can't help it. I'm about as excited about this race as I've ever been anything in my whole life. I can't wait!"

"I know how you feel, but you'll miss the whole thing for sure if you're upside down in some ditch somewhere. What time you got?"

Bubba looked at his old pocket watch.

"A little after nine, I think. Or is it a little before ten? Let's see, this thing loses two minutes a day and I set 'er last time on Wednesday, and now it says—"

"Look, the race is supposed to start at one, but I want to see if maybe they'll let us ride around the track some and check it out and see how the car does. I damn sure would like to get a feel for how she runs out there in that oval before we have to take on somebody else side by side in a real race."

"You really think they'll let us practice?"

"I don't know. I sure hope so. I need at least a couple of laps to make sure I have a good feel for the car and the track. This running around in a circle on purpose is going to be a new experience for me."

"Why? You run on dirt roads all the time around here, and with something a lot worse chasing you than some good old boys from 'crost the mountain in their daddies' cars. You think you can't run on this track? I ain't never seen a road you couldn't outdrive anybody else on."

"Bubba, all by myself except for a revenuer or two out there on a county highway in the dark of night is one thing. But going real fast and turning left all the time with all the other cars crowding in on you on all sides is a whole other breed of coon dog."

"Aw, Jodell, you can run laps around anybody else they is!"

Jodell appreciated Bubba's confidence. The big man always told anybody who would listen that Jodell was the best driver in that whole end of the state, whether it be wet, dry, dirt, asphalt, county road, or state highway.

"From your mouth to God's ear," was all Jodell said.

It was finally time to go, and Jodell was thankful. All the impatient waiting and nervous fidgeting with the car were about to get the best of him. Bubba climbed back into the dented hulk of his old Chevy while Jodell slipped back beneath the Ford's wheel. The engine kicked over again on the first turn and he once again put her in gear gently, almost like a caress. The flathead V8 rumbled reassuringly in response. She seemed tired of waiting and ready to move, too.

A cloud of whitish gray smoke belched from the back end of Bubba's car, and that let Jodell know he had managed to cheat the odds once again and get the old wreck to start for him. Bubba sat there, allowing the engine to smooth out on its own. He knew that when the Chevy's motor was hot, he had to let the smoke die down before driving or risk the car vapor-locking and leaving him stranded. And this was no morning to be stranded with a dead vehicle.

The two cars rolled down the driveway and onto the highway in tandem, Jodell leading the way. He sped up, then slowed down, listening carefully to the changing pitches in the sound of the engine like some choirmaster listening for flat notes and off-pitch singing. He still wasn't satisfied that he'd selected the proper jetting on the carburetors, but he knew it was probably too late to do anything about it now. There would be no carb rebuilding out there in the dusty field at Meyer's farm.

Jodell hardly noticed the scenery or anything else on the drive out. He was too busy listening for slight

misses in the engine, feeling for even the tiniest hint
of unresponsiveness in the steering. He imagined all
types of odd noises, squeaks, grumbles, and vibrations.

Finally he slapped the wheel and laughed out loud.

"This race don't start pretty quick, I'm gonna have
myself a nervous breakdown," he said to the disc
jockey who was chattering away on the radio.

Forty minutes later they were lining up behind a
queue of trucks and cars climbing a narrow side road
that led to the top of a tree-fringed hill. Cornstalks lay
at odd angles on each side of the road, left over from
the previous year. No one seemed to have been doing
any farming here lately, though. Weeds choked the
rows, and crows swooped and played at will. But the
road they were on was well graded and newly cherted.

Finally, they pulled into the freshly cut entrance to
the new track that had obviously been bulldozed from
a pasture on the hilltop. A shiny new fence surrounded the recent construction, and it was clear the
dirt was freshly turned. This had been a much
rougher track the year before, mostly a field beaten
down by the few amateur heats that had been run on
it, and the roadway leading to it had been not much
more than a rutted farm road, half washed away in
places. Obviously someone had put a lot of work and
money into upgrading it for this year.

Jodell was pleased to see that a large wooden
grandstand had been added down one of the straightaways. Spectators who wanted to could sit up high
and see the entire track from a position down the long
front stretch and along the start-finish line. Red,
white, and blue flags flew from posts above the growing crowd, festive streamers waved in the sun all
around the track, speakers were hung at regular in-
tervals for the public address system and were now

playing country music and the occasional Elvis or Little Richard song, and there appeared to be an actual press box set up atop a phalanx of telephone poles for reporters who might want to cover the races. There was also a covered concession stand with smoke pouring out a pipe over a grill, and a row of rest rooms were lined up on the back side of the grandstand.

It looked like a real, honest-to-God racetrack!

A couple of kids stood just inside the entrance, collecting the admission charge of fifty cents a head. The spectators parked outside the fence in a big field where the cornstalks had been cleared. The lot was already half full and a constant train of cars and trucks poured in even though it was several hours before the first heat was scheduled to go off.

Those who wanted to compete were waved on inside the fence and directed to a point just outside of the track's first turn. There were already twelve or fifteen cars sitting in this roped-off "garage" area when Jodell pulled the Ford over that way to join them. He could see a surprising number of spectators had already found their way to the grandstand, staked out the best spots, and opened their coolers and picnic baskets.

The sun was already hot, the air calm, but the quiet on the hilltop was occasionally broken by the staccato roar of a popping, full-throated, unmuffled engine someone would crank up and race. Sections of the grandstand would erupt in cheers every time, and whoever had cranked the engine would goose it, milking the cheers.

Bubba followed Jodell into the garage area, a small cloud of dust following them as they crossed the already worn route across the field.

"Welcome, neighbor," a man in bright red overalls

told Jodell as he pulled in to the roped-off area. "This here's your release you gotta sign before we can let you run. If you gotta make your mark, you better let me witness it right now, 'cause I'm gonna be busier than a one-legged man in a butt-kickin' contest directly."

Jodell simply signed the paper without even reading it. There was too much going on around him to take time to read all that tiny print.

The man in red overalls waved him on in and directed him to a parking spot. Bubba pulled to a stop beside him. The big man's eyes were wide, his face flushed with excitement.

"Lord, Jodell! You ever seen anything like this here?"

Jodell had been to a University of Tennessee football game down in Knoxville once, and that was about the only thing he could compare to all the color and people and noise and excitement on that high hilltop that Sunday morning. Everything seemed to be in motion at once, and the smells of oil smoke, gasoline, food, and hot dust were as intoxicating as anybody's home brew.

"It is something, all right, Bub. Let's get everything unloaded and then we'll see what we can find out about practicing."

Bubba took an old army blanket from his trunk and spread it on the ground behind the Chevy. They unloaded the toolbox and spare tires from the Ford, then the floor jack, a few spare parts, and a couple of jerry cans of water they had loaded in the Chevy. Last came the cooler and a croaker sack full of rags.

They each took a drink of icy water from a jug in the cooler and struck up a conversation with a couple of men who walked by and who appeared to be officials of some kind. They learned that the new track had been built by one of the Meyer boys. He had accidentally gotten into the race-promotion business while in the army back during the war. He'd volunteered to help a friend promote races on the West Coast after he had been discharged from the army. It had not taken him long to see how much money could be made from a bunch of loud cars running around in circles in the desert sand east of Los Angeles. Meyer had realized the business certainly beat dirt farming, his only other choice when he had returned home to take over his late father's place. And he knew such a track should do well here in the Tennessee mountains, a place where cars and speed were next to church and family in the grand pecking order of things.

Unfortunately, the men explained that there would be no practicing allowed since they didn't want to tear up the track before serious racing began. There would be heats that would be run before everybody raced in the main event. It appeared that Jodell's first competitive heat would have to be his first chance to learn what he could do, what the car could do.

That was when Jodell noticed Bubba was no longer paying any attention to their conversation at all. He had already been distracted by the aroma of the smoke from the concession stand, standing there with his nose in the air like a bloodhound on a wind-borne scent, with a distant look in his eyes.

"All right. What's the matter with you, Bubba?" Jodell asked, winking at the two men.

"I'm thinking I might had better eat me a bite of something before I have one of my sinkin' spells. You want anything?"

"Naw, I'm too keyed up to eat. Just make sure you

hurry back so we can have the car ready when they call us for the first heat."

"I won't be long. I just want maybe a couple of hot dogs and maybe a hamburger. Reckon they got doughnuts. I sure would like one of them jelly doughnuts."

"Go on and hurry up. We got lots to do yet. We gotta put the numbers . . ."

But Bubba was already gone, walking a straight line toward the food.

"Bubba Baxter will eat anything that don't eat him first," Jodell said, and the men laughed as they went on about their business.

He sat down in the dusty grass in the shade of the Ford and quickly surveyed the garage area. There didn't seem to be many local drivers there, as he had expected. He recognized only a couple of the cars, both whiskey runners from not too far away from Chandler Cove. But that was about it for locals.

Apparently the posted prize money and the opportunity to break in a brand-new track had drawn in drivers from some distance, drivers whose reputations had not yet reached this side of the mountains. Or maybe they had and that was why so few of the local folks had shown up.

Jodell could only assume from the license tags that most of them were from North Carolina, where organized racing was fever-hot already. There were a couple from South Carolina and even one, he noted, from Virginia. That would make the draw from a circle well over a hundred miles in radius.

Until now, racing in East Tennessee had consisted mostly of 'shiners and their whiskey cars chasing each other around and around in some abandoned pasture or tobacco field, simply so their friends could watch and bet some money on the outcome or settle some silly pool-hall argument. Lately, though, folks had been piling in their cars and driving down to the Carolinas to take in the real races. Then those folks had come back home telling tales of how wild and woolly the events had been, how daring the drivers were, how slick and rapid their cars had been.

Now they had grown hungry for races closer to home and were actually willing to part with the money to watch their favorites run. And if there were only some promoters willing to put up some serious prize money, take the risk in exchange for a big gate, then organized racing would surely catch on in the brushy mountains.

The garage area was now fast filling up with cars. Jodell was mildly surprised at how frantic the activity was in the roped-off domain. He and Joe had done most of their preparation the night before, but it seemed many of these fellows were just now tending to the big things, and with little regard for the little ones, the very things that had become such an obsession for Jodell.

Some of the cars seemed to have been half torn apart by some vicious beast that had now left them behind in search of other prey, the vehicles' insides spilled out all over the dusty grass. Tires and shocks and hoods lay scattered about in such a way that it looked as if there might have been some kind of explosion.

Some of the cars were jacked up and three or four men lay on the ground and worked feverishly at something above them, reaching out every so often for another tool or a can of beer. Most of the cars were spotted with rust, or they had had headlights busted out or windshields spidered with cracks, and they rode on patched, bald tires.

Just over the way, a large, shirtless, sweating man banged with a ball peen hammer on something under the hood of a rusty old Chevrolet, matching each lick of the hammer with a particularly vile curse. There was actually an air of desperation in the last-minute scrambling the men were doing.

Jodell choked back a laugh, but then noticed something not so funny. A clump of better-painted, better-tired cars were parked all to themselves farther down toward the first turn of the track. The tags on the bumpers showed them to be from North Carolina.

And the cars looked powerful and fast, as if they were already in motion, even though they were sitting there stone still. They appeared newer, in better shape, not a spot of rust or cracked glass on any of them. And there was an air of seriousness about the drivers and the others who had gathered around them to help or to cheer them on.

One man in particular caught Jodell's eye. He was of medium height, a stocky man but with a ruddy, cherubic face. He wore white khaki pants, black work boots, and a clean white T-shirt. The man stood relaxed and confident, leaning against his car while he talked easily with some of the others in the group who seemed somewhat in awe. The man appeared oblivious to all the frantic activity, the growing noise of the crowd, the roughly idling engines, coughing and backfiring. Even from this distance, Jodell could see how he exuded confidence.

A young boy was working hard under the hood of the car sitting next to Jodell.

"Who is that bunch over there in the corner?" he asked the kid, yelling to be heard over the racing of his engine. The boy let go the accelerator linkage and let the car idle down so he could answer.

"Oh. Them? That's that bunch from over the mountains, from Carolina. Most of 'em is from over in Wilkes County or thereabout, not too far from Boone."

"I take it they're supposed to be the hotshots I've been hearing so much about."

"Yeah, that's them. From what I hear, you and me might just as well go on home and not bother running agin' them boys. They have a pretty good ideer what they are doing behind the wheel of a car."

"You know any of their names?"

The kid pulled out from under the hood and wiped the sweat off his forehead with a dirty rag, leaving a long black streak of grease across his face. He studied the Carolina bunch with squinted eyes.

"The fellow in the white khakis is named Johnson. I've heered his friends call him 'Junior.' I don't know them other ones. That Johnson is tough as a hickory nut, though. They say he just got out of prison for something to do with 'shine. One fine race driver. Runs a lot of them Grand National races. I think he's trying to get back in the groove. He'll run anywhere, anytime. I've seen him before and he runs flat out and don't know how to back off. I hope to God I don't draw him in a heat, 'cause he'll run somebody right off the track iffen they get in his way."

"Looks like a fast car he's got."

"It is real fast. I saw him run it a couple of weeks ago over near Boone. He led the whole race till he had a flat tire on the last lap. Then I thought he was gonna win the danged thing on the rim after all."

"Hmmm," Jodell sighed, breathing in a lung full of smoke and dust. "What about you? You race much?"

"I've run a few races here and there, mostly just against my buddies out in the middle of some cow field, scaring the rabbits and crows to death. I run ever once in a while at the Hickory Speedway. That's where I heered about this new place over here. How about you?"

"Well, to be honest, this is my first time."

"Shoot, we all gotta start somewheres," the kid said.

"I've done a little bit of drag racing, but it ain't the same as this," Jodell went on. "I do a lot of driving for a living and I like to go fast, so I thought I'd come out here and see what I could do."

The kid gave Jodell a big wink. "I know exactly what you mean. Least if you lose here, you don't gotta go serve no hard time."

Jodell bit his tongue. He may have said too much, but the kid seemed okay.

"Sounds like you're about to get that miss out."

"I don't know. This old carburetor has about had it. Your engine sounded good when you pulled up. What you got there, a couple of deuces?"

The kid walked over, bent at the waist, and took a long, curious, admiring look under the Ford's hood.

"It's a flathead eight with three deuces. It's been ported and relieved and has a dual exhaust. I ain't bragging, but she's pretty quick."

Jodell polished the chrome cover on one of the deuces with the rag he held in his hand.

"Well, good luck this afternoon," the kid said, offering his hand.

"Same to you, friend. I'm sorry. My name is Jodell Lee from up in Chandler Cove, Tennessee. I didn't catch yours."

"I'm Ralph Earnhardt. I'm from over about Hickory."

The kid disappeared back under the hood.

Jodell was back under his own hood now, looking at every plug wire and belt for any sign of wear or breakage. He was in real danger of staring a hole in a hose, he was so intent on inspecting everything so thoroughly.

He checked his watch. Bubba wasn't back yet. Joe had not shown up yet, either, and it wasn't long until the first heat race would be called. As usual, he needed Joe for his mechanical ability. And for his good humor and common sense and his cheerleading abilities, too.

"Damn! C'mon, Bubba," he said under his breath. He needed the big man's strong, steady hand to paint the numbers on each side of the Ford. He had to have the numbers on the car to run. And he also needed Bubba to tell him again how sure he was that they would come out winners today.

Jodell had to admit to himself that the case of nerves he had had since crawling from bed that morning was now about to eat him up and spit him out. Watching the others in the garage, he had realized how little he knew about all this, how raw and green he really was. And in less than an hour, he would be out there in the middle of a pack made up of all those experienced, victory-hungry drivers who wanted that "nice trophy and fifty dollars" as much as Jodell did.

Man, what would it be like to actually beat the likes of that Johnson guy? To buzz around the track and come home, down the stretch out of turn four, zooming in for the checkered flag ahead of all those fast cars and hotshot drivers from Carolina? He stood there, staring down into the engine compartment of his Ford, and prayed that he might soon know that feeling.

Or at least, that he might live through it and simply finish the race.

"Drivers! Attention, drivers!" The metallic voice on the public address system brought him out of his thoughts. "We have about forty-five minutes before the first heat. Y'all might want to go on and finish up your prerace preparations."

Then it hit Jodell full force. He was a "driver." In less than an hour, he would be a real race car driver. The urge to compete had brought him here against all his better judgment. Now that undeniable urge was about to shove him right out there in the middle of a phalanx of rolling dynamite kegs, in front of more folks than he had ever been in front of in his entire life, football and basketball games, school plays, and church baptism in Caney Creek all rolled together.

His skin tingled, his breath quickened, and he felt cold sweat break out on his forehead and upper lip.

But there was such a delicious feeling of anticipation in his gut that he didn't mind at all. He absolutely couldn't wait to crank that engine and pull the car out there among the rest of them.

He now knew one thing beyond any doubt. He belonged behind this wheel.

He belonged out there on that track.

And he belonged up front.

WIND 'EM UP AND LET 'EM GO

hat you need me to do, Jodell?"

Bubba Baxter had come moseying back from the concession stand with a couple of hot dogs in one hand and a bottle of grape soda in the other. Jodell was so busy visualizing his victory move down the stretch toward an imaginary checkered flag that he didn't know Bubba was there. That is, until he touched the cold pop bottle to the back of Jodell's neck.

He jumped straight up and banged his head hard on the hood of the Ford.

"Lord A'mighty!" he spewed, rubbing his noggin and checking for blood.

"Sorry, Jodell. I was just trying to—"

"Aw, never mind. I need you to get the numbers painted on the sides of the car. We only have thirty minutes or so before the heat race starts. We gotta have old Fannie Mae here on the line, ready to go, or we don't race."

"What number do you want?"

"They don't give you much choice. We got thirty-four on the sign-up sheet when we came in. Here. Take this shoe polish and make it as big and pretty as you can. I want all them Carolina boys to know who I am when I go by 'em in a blur."

"Atta boy, Jodell! Now you're talking!" Bubba whooped.

He got busy, checking the numbers on some of the other cars for size and placement, then went to work with the white liquid, trying to draw the characters as neatly as he could. After he had finished the right-side doors, he stood back and observed his handiwork from several angles, serious as any artist inspecting his masterpiece. He was working on the other side when Joe Banker sauntered up, as casual as if he had been hanging around for hours, and looked crookedly at the numbers.

"Your three's a little bit skinny there, Rembrandt."

"What? Naw! She looks perfectly . . . Aw, Joe, shut up, will ya?"

"Where in hell have you been?" Jodell jumped in, obviously irritated. "We're almost ready to start this show and you turn up at the last minute like they're going to wait on you to wave the green flag or something."

"Hey, don't blow a head gasket, Cuz. I had to stop and pick some things up on the way."

Joe had a wide, conspiratorial grin on his face. There was no doubt he was up to something.

"What? What did you have to pick up? You know

we got everything we could possibly need. We double-checked everything last night."

"Well, what I had to pick up is right over yonder."

He pointed toward the rope fence, between the car and the grandstand.

"Where?"

Jodell squinted into the bright sun. The crowd, the flags, the streamers, were all a big blur in the shimmering heat and blowing dust.

"Right over here," he said, turning Jodell's head in the direction he needed to be looking.

The open hood of the Ford had been blocking his line of sight. He saw immediately what was so important that Joe had been late to the track.

Standing there by the rope were Susan and Betty Thompson. Each of the twins wore shorts, had a white blouse tied up at the belly, and carried a wicker picnic basket. Bubba had dropped his shoe polish bottle and was standing there, slack-jawed.

"Well, hi, ladies," Jodell finally said, sheepishly, still not sure that he shouldn't be mad at Joe.

"Hi, Jodell," they giggled back. "Hi, Bubba."

But Jodell had hardly noticed that someone else was standing there, half hidden behind the other two girls.

"Well, that's not being very polite," Joe said.

"Huh?"

That was when he noticed that the other person was Catherine Holt. She had been there the entire time and he had not even recognized her. He immediately blushed as crimson as the red convertible pace car that was parked behind them.

"Hi, Catherine. I'm sorry. I guess I've got my mind on the race."

"Well, you should, Jodell," she said, and then gave

him the most wonderful smile he had ever seen in his life. Bright as the Sunday sun was already, the entire hillside seemed to glow even more profoundly when she smiled.

"I'm glad you came," was all he could manage to say then, and even that came out husky and hoarse.

"Me, too. I wouldn't have missed it for anything, and when Joe offered to pick us up, I . . . well, I just had to be here, that's all. I hope you don't mind."

"I'm glad you came," he said again, drier and more hoarse than before.

He was still under the influence of her dazzling smile, of how beautiful she looked there in her shorts and white shirt and with her long, tan legs and blond hair and deep blue eyes. For that very moment, there might just as well have been nobody else on the top of that hill at Meyer's farm but Catherine Holt and Jodell Lee.

"How are you feeling?" she finally asked him, with obvious sincerity. Maybe he actually looked as goofy and addled as he felt on the inside right about then. And maybe that was why she was asking him how he felt.

"Just a little bit nervous. Can't you tell?"

He was hoping his face was returning to its normal color by then, wishing he could swallow. Joe piped up and thankfully saved him from any more mortification.

"Look, Romeo, why don't we let Juliet and the other girls go on back and get us some seats in the grandstand. I think they've got us some fried chicken in those baskets and we can eat us a bite after the first heat."

Catherine and the twins took their baskets and blankets and fought their way through the milling crowd toward the wooden grandstand. But as Jodell watched them walk away, Catherine suddenly turned, caught him watching, but she only smiled at him once more, mouthed a "good luck," then turned and followed the other two girls.

Jodell stood there as if he were frozen in place and watched them go. He couldn't believe the way he felt. Nothing, except the prospect of running the race that day, had ever sent such a cascade of conflicting emotions coursing through him.

When he had finally lost sight of them in the crowd, Jodell realized Joe was talking to him.

"I said, 'What heat are we in?' Get your mind off the girls and on the race."

"Oh. The first one. There are ten cars in each. I guess they'll have three or four preliminary heats. Then they have some old jalopies that will be racing for a case of sodas. And after that, it's the main race."

Joe nodded over toward where Bubba was standing, completely still, his mouth still open, still staring at the spot where the girls had disappeared into the mob. Joe tiptoed over and goosed him hard in the ribs.

"You don't hurry and finish, we're gonna be the number three car if you're looking at it from one side and the number thirty-four car if you're looking at it from the other. They won't know which number to carve on our winner's trophy."

Bubba grunted, took one more look at the mass of people, still trying to pick out Susan Thompson, then retrieved his shoe polish bottle. He worked on the rest of the number while Joe and Jodell went through the checklist they'd scribbled up last night for the umpteenth time. When they turned back around, Bubba was working on some lettering over the driver's-side door.

He had scripted out the name "Jodell Lee" on the roofline, the way he had seen it in the pictures in magazines, and the way some of the other drivers had done. It actually looked surprisingly professional.

But then something suddenly occurred to Jodell.

"It looks good, Bub, but I saw the photographer from the newspaper come by a while ago. If Grandpa sees a picture in the paper of a car that looks like his and it's got my name written all across it, I'm gonna be looking at the long end of a hickory switch."

Bubba thought for a moment.

"Well, sir. If it's your name you're so worried about, then let's just change it."

He wiped off the polish with the tail of his T-shirt and began painting something new there.

"Bob Lee," it finally said, in bold, white, cursive letters.

"Won't nobody know who you are now, and you still got your given name on there. Only not the whole thing."

Jodell grinned. Bubba was so proud of his work, he didn't want to hurt his feelings.

"I guess that'll be okay. I got other things to worry about right now anyhow."

Truth be told, Jodell actually thought the name looked pretty good there, all scripted out in a fancy signature. It was as if, by having Bubba paint his name on the car, he was actually a bona fide racer now. Having his name over the door of his car went a long way toward making it official.

And for some reason, "Bob Lee" sounded like the name of a racer.

The shoe polish had hardly had time to dry when

the call came over the PA to line up for the first race. They hurriedly closed the Ford's hood, then Joe had to block Jodell's way to keep him from opening it back up again to check something he had inspected a dozen times already.

Bubba moved the jack and all the tools out of the way while Jodell rolled down all the car's windows and Joe fetched from his car the hat he had picked up for Jodell to use as a helmet. It was a hat, all right. A coal miner's hard hat with a strap to tie under his chin. Thankfully, Joe had removed the light from on top and the carbide pack that was usually clipped to its side. Nobody actually figured the cars would go fast enough around the dirt track for anyone to get hurt anyway, but the belts and hard hat were required equipment.

"It'll work fine, so long as you don't get hit in the head," Joe told him.

"Thank you. I feel much better now."

"Well, it looks good anyway. And that's what's important if you are going to be a cham-peen race car driver. Looking good."

He gave Jodell another big, crooked grin as he straightened the hat on his head and helped him buckle the new seat belts. Jodell turned on the key and pushed the ignition button and heard her roar to life.

The big, black Ford, number 34 and with "Bob Lee" over its door, was ready to roll.

"Jodell, I don't guess I need to tell you to take it easy in the heat race. Just try to get a feel for what's going on. Don't tear up anything and try to be around at the finish. The feature race is the one we want to worry about."

Jodell nodded, his jaw set firmly.

"Sounds like a plan, partner. I'm going to school for a few laps."

"We'll be okay. Bubba will be down here if you need anything. I'm gonna walk you out to the track, then I'm gonna go see about the girls. We don't want some big ole Carolina boy horning in on 'em while we're down here working."

"All right. Let's do it."

Joe shook his hand, patted his cousin on the shoulder, then slapped the Ford's top for luck. Bubba stood back and grinned as Jodell raced the engine several times, pushing up the RPMs, listening to the engine sing its beautiful song. Sliding the gear into reverse, he backed from the slot where they had been parked. As he had cautiously eased out on the clutch, he realized how timid he was being, so afraid he would stall the engine and be embarrassed, or that he might pop the clutch too hard and break a cable.

"Loosen up, Jodell," he told himself. "Get out there and drive like you know how and you'll be all right."

He gunned the engine again as he rolled slowly through the grass, through the gap in the ropes, with Joe walking slowly alongside him. One of the officials, the man in the red overalls, grabbed Joe by the arm as they passed him, just before they were about to pull onto the track.

"You gonna be the scorer?"

"Huh?"

"Y'all need to have your scorer go on over to the scorers' box over there."

He was pointing to a group of folding chairs on a raised platform over by the fourth turn.

"Scorer? What the hell's that?"

Jodell couldn't hear any of the conversation over

the noise of all the cars' engines, but he could see the puzzled look on Joe's face.

Oh, Lord. Now what?

It had never occurred to either of them that there had to be some way to keep up with each car's lap time. Their ignorance was beginning to show.

"Look, here's the deal. Either you, or maybe a wife or a girlfriend, has got to score the car if you're going to race. No scorer, no run. And you damn well better get somebody up there or you'll miss the start. And that's it."

" 'Preciate you letting us know, neighbor. Thanks."

Joe gave Jodell a big thumbs-up and a wink, then scurried off to find the girls. He wasn't looking forward to telling Betty that he couldn't sit with her and enjoy her delicious bread-and-butter pickles she had made just for him. But he had no choice. He didn't trust Bubba to do something as important as this scoring thing appeared to be. Somebody walks by with a sack of burgers and he'd miss three laps.

Out on the track, a ragged old farm truck rigged with a big tank was making laps around the dirt surface, dribbling a pitiful stream of water on the powdery dust. It appeared to be a futile effort.

The cars selected to run the first heat race were gathered in a line outside of turn one, the drivers trying not to look at the huge crowd that would watch them. The grandstand was now packed, and more people had crawled up on the hoods of their cars or spread blankets on the grassy hillside behind the stands. The sun was hot and bright, the sky still perfectly cloudless, and what precious breeze there was did no more to cool things down than the wheezing old water truck did to douse the dust. But no one seemed to notice. The spectators were primed, ready to see some racing, and were wildly cheering everything that went on out there on the track.

Joe finally found the girls clinging to seats at the far end of the grandstand. They were obviously enjoying the spectacle that was going on around them, although the twins had almost begged off coming. They hadn't wanted to spend all day getting a headache from all the noise or risking a nasty sunburn. But the opportunity to see Joe and Bubba had convinced them to come anyway.

Catherine had been excited from the start. She couldn't wait to see Jodell drive.

"Everybody having fun?"

"It's so loud!" Susan complained.

"And it's hot!" Betty added.

"It's wonderful, Joe!" Catherine sang. "Are they about ready to go?"

"In just a couple of minutes." He turned on his best sorrowful face. "Look, girls, I'm sorry. I can't sit with y'all 'cause they say we need a scorer. I'm going over there and score Jodell, but y'all better save me a drumstick for when I get back."

He ignored the disappointed look on Betty's face and talked on.

"We didn't know we needed a scorer, but they said we couldn't race without one. They told us it was usually the driver's wife or girlfriend that scores for him, but since old Jodell ain't married and all, it looks like I'll have to do it."

Catherine Holt surprised them all and started to stand up. "I'll do it."

Both twins looked hard at her.

"What do you know about scoring a car race, Cath?" Betty asked.

"Looks like about as much as Joe does. Just show me where to go and what to do."

"Aw, Catherine. I couldn't let you do that. Jodell would kill me if he found out I made you do that. This is our adventure, mine and Bubba's and Jodell's. Y'all just sit back and have some chicken and enjoy the race."

"You listen to me, Joe. I want to score Jodell. I'll help y'all out where I can. He might need you during the race anyway, and you need to watch the car and see how it does out there. You don't need to be worrying about anything but him and that car."

Catherine could plainly see the other women in the scorers' box. Surely they could tell her what she needed to know. How hard could it be?

Joe finally raised his eyebrows with a surrendered look crossing his face.

"Well, all right. If you insist. One of us has got to get on over there or they're gonna pull old Jodell off the track here in just a minute."

She quickly made her way to the box, obviously excited to be an integral part of Jodell Lee's big day. She told them she was there to score number 34. Several of the women pitched in and politely showed her what she needed to know.

"Baby, all you got to do is mark the right boxes on that there scorers' sheet," one of the older girls told her through her cigarette. "And then you gotta be sure to let your man cry on your shoulder when he wrecks up or gets outrun out there."

All the other women cackled. Another girl, about Catherine's age, said, "Just put the car number here . . . thirty-four . . . and there's a box for each of the ten laps in the heat race and fifty boxes for the feature."

"And you gotta give him enough sugar tonight so's he forgets about gettin' bumped off the track, honey," the older woman was saying. Everyone giggled again.

"If you ain't noticed," another older woman chimed in, "he's gonna love that old car lots more than he does you anyhow, so you may as well learn to play second fiddle."

Several women nodded and murmured their agreement. The younger girl simply smiled and touched her arm.

"Don't listen to them, hon. If you really love him, you'll love racing as much as he does anyway. Just be thankful there's something he's interested in that you can share with him."

Catherine returned the smile and thanked her.

"How many of y'all have had a carburetor boiled out in your kitchen sink?" the older woman was asking, seeking a show of hands.

But at that moment, the cars began to roll out onto the track in double file, two by two and five deep, so Catherine could turn and watch what was happening on the track. In the stands, Joe Banker was trying to explain to Betty and Susan that most of the cars were basically stock, maybe souped up some, but usually right off the street. But then again, a couple of the ten cars were obviously modified strictly for racing. Those would be the ones to beat, he pointed out.

The regiment of cars marched slowly around the track in the lock-step order in which they had been lined up, strictly by the luck of the draw. After one trip around, they rolled to a stop in front of the grandstand and shut off their motors. The lead cars had halted with their noses directly on the invisible line between the two wooden poles marking the start-finish line.

The starter, the familiar figure in his red overalls, climbed up a rough wooden ladder to a small platform mounted to the side of the pole. There was a box nailed there which held an assortment of flags he would use to direct the race, including green, yellow, red, black, white, and checkered ones. Walking among the race cars, another official checked a clipboard and made sure the cars were lined up in the proper order.

A gospel quartet from Bryson City stepped to the PA microphone and sang "The Star-Spangled Banner." Most of the crowd stood and sang along, with their hands on their hearts.

Over in the roped-off area, Bubba Baxter held a hot dog over his heart and sang along loudly, terribly off-key.

Back up in the stands, Joe Banker took advantage of the song's finish to give Betty Thompson a huge kiss.

Down on the track, Jodell Lee didn't hear a thing. He was too nervous to listen. He only hoped he could hear the command to restart the engines. And that he would remember which way to turn the steering wheel to make the car turn left.

The red convertible pace car pulled onto the track from behind the stands and made a quick lap of the track, raising a fair-sized fog of dust despite the water truck's best efforts. At the end of the lap, the convertible pulled in front of the line of cars and the PA announcer introduced a politician from some nearby town.

The man yelled into the microphone, "Boys, are y'all about ready to wind 'em up and let 'em go? Well then, gentlemen, start your engines!"

The ten powerful motors bellowed like caged ani-

mals, the din rolling across the track, over the grandstand and down the hillside, through woods and fields,
reverberating off mountains, letting folks for miles
around know that racing had come to town for certain, like it or not. The engines rumbled like continual, captured thunder, blue smoke billowing from the
rear ends of a few of the ten.

Those in the crowd who had not attended a race
before could only imagine how loud it would be when
all forty or so racers were on the track at once later
on. The cars themselves looked as if they were straining impatiently, stretching, ready to be turned loose,
given their head to circle around the track.

"Why is it so loud?" Betty yelled into Joe's ear
while he hugged her close.

"See that number twenty? And the seventeen car?
I know they're running straight pipes, right off the
headers."

"Oh," Betty said, but anything else she might have
said was lost in the wall of noise.

On the command, Jodell had reached over and
punched the starter button. He had revved the engine
once or twice, then let the RPMs drop back down to
a fast idle. Some of the other drivers kept revving their
engines, and he could feel his own car vibrate with
the noise. He thanked the Lord he had thought to rob
every aspirin and medicine bottle in Grandma's house
for wads of cotton. He had his ears stuffed full of it.

But he worried that he would not be able to hear
something amiss with the car, the subtle changes in
the pitch of the engine or rumble of the tires that
might indicate something was wrong. Well, no matter.
With all the racket from the other cars, he wouldn't
have been able to hear such things anyway. And there

was no point in being deaf for the next week or so for no good reason at all.

He pulled the car down into gear and waited for the signal to roll off the line. It seemed like an eternity, but slowly, maddeningly slowly, the bright red pace car began to ease forward, as if teasing them. The two lines of cars jerked and bounced as they rolled out in formation behind him, each driver seeming to be doing all he could do to hold back his machine, to keep it from bolting ahead of the pace car and leading it around the track.

Jodell worked the clutch and gas pedal, moved the steering wheel slightly from side to side, trying to get some feel for the dirt track that rolled beneath him. The car lurched ahead with each stomp on the accelerator, and he could easily feel the tires lose traction in the loose soil. He sensed, too, that much more than a light touch on the gas would cause the rear end of the Ford to break loose and send him skidding toward the outer edge of the track.

Gotta be gentle, he told himself. Gotta take it easy on the gas.

"He's gotta be easy with her," Joe was saying to the twins. "Gotta be careful he doesn't fishtail her."

"Huh?" they asked in unison.

"Gotta give her all you got from the git-go, Jodell! Stomp that thing!" Bubba Baxter was screaming from behind the ropes in turn one.

The cars made two circuits around the course, the dust already boiling from beneath their wheels. The starter held up one finger the first time they passed him, a signal to the cars they would be turned loose the next time past. The cars moved closer to each other, some touching bumper to bumper ever so gently.

As the field grumbled off the fourth corner for the second time, the red convertible sped up and pulled off the track into the interior of the oval. The starter swayed back and forth in his box, checking the lineup, the green flag already in his hand but still tightly wrapped.

Then, satisfied everything was in order, the field of cars quickly approaching him down the stretch, he unfurled the flag and gave it a vigorous wave.

Everyone was immediately into the gas while every soul in the crowd was on his or her feet, screaming as if anyone could actually hear over the impossibly loud engines. Dust and dirt flew everywhere, with the back four or six cars almost lost in the cloud. But the entire bunch plowed hard, picking up speed for the first turn.

The first two cars stayed side by side, as if bound together as one. The rest of the cars stacked up tightly behind them. In the turn, the car on the outside suddenly broke loose and swung wide, sliding wildly high on the track. A couple of the cars behind him took advantage of the slip to ease underneath and gain a spot.

Farther back, Jodell was tied up in the middle of the pack of cars, eating dust, with nowhere to go except to follow the guy that was leading him. He concentrated on trying not to run up the tailpipe of the two cars directly in front of him. And to do all he could to not allow the cars in his rearview mirror to climb all over him.

By the time the field had hit the third turn, the two-by-two formation had become mostly single file. Jodell was in a sandwich, caught between two slower cars in the seventh position. At least, he assumed that that was where he was. The dust was so dense he couldn't see much beyond his own hood.

As the drivers pushed the cars off the fourth turn, Jodell thought he saw the opening he had been looking for. He barely nudged the wheel to the left, taking the Ford inside the car directly in front of him. He knew he was faster than the car he was following, but he couldn't seem to get the line he needed to pass him. As soon as he thought he might be in the right spot, almost beside the other car, ready to nose in front of him, the next turn came up quickly and he had to back down when the driver cut him off.

They stayed in formation for two more laps, no one able to pass anyone else. Just as Jodell was, the other drivers were slipping and sliding on the dust and dirt as if it were ice. Traction was a scarce commodity. And it was obvious that many of the drivers were as inexperienced as Jodell, too, and were feeling their way. Few seemed to have a handle on how to take what the track gave them.

Then Jodell began to note the way the car in front of him was getting around the track, the line it would take through the turns. He had no choice but to study him. He was taking up most of the Ford's windshield. The guy had begun to block him any way he tried to pass. The only way he was going to get past him appeared to be to make some kind of risky move. Or to simply bump him out of the way. And Jodell wasn't sure that was allowed. Or right.

Then, on the fourth trip around the track, Jodell really went to school. And he came close to flunking out entirely.

As they raced into the third turn, Jodell decided to go for broke and tried to drive the car deeper into the turn than he had been doing so far. He had planned to brake out of the slide once he was past the blocker.

But the Ford got into a wider slide than he had anticipated. Jodell tried to pour on the power, to keep the car in a broadside slide all the way through the turn, then pull it out once he was headed into the straightaway.

But it was almost more than he could do. The wheels spun wildly beneath him all the way through the turn, and he half expected to suddenly flash around, to see the cars behind him but now through his windshield, all of them coming down on him full bore while he sat there helpless. Or to find himself in a billow of dust in the old cornfield outside the track with nothing but the cows and crows watching him.

Jodell realized immediately what he had done before he had completely lost control of the slide. Then he burped the gas, causing the wheels to catch some semblance of traction. Next, he lined the car up just close enough to straight that he was back under control down the front stretch. But the slide had caused him to drop back, to lose at least five car lengths on the driver in front of him. It took another full lap to get back up, close on the car's rear bumper. And it took almost that long to regain control of his own breathing.

In the stands, Joe had long since turned blue. He had held his breath for most of the last four laps, and the near-fatal slide had left him on the verge of blacking out.

"Was that good, Joe? Was what he did good?" the twins kept asking.

He didn't have the strength to answer.

Down in the scorers' box, Catherine realized immediately that Jodell was in trouble. And she also recognized he had done something near miraculous to pull out of the slide he was in. She dutifully entered his lap when he passed the start-finish line, but her hand was shaking as she wrote.

The rest of the grandstand was screaming, cheering, loving the action out there on the slippery track. But Jodell and the other drivers couldn't hear their noise. They were driving as hard as they could muster, and Jodell was concentrating on the lesson he had learned, trying to figure another angle.

Next time in the turn, he got on the gas an instant earlier than he had before, boldly swinging out to come alongside the car again. But this time he used the raw power of the flathead to keep him there. He glanced over and saw the wide eyes of the driver, not believing that Jodell would try it again.

But now that he had gotten the spot, it was simply a matter of setting the line through the corner, holding the spot through the turn, and then nosing in front of the Buick. This time it worked, and Jodell had ended up exactly where he needed to be, barely under control the whole way.

Jodell Lee had made his first racing pass.

The laps wore down quickly. It seemed to be almost over before they had even gotten warmed up. Save for a couple of spins in which the drivers were able to quickly get going again, there was no crumpled sheet metal. The starter waved the white flag, indicating one lap to go after the lead car passed the flag stand.

Jodell now felt more confident, ready to try to make another move. Five cars had moved away from the other five, with Jodell the last one in the front pack. As they came off the first corner on the last lap, he steered the car underneath the Hudson that was running directly in front of him in the fourth spot. It was the same identical maneuver he had successfully used earlier, a controlled slide into the corner, establishing the line on the other car, then using the power he had available to him to pull out of the slide and into the straight chute of the track ahead of the car he was passing.

This time, though, the other car apparently had some power to play with, too. It stayed beside him, seemingly locked to his door handle, all the way through the corner. Jodell tried feathering the throttle slightly, hoping he could get the underinflated tires and heavy car to find some bite, any bite, in the dirt of the track, enough to get any kind of slight jump on the other car.

But the heavier Hudson never faltered. It seemed to be rooted to the track as they raced back to the finish line. The driver hunched over the wheel, concentrating totally, working the throttle just as skillfully as Jodell was.

But then, thirty feet from the line, Jodell goosed the accelerator one more time and felt the rear end swish slightly, then, gratefully, grab hold. That surge of power, that bit of adhesion, was all it took to send him the width of a bumper ahead of the Hudson as they roared past the checkered flag.

Jodell whooped and pounded the steering wheel. It was as if he had won the feature race with that final move, not finished fourth in a heat race.

Up in the stands, Joe collapsed and almost didn't have to fake a faint. Bubba danced with everyone he could grab in the roped-off garage area. Catherine dropped her head, exhausted, as if she had driven the ten laps instead of Jodell.

As the cars slowed and made one last turn around the track, Jodell tried to calm his breathing, to slow his racing heart. If he had not felt it before, he certainly did now. Slipping past the old Hudson for fourth place had been the most wonderful experience of his young life.

He wished he could merely keep circling, blend into the next heat, jam his foot to the floorboard for the main event, and keep on running for the front without ever stopping. All fears of wrecking his grandfather's whiskey car had faded.

Now all he wanted was to keep right on running, keep trying to lead the pack of thunder-throated race cars out of the turn for the checkered flag.

There was no doubt about it. Racing had its hooks in Jodell Lee but good.

GOING TO SCHOOL

The cars that had been circling the track slowed
down gradually, almost as if they didn't want
the race to end either. They made one last circuit around the speedway, then headed back to the
roped-off area, their jobs done for the time being.

A breeze had kicked up from out of nowhere and
was strong enough to instantly clear the clouds of fine
dirt away. The water truck lumbered back out onto
the track as the last of the cars pulled off. It was going
so slow in relation to the cars that had so recently
buzzed around out there that it almost seemed to be
backing up.

Already the next group of race cars sat, lined up
impatiently, panting, just outside the first turn, waiting
for the water truck to finish so they, too, could have
at it. For those spectators gathered all over the hillside,

the brief pause gave them a moment to stand, to get another drink to wash the powdery dirt from their throats, to give their ears a rest from the accumulated clamor of the engines.

Jodell pulled easily into the spot where their tools and gear waited. Bubba Baxter jumped up and down excitedly, as if on a pogo stick, half waving him into the slot, half dancing in glee. Jodell couldn't help but laugh. The huge man looked as if he had been dusted with flour, ready for frying. The dirt covered him from cowlick to boot bottom.

"Whooee!" Jodell screeched as he climbed from the car and slapped the Ford's top with affection. He checked his own face in a side mirror and almost didn't recognize himself. He swiped at the grime and grease with the rag from his back pocket but only managed to smear on more grease while turning the sweat and dust into mud. His voice sounded high and shrill in his own noise-weakened ears. He talked extra-loud to make up for it. "That was wild, Bub! Wild as all get-out!"

"You ain't telling me nothing, Jodell! Man! That was the greatest!"

The big man was showing more emotion than Jodell had ever seen. There was a real possibility he would jump clear out of his jeans the way he was hopping around, first on one leg, then the other.

"Now, that, that was some real fun. Old Suzie drove like a dream, but I gotta admit, it's gonna take me a while to get the hang of driving in a circle like that. And in that dirt. It sure ain't like running from the revenuers out there on the blacktop highway."

"You did great, Jodell. Looked like you was having a little trouble passing sometimes. But man, there at the end . . . whoooee!"

Bubba still danced, but now he was at least standing in one spot when he did.

"Yeah, the cars can't get a good grip in the dirt like they do on asphalt, and especially when you hit the gas hard. It's like you're in mud for a split second. Then once it starts sliding around, you have to stay in the gas and do a sort of controlled slide all the way through the corner or you lose it."

Jodell demonstrated his point with his hands, showing the effects of a slide on the car.

"How'd the car handle besides that? Okay?"

"It handled all right, I guess. Hard to tell in ten laps. Seems like she still likes to sway over to the side in the turns. Thank goodness for those heavy springs and shocks on the right side. They seem like they made a big difference. Near as I could tell, the car wouldn't start to really roll until she got up into the middle of the corner. Once she hit the center and started out of the next turn was when it was the worst. Wasn't only me, though. It looked like most of the others were having a lot worse time with it than I was."

"Any other trouble?"

"Naw. I just need to get some laps under my belt and get the hang of this thing. All this is still new to me, like the first time I rode a bike without the training wheels. Skint my knees a time or two, best I can remember. Where did you watch from?"

"Right over there by the rail," Bubba answered, pointing to a thin slab railing that had been tacked up along the backstretch of the track.

"Looks like you been wallowing in the gristmill, buddy," Jodell laughed, pointing.

"Hey! I ain't caring about a little dirt. That was one helluva race and I had the best seat in the house."

Bubba started slapping at his clothes anyway, trying to knock off some of the dust. But about all he managed to do was stir up another mini cloud that seemed to settle right back down onto him like magnetic attraction. But the big man's teeth still shone white as he grinned through his grimy face.

"Where's Joe?" Jodell asked.

"He had to go score the car. I think that meant he had to keep up with the laps or something like that. But I can't swear to it."

"If I know him, he's right up yonder in the stands where the girls are. Here, help me get these air cleaners off. We need to get them cleaned out before we line up for the main feature."

The two men popped open the hood and went about cleaning as much of the dirt out of the air cleaners and the front of the radiator as possible. Luckily the wire screen they put on the front end kept all the rocks out of it. Beneath the hood was a dirty mess, with grit everywhere. Jodell winced when he thought of the oil filter and all the other nooks and crannies that the grime had probably found a place to hide already. But there was nothing he could do about dirt he couldn't see.

Joe sauntered up while they were still cleaning up the engine compartment.

"Good job," he said as he slapped Jodell on the back. "That sure didn't look easy. The guys driving those front two cars seemed to know what they were doing."

Jodell ducked out from beneath the hood.

"And I'll be the first to admit that I didn't. But man, that was some kind of fun. I never thought I'd say this, but it makes hauling whiskey dull in comparison."

"Yep, but I can imagine how tough it was to keep the back end from passing you and going that away off the track. You did a good job keeping it going frontwards instead of sideways. That dirt sure seems like it makes it hard to get around whoever's in front of you."

"You got it. The passing was a lot harder than I thought it would be. Hardest thing about it. I figured I could just stand on the gas and outrun all of them. Boy, was I wrong!"

"What did she do when you showered down on it?" Joe asked.

Like Jodell, he was learning, listening as if he were taking notes from a professor's lecture. He knew most of the cars seemed to have hot engines lurking under their hoods. But he also knew few of them could probably run with the Ford on a straightaway drag race.

"Well, I found out in a little bit that the power works against you in the dirt. You get on the gas too hard and the car gets away from you before you know it. Too easy on the throttle and the other cars will leave you eating their dirt. It seems like the handling is going to be a bunch more important than the sheer power of the engine."

Joe nodded his head, immediately understanding what Jodell was telling him. The knowledge they had learned in ten laps of dirt racing would stand them in good stead from then on. An underpowered motor might not win races, but if the car handled correctly and the driver knew what he was doing, he could make up for the lack of horses. Most drivers, and especially 'shine haulers, instinctively tended to want to stand on the gas pedal. They soon found themselves spun backward, looking at the rest of the field coming at them from their windshields.

A good-handling car would seem to flow smoothly around the track, with no push causing the front end to want to head for the outside edge of the track, or without being so loose in the corners that the rear end would want to break free. And an underpowered motor also made it harder to spin the rear tires unnecessarily.

"Know what I'm coming to think, Cuz?" Joe offered, massaging his chin thoughtfully, ready to do some lecturing of his own. "Power don't really matter so much on a short track like this one. The key is gonna be how much torque the car gets coming out of the corner. The engine needs to be able to make some power in the low ranges of the RPMs. Then you can get a burst of acceleration coming off the corner. Specially on this danged old dirt. You don't need so much power that you break the wheels loose and lose traction."

Jodell agreed, then all three of them dived back under the hood and continued their cleaning job, still talking, comparing notes about what they had learned in their first experiment on a real racetrack. But Jodell did attempt a glimpse at the grandstand a time or two. No matter how hard he tried, though, he couldn't find Catherine and the twins in the sea of sunburned faces. He almost asked Joe, but he didn't want to appear to be thinking of anything else but the feature race.

And he honestly tried not to. But it was as difficult a task as keeping the Ford's rear tires from spinning in the track dirt.

The second heat race took a while to finish, half as long again as the first. There were several collisions, whittling the field down from twelve cars to eight by the time it was finished, and some of the ones who survived were dented and scratched like they had been in a battle. Several others had more substantial damage, noses punched in, fenders crumpled against tires, rear bumpers dragging.

One or two might could be patched together in time for the feature race. Most of the worst-wrecked cars were clearly done for the day, though, with some serious doubt about how they might be able to limp to wherever home was.

The third and fourth heats were quicker, more incident-free. There was plenty of beating and banging, paint-swapping and door-banging, going on, though. And it was clear to everyone, from the makeshift garage to the grandstand, that a few drivers' tempers were getting hotter than their radiators.

Jodell, Joe, and Bubba watched what they could of the heat races, trying to see which cars could do what maneuvers on the track. Twenty minutes after the end of the last heat, the tinny voice on the PA began to impatiently call the cars to the starting line for the feature. The day was getting late and there were fifty laps yet to be run.

Bubba was still buried under the hood of the Ford checking the advance on the timing when the call came. Jodell was underneath the car, flat on his back on the army blanket, driving a couple of wooden wedges into the passenger-side springs, doing all he could to try to stiffen up the right side even more. He figured that if he could toughen up the car only a little bit, then he could pick up several tenths of a second in the corners. And several tenths of a second in each of four corners over fifty laps could be the difference between winning and finishing back there in the smoke and dust.

Meanwhile, Joe had done all he could do without getting too dirty, then had wandered back toward the grandstand. Jodell assumed he was headed to the scorers' stand, but he was too busy with the springs to watch him go.

Jodell and Bubba had to hustle to get the car up to the line for the start of the feature. Most of the competitors had played around in the pits between the heats, the drivers bragging about their daring feats out there on the track, the mechanics talking loudly about their hot engines that had enabled their drivers to finish high despite an obvious lack of driving ability. There was plenty of beer and jugs of moonshine passed around among the crews.

It seemed as if only Jodell, Bubba, and Joe and the boys from Carolina worked on their cars between the heats. The Carolina boys seemed deadly serious. They were methodical and precise as they went over their cars from rear bumper to hood ornament. They seemed to know exactly what they were doing, to have an order to what needed to be done to the cars.

They didn't seem as friendly and lighthearted either. They kept to themselves, oblivious to all the turmoil swirling around them. It was clear. They came to Meyer's farm to race. And they raced to win.

Jodell studied them carefully out of the corner of his eye, soaking in what they were doing, how they did it. These were the cars and the drivers he would have to beat in the feature. And with any luck, he would meet them some other day, somewhere else.

He immediately noticed that they worked mostly under the front ends of the cars. They knew that the engine was not the most important element in winning races on a track like this one. It was the handling. And the driver, of course. How he drove the car could make the difference between winning and losing.

The officials came by a second time, chiding them,

giving the cars a final call to the starting line. Jodell and Bubba hurried to get the Ford buttoned up and ready. There was some consolation in noticing that the other cars that were late getting to the line were the Carolina cars, the ones that had been getting earnest treatment getting ready.

"It's as good as we can get it, Bub," Jodell said. "We work on 'er anymore, we're gonna wear the bolts round."

"You're right, Jodell. Good luck. And be careful."

Bubba stood there solemnly, waving 'bye.

Jodell revved the engine and felt the vibrations of the powerful engine, responding in front of him.

"Ready as we're ever gonna be, Suzie," he said.

The Ford answered with a deep-throated surge forward as he lifted the clutch and headed for the starting line.

FEATURE

Finally the cars were lined up, more or less in the proper positions for the start of the feature race. Bubba made his way back down to the railing in turn two and found a good spot to stand and watch where the dipping sun wouldn't be in his eyes. He didn't want to miss a second.

Jodell sat there in the car waiting for the command to start the engines. His nerves were starting to get the best of him, no doubt about it. He wondered how many of those folks over there in the grandstand had recognized his car. And whether any of them might tell Grandma or, worse yet, Grandpa. Thank God he had caught Bubba before he had painted his given name on the roof with the shoe polish.

He picked up the sweat rag off the seat next to him and wiped his brow. Back there behind him, the starter was still trying to get the last of the cars lined up. Jodell was on the sixth row, in the twelfth spot, with thirty more cars behind him, all sitting there that very minute, vowing to pass him the first chance they got.

It was now jungle-hot in the cab of the Ford. The late sun shone directly into his eyes and made the car feel like the inside of a kiln. The sweat rag was doing him little if any good now either. It was soaked completely through, greasy, gritty, scratchy, when he tried to use it.

Again he tried to pick Catherine's face out of the crowd, but couldn't. He'd finally found the Thompson twins and Joe Banker's black mane, but no Catherine. Could Joe do his scoring with an arm around a girl like that?

Where was she? Surely she hadn't gotten so disgusted with his racing, so offended that he had paid her so little attention all afternoon, that she had caught herself a ride home. Well, if she had, then so be it. He had come here to this mountaintop to race. Not to flirt. Maybe she just went to get a Coke from the shack that served as a concession stand.

But there was still a flutter in his stomach that had nothing to do with the thirty cars staring at the back of his neck. Nor with the eleven vehicles lined up ahead of him, boxing him in, blocking his way to the front.

Finally, after what seemed like an hour sitting there in the stifling car, Jodell saw the starter take one last look over the field of cars. Then, satisfied there was some order to the way they had been arranged, he climbed slowly up the pole to the tiny platform that served as the flag stand. The official on the track gave the wind-up signal, telling the drivers to crank their engines.

The crowd in the grandstand responded, rising to their feet one more time with the sound of the forty or so cars coming to gruff, rumbling, noisy life. The engines raced up and down through the RPM ranges as the drivers warmed the cars up once again, making sure oil quickly got to all the right places.

The Thompson twins stood along with the rest of the crowd, waving wildly at Jodell from their position near the top of the stands. Joe stood too, already awash with nervousness again, wondering if Jodell could actually keep from getting run over by the swarm of cars that surrounded him.

But down there, behind the Ford's steering wheel, Jodell Lee had stopped looking in the stands, quit wondering where Catherine might be. He had become oblivious to anything else but the sound of his own engine. Finally, before they rolled off the line, he gave one more critical listen, decided everything sounded just right, and focused in on the task at hand. It was time to go out and win him a race.

He stuffed the medicine-bottle cotton back into his ears just as the starter waved the curled-up yellow flag wildly, urging the field to get moving. The cars rolled away, easing slowly, deliberately, around the track. In his rearview mirror, Jodell saw that a tow truck had to move up behind a couple of the cars and give them sharp nudges to get them under way. He whispered a prayer, thanking God that he and Joe and Bubba had been so fastidious about getting the Ford ready to go. The smooth vibration of her engine was reassuring, even if he could only hear her as a dull rumble through all the aspirin cotton.

It took two circuits around the track to allow time

to get all the cars pushed off and running. Jodell was thankful for the cool breeze through the windows, even if it carried the billowing dust that already had him tasting grit. The field stretched out raggedly around the track in two-by-two fashion, with the last cars in line barely half a lap ahead of the first two.

The first time the parade of cars rolled by the starter, he held up two fingers signaling two laps to go until the green flag would drop and send them off. The drivers revved their engines, doing the only thing they could to keep their spark plugs from fouling. In the case of some of the junker cars, goosing the engines was the only way to keep the things running, and even then, they belched smoke and backfired with deep bass-voiced booms.

Catherine sat in the scorers' box, getting the last-minute word from the official who oversaw the scoring. She could already feel the thrill returning. The heat race had captured her completely, kept her spellbound even as she marked the laps down on the scoring sheet. She tried to watch every move Jodell made out there on the track. With one lap to go before the start, she took a deep breath, said a quiet prayer, gripped the pencil as if it might try to wriggle away if she didn't, and followed with her eyes the snaking line of cars as they wound into turn one.

Jodell was keeping his own eyes on the two cars immediately in front of him while still trying to watch the starter. He could see that he was holding the green flag still curled and with one finger in the air, signaling one more lap to go. Jodell passed the flag stand and tried to clear his mind of everything. Everything but the coming start.

He strained to pick up sight of the flag from the backstretch, then again as he approached the throat of the fourth turn, ready to get into the throttle as soon as he saw it waving. Finally he could see the motion as it was raised high in the starter's hand.

As the flag fell, he jammed the accelerator to the floor and felt the Ford leap forward beneath him as it got a good bite off the corner. The power from the flathead eight pushed him deep into the seat as he raced off toward the first turn.

Thankfully, the cars ahead of him got a good jump on the field, too, or he would have been boxed in by the traffic or up somebody's tailpipe. The racers behind, though, seemed to immediately fall several car lengths behind. The faster lead cars raced off, side by side, down into the first corner.

The driver on the inside took a small, tentative lead, getting a better run off the turn as they steered through the second corner and as the outside car had trouble holding his own line. The wide, arcing swing allowed the third-place car to pull up alongside him, to get a nose in where he needed it to be, then to pull ahead as they hit the backstretch.

Jodell quickly found himself trapped between two cars, both going slower than he thought he could go, just as he'd been in the heat race. He rode along on the high side of the track, boxed in, and then sensed that he was dropping back in the field as other cars managed to slip inside of him and the two others.

Getting passed by several cars stuck in his craw worse than the dust.

His patience lasted less than a lap. He punched the accelerator just enough to give the car in front of him a friendly little love tap on the rear bumper. But the kiss was just hard enough to get the car loose, his rear end shimmying as they entered the next turn. The driver had to fight the steering wheel, to run deeper into the corner than he wanted to as he tried to gather the car back up beneath him after Jodell's pop to the rear.

But that slightest of slips in the corner was all Jodell needed to slide past the slower car on its inside. And that pass freed him to move down the track, allowing him to settle into the inside line around the raceway. From there he was able to finally start picking off the cars in front of him one by one. The power of the Ford up off the corners, along with the stiff springs, was more than most of the stock model cars in front of him could handle.

The cars in the back of the pack were fighting fiercely for position, knowing that getting lapped, even so early in the race, would assure they would not take home any prize money this day. They were stacking up, two and three wide, going into every corner.

And there was some vicious beating and banging going on as the cars rubbed fenders, swapping paint and cuss words, as they slid through the corners side by side. Those up front were oblivious to all the mixing up going on in the back there as they tried to get in line and put as many car lengths as they could between them and the big knot of cars that followed in formation, as if they were bolted together.

They knew not to try to win the race on the first lap. There would be ample opportunity to race for the win once the faster cars got sorted out from the back-markers. For now, it was smart to stay out of trouble, find the car's best groove in the dirt track, and keep the leaders in sight.

Suddenly, back in the fourth turn, cars were spinning everywhere. Three of them had tried to enter the third turn side by side, in a spot where there was hardly room for two. The driver on the inside found it impossible to hold his line as he tried to pass. His vehicle had slid upward enough to bump the middle car, sandwiching it with the one on the outside of the trio. That sent the outside driver off the track, into loose dirt and gravel that had been kicked up there by all the racing. He did all he could to get control, but his efforts only sent him back onto the track. And when he swerved back into traffic, he banged into the other two cars once again.

Before they could get a grip on their spinning steering wheels, the three cars had ended up sideways, momentarily blocking most of the track. Several more cars piled into the mess before the rest of them could get slowed down to thread their way through the crumpled, steaming wreckage.

Luckily, Jodell was ahead of the wreck. He saw all the dust kicked up by the melee in his rearview mirror and then caught the yellow flag waving as he went into the first turn. He stayed out of the gas as he came out of the second turn, still not sure how far ahead the wreckage might lay. All the while he waved his hand to show the drivers behind him he was slowing down.

As he wove past the demolished cars, he was surprised at the damage a couple of them had suffered. The outside car, the one that had left the track momentarily, was chewed up as surely as if it had quarreled with a bulldozer. Another car had obviously been T-boned squarely in the side with serious damage in the passenger-side door. The one that had struck him sat there, still motionless, its front fenders crumpled and the cracked radiator sending up a plume of hissing steam.

Jodell eased between the wrecked cars while some of their drivers struggled furiously, trying to get them going again. He hated the other drivers' bad luck, but he was thankful for the opportunity to finally catch his breath, to ease his choke-hold on the steering wheel, as they circled under the caution flag. He tried to spit out some of the dust that caked his mouth, but his mouth was too dry.

As he passed the start-finish line, he was surprised to see on a chalkboard sign someone was holding up that they had traveled only eight laps so far. He would have sworn they were well past thirty. The drivers had been told that the laps run under caution wouldn't count in the total. That meant there were still forty-two laps left to go.

It took another slow lap or two to allow the wrecked cars to be cleared out of the way. All but two were apparently able to continue the race. But the car that had been crunched in on its side also had its rear end knocked out of line. It made a sorrowful sight, its butt cocked off to one side as it sidled down the straightaway.

The wrecker finally got the car with the busted radiator towed from the middle of the fourth corner and out of the way, so the race could resume. The cars at the front of the field were already impatiently bunched up for the restart while those farther back were strung out single file, stretching halfway around the track like a leisurely funeral procession.

Jodell had already managed to pass six or seven cars in the first eight laps, leaving him back in tenth position after his slip. They clearly had the car's handling and suspension set up well for the track, and he was also beginning to feel comfortable with what he was doing out there in the midst of the storm. Before, getting boxed in on the high side on the start had kept him from getting by several of the cars in front of him, cars that were slower than he was. Now that they were single file, he figured he should be able to have a decent shot at passing them.

The convertible pacing the field pulled off the track as the cars took the one-lap-to-go sign. As the field came out of the fourth turn onto the front stretch, the flag man once more waved the green banner, sending them on their way again. The leader obviously knew what he was doing and was into the gas way early. He got a sizable jump on the cars behind him and pulled farther ahead.

Jodell didn't know who the guy was, but he suspected it was the Johnson character from North Carolina who was setting the pace for the rest of them. Whoever it was clearly knew how to drive a race car.

Jodell saw the green flag wave while he was still deep in the fourth turn. He, too, jammed down hard on the gas and swung inside the car in front of him as he came out of the corner. With the stiff shocks and the wedges in the right-side springs, he was able to get enough bite off the corner to get a fender alongside the Chevy that labored along directly in front of him. Once the cars hit the straightaway and roared past the start-finish line, the power of the Ford had kicked in and he easily swept past the slower car.

The corners were noticeably slicker as the continual traffic had worn the dirt down to a polished, rutted surface. Most of the loose dirt had been kicked aside or blown away as dust in the breeze. And a good portion of it now covered those who watched from the bleachers with a fine powder.

Gradually, as the laps mounted, Jodell began to find a groove in the track, a line where the car seemed most comfortable. He began to move up even farther through the pack, picking off cars one at a time, driving as steadily and smoothly as the adrenaline pumping through his veins would allow.

It was just like keeping ahead of the revenuers, Jodell thought. Stay ahead of them until you can find a place to pull off and hide. Same principle, only now he wanted to hide right up yonder, in front of the pack.

Then, suddenly, just as the race seemed to have settled into a routine, a car spun directly in front of him, going wildly out of control. Jodell feathered the gas, avoided the natural impulse to hit the brake, and then swung the steering wheel sharply left, cutting the car down to the inside of the track. The spinning car climbed the low plank railing that had been built along the curving turn, and then it hung there, rear tires off the ground, unable to get back off.

That wreck once more caused the yellow caution flag to wave furiously, forcing the cars to slow down again while a wrecker pulled up to shove the car off the rail. Jodell relaxed, slumped slightly in the seat, and was amazed at how drenched with sweat his clothes were. He had not had time to notice how hot it was in the car.

In the scoring box, Catherine Holt took the opportunity to catch her own breath as well. Someone handed her a soda out of a cooler. She gladly took it. In the swirl of excitement, she had not noticed how thirsty she was. And she was surprised to see she was covered with dust all over her nice new blouse.

"I must look like a mess," she said, to no one in particular.

"Here, honey." The younger woman sitting next to her offered her a damp cloth. "I always bring some rags to dip in the cooler to stay cool and to help keep the dust off."

"Thank you very much. I guess I'll learn some of these things for my next race."

If Jodell would want her to go to another one with him, that was.

"Well, honey, you're doing just fine. Which one's yours?" The woman nodded toward the track.

"Number thirty-four," Catherine said, pointing to where Jodell was just then entering turn two.

"Husband?"

Catherine was certain the woman could see her blush, even through the grime. They could probably see her glowing all the way from Knoxville.

"No. No, no. Boyfriend. Sort of. We've only been out together once. I came to the race with my girl-friends and his cousin. I've always wanted to see one of these things, though. It really is exciting."

One of the older women had been listening. She squinted her eyes conspiratorially.

"Yes, ma'am. They're fun, all right. So long as no-body wrecks too bad or there ain't no fights."

"Fights?"

"Yeah, boys will be boys, you know. They gotta show how tough they are. Somebody bumps some-body a little too hard and spins him out. Then the one who got spun out bumps the one who bumped him and spins him out to get even. Then the next thing you know, they're out of their old cars, going at it down there in the middle of the track or out in the parking lot when the thing is over."

"Everybody seems so nice, though," Catherine said.

"Oh, they are nice. They will fight today, then be best buddies later on tonight over a beer down at the pool hall or at the burger stand. That's the way they are. Maybe it's the gas fumes getting to their brains. Or maybe that's just the way it is with men in general."

The women all laughed in agreement. Catherine only wiped at the dust that she was succeeding in smearing all over her face.

On the stand, the flag man gave the one-to-go signal. The women went back to concentrating on their own score sheets, but still shaking their heads over their silly-acting men. Catherine took a last sip of the cold soda, then picked up her pencil and clipboard, serious again, ready to go back to work. She quickly found Jodell again as he circled the track.

She was all ready to begin worrying again, too. While the speed and door-to-door driving certainly made things exciting, it also concerned her mightily. The cars were going fast enough that someone could obviously get hurt. She thought too much of Jodell Lee to see him get crippled up in some old wreck.

The cars came around and took the green flag yet again, racing off into the first turn. Jodell made the same move he'd made several times already, trying to get around the car directly in front of him. But this time the car ahead didn't give up so easily. It was one of the North Carolina drivers and he clearly wanted to hold his spot. And even more clearly, he had the car and the ability to do just that thing.

Okay, then I'll just do what I do when the Federal men are on my tail, he thought. I'll stay back and wait for you to slip up, then I'll make my move. What was it Grandma was always saying? Patience is a virtue?

It took another three laps. That was when the driver tried to outrace Jodell into the corner, to put a little distance between himself and the Ford on his bumper, but he ended up slipping high into the center of the turn. Jodell's eyes were wide when he saw the slight bobble. He powered underneath the car on the low side coming out of the second turn and seized the position he felt was rightfully his already.

He could now count four closely bunched cars ahead of him. The fourth-place racer was now three car lengths away. It took another full lap of concentrated driving to close that gap and to ride on the car's rear bumper. Jodell could see that he had more power at his disposal than the other car, but the driver was covering his inside line well. There were only two ways around him. Sit back again and wait for him to slip, as the other driver had done. Or go around him on the high side.

Jodell took several peeks to the outside, trying out the line, seeing how the Ford would handle up there. Then, confident he could stick to the track, he managed to get alongside the other car, pinching him down as tight as he could coming off the fourth turn. Then he used the power of the flathead to outrun him down the short straightaway past the grandstand.

He thought he saw people on their feet, waving him on. Or maybe they were only swatting at the thick fog of dust that seemed to be everywhere.

At any rate, he didn't have long to survey his fans. In making the pass, he was forced to drive into the corner much harder than he had planned, and he could feel the rear end breaking loose, sliding deeper into the corner. Again, his nonracing instincts told him to ease up on the accelerator, maybe touch the brake to try to get full control of the car again. But his much-more-reliable racing instincts, born on so many lonely stretches of highway under a grinning moon, screamed for him to stay in the gas, to let the power seize the track, and to hold his hard-earned ground.

It worked. The car hugged the corner like a bobsled on a closed course. Jodell felt the thrill again of a learned move, accomplished in a good machine, leaving him exactly where he needed to be.

Next, he set his sights on the third-place driver, now only a couple of car lengths ahead of him. This one didn't fall back so easily as the others had. It took another ten or so laborious laps of intense racing to get past him, then another five or so to ease under the second-place driver.

With only six laps to go, Jodell was near where he wanted to be, behind the leader, that Johnson boy from North Carolina that everybody thought was such a hotshot driver. They weren't lying. Johnson was clearly smoother and faster behind the wheel than anybody else on the track. He never made a bobble, always held his line perfectly, kept the car exactly where it needed to be to circle the track most efficiently.

Jodell did all he could do to close up on Johnson's rear bumper. He was so close, so near the front, that his heart pounded in his chest like a piston as he sawed back and forth on the wheel, doing his best to stay in the other car's shadow.

But try as he might, there seemed to be no way he could get past this last car between him and the front. Even with everything working the way it was supposed to, there was simply not enough power to clear him.

Now, up ahead, Jodell could see a single-file line of slower cars. That might give him a chance. If the slow cars would only stay to the inside, that would force him and Johnson to the high side of the track. And he was reasonably sure that the Ford would be faster than Johnson's Chevrolet in the higher route around the track.

With two laps to go, they caught the line of weaker cars as they slowed down even more for the first turn. Sure enough, Johnson had to swing high to go around them. One of the cars on the inside, reacting to the sudden appearance of the car to his right, drifted a few feet high, forcing Junior to move a bit to his own right, out of the line he wanted to follow through the turn.

Jodell held his breath. He kept the wheel steady, maintaining his own preferred line, hoping the inside driver would gather his slower vehicle back up, leaving Jodell room to dive between the two cars.

Then it happened, exactly as he had pictured it in his mind in the split second before. The slower car drifted back low as they swept through the corner. That left the narrow opening Jodell was looking for, the opening that gave him his only chance to win.

He shoved the Ford through the hole, a gap that had at first seemed much too shallow for the width of the race car, but there he was, directly alongside Johnson's Chevrolet. They raced that way, side by side, all the way into the third turn. That was where they caught another slow car, one of the wrecked hulks that was obviously having trouble keeping itself on the track. But before Jodell knew it, they were racing off three deep, with Jodell now half a car length ahead of Johnson.

"Whoooooeeceee!" he yodeled, screaming at the top of his lungs. He was leading the race! His first real race and he was leading one of the North Carolina drivers toward the white flag, one lap to go.

Jodell caught himself, hunkered down even harder over the steering wheel, and concentrated on holding on to the car as it swept out through the corner and headed for the start-finish line for the next-to-last time. The flag man was already waving his white flag. If he could work around the rattletrap to his left, another foot or so, then block Johnson from passing him back, he would actually win this thing.

Jodell Lee could smell the checkered flag already.

Then, suddenly, the inside car drifted up six inches. Not a bit more. But that was plenty enough to clip Jodell and the whiskey car on her left rear. The back end of the Ford whipped sharply to the right with the touch, and she was instantly broadside, right in the middle of the oncoming rush of cars racing for position on the last lap.

Two of the cars swerved hard and cleared him, their tires spinning uselessly as they went on past. Thank God those Carolinians knew how to dodge as well as they did! For an instant, Jodell thought he might be able to gather the car back up and save his second-place finish.

But the next car, probably blinded by all the dust, was a split second too late in making a duck to the outside. His bumper clipped Jodell's left front wheel and fender hard. Jodell felt the steering wheel jerk sharply in his hands as if some giant had taken the front tires and given them a vicious twist. The impact made the car spin in tight circles, but, thankfully, up and out of the way of the rest of the oncoming traffic.

Jodell stood on the brake pedal with both feet as he slid on down the front stretch. He waited for more impact, another car slamming into him, maybe kicking him off the track and toward the grandstand. But there was none. The Ford finally slid to a stop, just off the track, its engine dead.

Everyone else raced on around Jodell as he sat there, watching. Junior Johnson took the checkered flag as the winner. Jodell could only sit there, dazed, his heart still thumping.

He was amazed at how fast it had all happened. Going for the lead in one instant, sitting there crumpled and stalled the next. Reluctantly he finally unbuckled the web belts-turned-seat belts and climbed out through the open window to survey the damage.

It had obviously been a hard lick. The damage confirmed it. So did the bruise just beneath Jodell Lee's knee on his left leg where it hit the steering column. The car had hit him squarely in the tire, leaving the wheel cocked off at an odd, sharp angle. The fender was smashed inward and the sheet metal had cut the tire, leaving it flattened.

Jodell felt helpless as he stood there, looking at the wounded whiskey car. She looked so pitiful with the smashed-up fender, the ruptured tire, and all covered in thick grime. It was as if someone close to him had died a painful death.

Then he heard something heavy and panting coming his way at a gallop. Bubba Baxter.

"I seen it all from where I was standing, Jodell!" he said. "I knew he hit you hard, but man . . ."

His voice trailed off as he saw the damage.

"Well, Bubba, what do you think about this racing thing now?"

Bubba stood there, scratching his head, one eye closed as if he were tallying up the havoc.

"She took a pretty good lick, but we can fix her,"

he said with all the confidence in the world. "No problem. We can get her fixed."

"Shoot, Bubba. I just hope we can get her in some kind of shape so's we can get her back to the house."

"We can fix her. No problem," Bubba repeated, but he was still scratching his chin as if he was not so certain now, the longer he looked at the crushed mess of metal.

The wrecker wheeled up then to give the Ford a pull back to where the tools and the spare tires were laid out. Bubba helped the wrecker driver get the hood open and the car hooked up. Joe was standing there waiting for them as they snaked the car into its slot.

"Whew, it looks pretty tore up, Jodell. Do you think we can fix it?" Joe asked.

Jodell looked at Bubba, who chimed in, right on cue.

"We can fix her. No problem."

"Well then," Joe agreed. "If Bubba says we can fix her, that's it."

Jodell still wasn't so sure. He couldn't believe how quickly he had fallen from the top of the world to rock-solid bottom. From leading the first race he had ever run to sitting here on the trampled-down grass looking at the mess that had been his grandfather's whiskey car. Then there was the shadow of someone else who had walked up.

"You were great, Jodell." The words were quiet but sincere. Catherine stood there, eclipsing the late-day sun. "Sorry about the way it ended, though."

"Thanks," he said weakly.

"That guy came up and just ran into you. He oughta be . . . I don't know . . . whipped, I guess."

"If I had the energy, I might. But right now I've

got to get this car fixed up enough to drive it home or my granddad'll be the one doing the whipping and I'll be the whippee."

He dropped his head. He had not been joking.

"Anything I can do?"

"No, Catherine. I appreciate it. How did you like my brilliant but short racing career?"

He looked up again into a dazzling smile.

"It was the most exciting thing I've ever seen. I hope you'll let me score your next race, too."

"Huh?"

But before he could wonder what she was talking about, she bent and gave him a quick kiss on his dirty forehead.

"I hope you'll call me sometime, Jodell."

"Certainly I will. And thanks for coming. I do believe you brought me good luck. If not for you, I might have got banged around like a pinball on that wreck. As it was, we got out with just this little old damage here."

She smiled again, then finally wandered away with the twins, headed for home.

Somehow, sitting there in the still hot sun, sweat running down both cheeks, leg aching from the impact of the wreck, surveying the mess that had so recently been a fine race car as well as the means to much of his family's income, he still felt a strange but powerful sense of euphoria welling up inside him.

He had led the race. He had beaten three dozen other cars to the white flag before some old boy got careless and knocked him out. That could have happened to anybody.

And Catherine Holt had told him that she had

loved watching him race, that she wanted to watch him do it again.

Maybe Bubba was right. Maybe they actually could fix her.

No problem.

IN THE "PITS"

I t was threatening to get dark on them before they could make much progress on the car. They spent most of the few remaining daylight hours working on the front end, trying to get it straightened out enough to be able to drive the car home. None of them had money for a wrecker, and Grandpa would certainly see them if they had the Ford towed in.

The left front was a mess. The tie rods were bent badly, along with the rim that was holding the flat tire. The front fender was smashed up tight against the wheel.

It was not a pretty sight.

The three of them took turns with the hammer, beating the fender outward until it was no longer touching the tire. They removed the bent rim and disassembled the tie rods. Some kind soul loaned them a sledgehammer and they used it to try to straighten the tie rods out enough so they could at least limp home with the car. Then they had to reassemble them.

Finally, with darkness falling all around them and lightning bugs long since out, they were finished doing what they could do. But it was a long, slow, sorrowful ride back to the barn shop.

They stopped in the middle of the ford across New Canaan Creek, pulled off their shoes and rolled up their pants legs, and used the cold mountain water to wash the dust from the car. That helped her looks but not the way she drove.

Jodell could hear the painful groaning from the left front as he fought to keep the steering wheel straight and the car heading forward in some semblance of a straight line. The spare tire was completely worn out by the time they got home. It wobbled horribly the entire way and the asphalt simply chewed it up.

It was too late then to try to do more on the car, and they would have to find parts on Monday anyway. Jodell could only hope his grandfather didn't get curious and come give the car a good look. He would notice the crumpled fender and used-up tire right off.

The newspaper on Monday morning had an article about the race and carried a set of small photos. One showed the winner, the smiling Johnson boy, with the checkered flag held behind his head, standing there, beaming, beside his race car. The second showed one of the wrecked cars. The caption beneath the picture read, "Local boy has bad day as driver Bob Lee wrecks his car on last lap of yesterday's big race."

Joe tracked him down in the upper hayfield to show him a copy. Jodell's stomach turned over when he saw him coming, the newspaper in hand.

"Well, you're famous now, Mr. Bob Lee," Joe said, then took a seat on the front tractor wheel while Jodell read the story and checked out the photo.

The picture clearly showed the damaged front end of the Ford, and there was no problem reading the name in shoe polish that Bubba had scripted across the roof above the door.

"Reckon Grandpa's seen this?" Jodell asked when he had finished.

"Probably so. You know he reads the paper religiously first thing after he does the feeding in the morning."

"Surely he would have come up the stairs after me if he had. Or else he's so mad he's out stringing up a hanging rope for the both of us."

Joe's eyes widened and he swallowed hard. He was actually considering the possibilities.

"Shoot, Jodell, it's not even a full shot of the car. He might not even recognize it."

"Maybe not. Keep your fingers crossed. With all the damage on the front end and with it only showing back past the front door, maybe he won't," Jodell answered, trying to convince himself as much as Joe. "Course, he's probably gonna be trying to figure out which one of his kinfolk this 'Bob Lee' is, too."

"Good thing there's more Lees in this county than there are pine trees."

"I think I'm still gonna stay out here as long as I can today anyhow. You wanna ride into town with me to get the parts for the front end? We got to have the thing fixed by Wednesday. Grandpa is gonna be expecting me to make a run for him that night."

"Yeah, I'll ride with you. I told Daddy I was gonna help you get this hay raked and hauled for Grandpa so he won't be wondering where I am. Main thing is, we better get that old Ford fixed or you may have the shortest racing career in stock-car history," Joe said, standing and stretching. "And besides, I'm too young and good-lookin' to die!"

As soon as they could get most of the hay raked, forked onto the trailer, and then tossed into the old storage shed below the back pasture, they headed for Chandler Cove and Findlay's Auto Salvage. Behind the big wooden fence they found a wrecked Ford, its rear end smashed but the front parts still in good shape. It was even the same color, so the fender would match without repainting. They began disassembling what they needed and left Chester Findlay five dollars for what they had reclaimed.

Jodell dropped Joe off at his house, then headed back home. It was already dusky dark when he got there. Supper was waiting and Grandma fussed about having to keep it warm for him.

"This cornbread had done got tough and the beans are too mushy. They won't be fit to eat," she complained.

Of course, it was all delicious, but Jodell ate hurriedly. He had to get the car fixed that night, if it took till dawn to do it. Grandpa had plans for him on Tuesday night, and, of course, there was the run to make Wednesday night. And this week's run was all the way across the big mountains into western Carolina.

The car would have to be right. There was no two ways about it. It would have to be good as new by the next morning.

Grandpa was in the parlor, listening to his old upright radio. He hadn't seemed to hear Jodell come in or seen him go past him on the way back out to the shop. Surely, if he had noticed the car or recognized it in the paper, he would have cut loose on him by now. Or else he was merely prolonging the agony.

Jodell had unloaded the parts from the truck and had most of the tools laid out when Bubba showed up to help. Joe was supposed to come, too, but he hadn't shown, so they dived in without waiting for him. Neither man stopped, even for a drink of water, until it was well past midnight. Finally they ran a string alongside the front and rear tires to check the toe-in on the left-front-wheel geometry. Thankfully, it showed it was true and straight, but the only way to know for sure was to take it for a spin.

Jodell followed Bubba as far as the turn to his house, blinked the lights to show him all seemed well, then cruised up and along the top of the ridge, through pockets of mist and past dark houses. He listened critically for any noises that weren't supposed to be there. He held the wheel gently, let the car have its own way on the smooth straightaways, and watched for any sign of pull or shimmy.

The Ford seemed to drive good as new, forgiving him completely for what had happened to her the day before. Jodell smiled, patted the wheel affectionately, appreciatively, and then let her prowl extraswiftly on the ride back toward home.

He was so tired when he finally got back to his room, he could only take a quick bath and was asleep almost instantly. But lying there, before fatigue claimed him completely, he could still feel the smoothness of the repaired car's front end, the way the tires rolled so fluidly along the road.

He dreamed then, of racing, of passing, of winning.

THE FAMILY BUSINESS

The night was black as chimney soot. The full moon had already long since given up and retired for the evening. A heavy overcast obscured the night sky anyway, like a dark canopy, shutting out even the faint, shimmering starlight. Even though it was still only late August, there was a coolness to the air that already hinted of fall and rainbow leaves and brittle frost. The damp air was thick and still, the tall pines that scored the steep hillsides were motionless, silent.

The night seemed even blacker still up one of the especially deep hollows that ran off Short Mountain. It was a perfect night, the perfect place, for the devil's work. Some, even in that part of the country, would not approve. Others would never understand. But this particular devil's work had been getting done in the hollows of these mountains for nearly a hundred and fifty years. It was as much a part of the lives of the people who had settled there as trying to farm the rocky, slanting hillsides, as it was to go worship in the dozens of white church houses that centered the coves and crowned the hilltops.

The acrid smell of boiling mash hung thickly in the cool night air. The heaviness of the humid air pushed the aroma for a couple of hundred yards down the hollow toward the rough trail that wound back into these woods for several miles from the nearest dirt road. The smoke from a fire mingled with the sickly-sweet smell of the cooking mash. The fire itself was hidden by the pit in which it was contained. Several pack mules stood patiently off to the side, munching on corn from a feed sack that was drooped around each of their necks.

In the pit, almost in the fire, a man worked. He was lean, bent with age, and his face, illuminated in the firelight, was weathered and wrinkled.

A much younger man suddenly stepped out of the shadows with another armload of firewood. Jodell Lee crouched and carefully placed a stick or two of wood on the fire. He wanted to avoid setting loose any sparks into the night sky. Sparks could be seen from miles away in the almost complete darkness and against the blackness of the mountain that rose upward behind them.

The two men were mostly silent as they tended the fire, just as many other men, some kin, others not, had done for generations before them. They kept a close eye on the large copper mash kettle that rested over the fire. The smell of the mash in the pit was almost overpowering, but the two men were accustomed to it. As used to it as they were the essences of fresh-turned earth or honeysuckle, work sweat or mountain laurel.

Jodell and his grandfather stood there side by side, gently stoking the fire with their long sticks. They slowly stirred the coals and added more of the split sticks of oak as they were needed. The two of them worked with a practiced eye, keeping a steady temperature on the boiling mash.

They had been there, high up on the mountainside, since midmorning, and now it must have been an hour or two past midnight. It had taken them the better part of an hour to uncover the still from beneath all the branches that had been piled over the top of it, then to carefully reassemble it.

The fire was started in the late afternoon. While it grew hot, the mash was moved into the giant kettle from the two wooden barrels where it had been fermenting for almost a week. This was to be a hundred-gallon batch, but it would be a while before it would be ready for consumption. The coming night, Jodell would deliver a load of previously finished product in the Ford to several bootleggers on the other side of the mountains. The two of them had no idea where their product would end up from there. That was not their concern.

"Jodell, I sure wish that wind would pick up some." Grandpa Lee spoke in a low voice. He knew any sound could carry for miles on such a still night. "A revenuer could smell us in a second if they happened along about the mouth of this hollow."

"Yeah, Papa Lee. I know you're right. This smell is probably carrying halfway to Bristol tonight."

"I don't like it a'tall. Not a'tall," Grandpa Lee grumbled, adding a couple of more sticks of oak to the fire.

"Aw, you worry too much, Papa Lee. There surely is nobody way out here snooping around. We're so far from civilization, they probably have to pipe in daylight. How long you figure it'll be before the boil is ready?"

Grandpa still was the only one who could tell when the brew was done. It was his recipe. His own concoction, adapted from what had been handed down to him as surely as his looks and ways had been. And he was the only one who knew when it was ripe. That was why no one else could quite make such good quality 'shine as old Robert Ezekiel Lee could brew up.

"Well, it looks like it's just about time to get the lid on this thing. Notice how the smell is changing? The water is startin' to roll over real steadylike."

"I see the roll, but what do you mean about the smell?"

"It's losing some of its sweetness. That means it's starting to steam. Most folks been 'shining all their lives can't smell the difference, but to make a good batch you got to time it just right. Take a whiff. See what I mean?"

Grandpa might as well have been some fancy chef, sampling the aroma of a delicate soufflé. Jodell leaned back and breathed in the familiar perfume of cooking corn mash.

"You know, I think I can tell some difference."

"You have got to get your nose right down here close," the old man said, gently lecturing his apprentice. He was putting his nose almost down into the boiling, swirling mixture.

Jodell bent over as close to the pot as he dared and inhaled again deeply. He had been helping his grandfather for four years now and could actually appreciate the richness of the smell of the brew. But tonight, for the first time, he also finally noticed the subtle change in the aroma as the mash began to really turn over in the pot.

"I see what you mean, Papa Lee. I think I can tell the difference now."

"Good. If you're going to learn how to make a batch right, you've got to pay attention to the little details. I don't make bad whiskey and neither will you. Learn to make it right if you're ever going to do it. That's what the customer expects. And that's the way this family has been making it for well over a hundred years, boy."

Jodell paused a moment before he said anything.

"I do want to learn it right, Papa Lee."

But he sensed that his words lacked conviction somehow. It was not the first time Jodell's grandfather had impressed upon him the burden of his heritage. But the old man didn't seem to notice that Jodell was anything less than enthusiastic.

"Good. Good. Now help me get the lid on this pot and the steam lines hooked up. This batch looks like it's just about ready to go. We got a lot of cooking to do before daybreak."

The two men worked together until the first drops of whiskey slowly began to drip out the end of the copper pipe as the steam cooled inside the copper coil. The coolness of the night air actually helped to move the process along. After a while, the liquor came out in a thin, steady stream, first splattering in the bottom of the two charred oak collection barrels, then slowly filling them.

Once the barrels were full and covered, they would sit for a week or two to let the 'shine settle out, to age. The longer it could sit, the better the finished product would be. But it was not practical to allow it to sit for long.

Once the whiskey had settled in the barrels as long as they could let it, the two of them would siphon it off into Mason jars, canning jars, syrup jugs, or anything else glass that they could get their hands on. Then Jodell could make his fast run to wherever the buyer waited, returning with cash money in his jeans pocket.

While the family still farmed for a living, whiskey-making had actually been their lifeblood for generations. Since most of the counties in that part of the state were "dry," not allowing the legal sale of alcohol, business was good. And that was especially the case since many of the old-guard whiskey makers were beginning to die off or get too old to work late nights on chilly mountainsides. And it seemed that many of the younger folks were more interested in leaving for good jobs in Knoxville or Atlanta or Charlotte, leaving the dirt farms and whiskey stills behind for good.

Grandpa Lee, though, was determined to pass along his whiskey-making skills to Jodell. He had wanted to bring in Joe Banker, his other grandson, too, but the boy's mother, even though it was her own father, had absolutely forbade him to get her boy involved in the "family business."

The delivery for this particular batch was scheduled for two weeks from Wednesday. That way the bootleggers would have it in plenty of time for Friday night, payday at the mills and their biggest night by far. Papa Lee usually ran off one or two batches a month. Then, every other week, Jodell would make his delivery runs, usually on Wednesday and always at night.

Most of the revenue agents were still timid about

poking around high up on the mountainsides. There was a time when some of them had gone out looking for stills, then had not come home, with no trace of them ever turning up.

"Bears got 'em," was usually the explanation of the mountain folks, and always said with a knowing grin.

The agents had long ago learned it was much easier to intercept the whiskey runners and stop the flow of the illegal brew that way. That meant a fast car and nerves of steel were required to keep the drivers from getting caught.

Papa Lee certainly didn't have the driving skills anymore. Old age and good sense told him to leave the driving to someone younger. And that was his grandson, Jodell. And the boy also worked on the whiskey car and farm equipment down in the big old barn.

For Jodell's part, he certainly wanted to help his grandparents any way he could. They had taken him in when his father had been lost in the war and when his mother had left so abruptly. They had raised him as their own. He owed them for that.

And he certainly felt the heritage of whiskey-making that was his birthright. Even if his granddad had not preached it to him since he was a boy, he still would have known how important the industry was to the folks in that part of the country. How much they resented the interference of the federal government in what they felt was a God-given right. How much a part of his fiber the industry actually was.

He willingly drove the whiskey car for those reasons. But he drove it, too, because he loved the speed, the danger, the self-satisfaction when he made a good move or did some trick to finish ahead of the pursuing revenuers. He lived for that feeling more than he ever did to deliver the odd, assorted jars and jugs of clear 'shine to some bootlegger in the dark of the night.

But tonight was different for some reason. As he stood there, shoulder to shoulder with his grandfather, working hard in the heat and eerie light from the pit fire, he couldn't help but think about the new excitement he had discovered. He felt almost sad as he watched Papa Lee stir the mash, then struggle to maneuver the barrels to catch the liquid as it condensed out.

Somehow, he knew this could well be one of the last times he would be here in this spot, breathing the sweetness of the mash. And excited as he was about pursuing racing, he was almost overcome with the sadness that swept over him.

Somewhere, off down the mountain somewhere, a dog howled mournfully, and the sound sent a shiver up Jodell's spine. His grandfather seemed so old, so frail, bent over the copper coils. The fire gave his face a ghostly look, and made his eyes look black and lost. His hands were gnarled with arthritis and he had to struggle to grip the valves on the tubes.

Then the guilt over what had happened to the whiskey car seized Jodell like a strong hand around his throat.

"Papa Lee, there's something I need to tell you about."

And he moved closer, so he could talk low as he explained what he had done, and so his voice wouldn't ride down the hollow like the sweet smell of the whiskey they were brewing together.

Grandma had fixed Jodell an extrabig supper. She knew where he had been all the previous night, why he had slept most all day. She knew, too, where he would be going that night. But she never said a word to him about it. She only apologized for the biscuits, which were simply delicious, and for the fried chicken, which was nothing but wonderful.

"Grandma, you ever cooked a meal you were satisfied with?" he asked her through a big bite of luscious mashed potatoes.

"I reckon not. Them potatoes are lumpy, too. I oughta just throw them out to the hogs."

Full, rested, and ready, he finally stood and strode out to the back porch of his grandparents' house. He watched the afternoon sun disappearing quickly over the spine of the mountain that ran behind the house. That was a sure sign fall was imminent, the sun diving behind the mountain so soon after supper. But as always, he paused to savor the view from the porch. He always did that before a whiskey run. He never knew when it might be his last.

He grabbed his black slouch hat off a hook by the back door and made his way to the barn. The Ford was there, waiting. Jodell rubbed a hand down along the side of the gleaming black automobile and whispered softly to her.

"How's Miss Delilah tonight? We've got a big night ahead of us, honey, and I hope you're feeling all right." He opened the door and slid into the seat. "We need to be fast and mean tonight, my sweet lady."

With that, he turned the key on, then reached over with his left hand and punched the starter button. Under the hood, the engine roared to life. Even muffled, the motor was loud inside the barn. The flathead eight sounded as powerful as she was as he gently pushed the gas pedal to the point where the engine did a fast idle to warm it up. Atop the engine, the three deuces sucked in air through the chrome air cleaners, inhaling with a loud whoosh. The slightly muffled tailpipe belched a throaty roar.

Jodell allowed the engine to drop to its normal idle. The deuces sucked and gasped harder as they pulled in more air. The mechanical fuel pump clicked along in time with the rest of the engine.

Finally, satisfied with how everything sounded, Jodell pumped the accelerator one last time before he pulled the column shifter down into first gear and eased off on the clutch. The clutch caught an inch off the floorboard and the car rolled out of the garage into the turnaround in front of the barn.

Once onto the highway, he punched the accelerator and the Ford took off with a bellow. He raced quickly to a farm road that meandered off at an angle about three miles down the highway. It ran from the blacktop up a steep ridge, then circled farther up the side of the mountain. He turned off, dropped the car into low gear, and started up the road, climbing slowly just as darkness began to seriously settle in on the mountain.

He finally came to a logging road that took a quick dip away from the rutted dirt lane he had been following. It was mostly overgrown by Johnson grass and kudzu. Someone who didn't know it was there could have easily missed it entirely. But Jodell turned down it, picking his way slowly.

This road ran along the back side of Grandpa Lee's farm and ended up on land owned by a timber company from Knoxville, and had once given access to loggers harvesting trees from the adjacent property. A half mile down the logging road, Jodell stopped, backed the car into a small clearing, and shut off the engine.

He climbed out of the car and leaned casually against the back fender, listening for the sound of another engine, any indication that he might have been followed. He could only hear the quiet popping of the Ford as she cooled down, though.

He patiently waited a full five minutes, heard nothing suspicious, and then started walking down the side of the ridge in the general direction of Grandpa Lee's house. But after several hundred yards, he came upon a dense thicket. He looked around, saw no one, then hopped into the brush and was instantly swallowed up. No one could have seen him from the clearing then and he had lost sight of the Ford already.

He worked his way through the thicket, concentrating on the almost invisible trail at his feet. Then, about forty yards ahead, he could see an old cabin, almost claimed by the vines and thick underbrush. The blackberry briars formed an almost impenetrable wall, so the going was slow, the stickers snatching at his clothes. He was nearly through the jungle when he misstepped, tripped on something, and, as he caught himself, grabbed hold of the only thing he could reach, a dead tree branch. It snapped with a loud crack, like the report of rifle.

Kaboom!

Something hot and mad came whistling over his head from out of nowhere.

Jodell dropped to the ground as if he had actually been hit. Two seconds later, there was another boom and he could hear more bird shot sizzling overhead.

"Get off my property or they'll have to carry you off!" The voice came from somewhere near the cabin. So had the shotgun blasts. "Another step this way and I'll fill your rear end so full of buckshot you'll point to true north the rest of your days. Now, get the hell out of here."

Jodell could clearly hear the breaking of the breech on a double-barreled shotgun, the thud of now empty shells hitting the porch of the cabin, the sound of two fresh shells being rammed into the chambers, and the sharp click of the gun closing.

"Papa Lee!" Jodell cried out. "It's me! Jodell Bob!"

"Who is it?"

He could hear the ominous click of the double hammers being drawn back.

"Damn, Papa Lee! It's me! You trying to attract

every revenuer within a hundred miles? Not to mention, blow your grandbaby's head off!"

"Well, 'Dell. Shoot fire! You way early, boy."

Jodell stood up and dusted the straw off his shirt
and jeans. Thankfully, Grandpa Lee released the
hammers and dropped the twin barrels of the shotgun.

"I got a long way to go and wanted an early start.
Tell you what. If you promise not to kill me, I'll come
on in and help you."

"Aw, boy, if I was intending on shootin' to kill,
you'd be gone to the Lord by now. I thought you
might be some of them Yankee revenue agents I saw
in town yesterday. I hear they've been asking lots of
questions lately. C'mon. We got plenty to do."

"Okay, Papa. Where are the mules?"

"Waiting patiently out back. They love to work.
Can't wait to get in front of a load. It's bred in 'em.
Wish we could do that with people. We'd get a lot
more done. We just need to hook up the sleds and
we'll be ready."

Grandpa led the way through the old cabin and
out onto the back steps. Otto, Frank, and Jesse, the
three mules, stood, tied to a tree limb, munching on
some grass. Three pole sleds were stored in a rough
shed, practically covered with brush. The mules stood
still as they hooked them up to the sleds.

Then the two men and the mules started slowly up
the mountain, feeling their way in the deepening darkness. They climbed higher and higher, stopping every
so often to listen for any sound of someone following.
But there was nothing but the lonesome call of a
whippoorwill and of the mules, trying to get their
breath from the climb.

A couple of hundred yards from the still, the two

men deliberately stopped, dead motionless. Jodell moved on ahead to take a look at the site. All the years he'd spent hunting in these woods now served him well. He moved silently, circling the clearing where the still sat. From fifty yards out, he saw no signs of anyone else having been there. He made his way quickly through the darkness back to where Grandpa waited with the mules and gave him an all-clear whistle. The old man returned the whistle, the whole exchange sounding exactly like a couple of mockingbirds flirting.

Jodell lit two kerosene lanterns and set them out. They cast a pale glow over the bowl in the hillside where the still rested, covered again in leaves and thick brush. The slight depression in the side of the mountain and the dense foliage effectively hid the dim light of the lanterns. From any more than thirty yards away, they could not be seen.

The mules rested peacefully in the shadows off to the side as if they knew there was harder work to be done shortly. Jodell and his grandfather went to work, uncovering the two oak barrels that contained the batch of moonshine that was ready to move. The barrels were kept in a rock cellar that had been cut into the side of the mountain. It was capped with a wooden top, then covered over with dirt and leaves so it was almost impossible to see. Even if someone had found the still fifty feet away, the storage area where the more valuable whiskey was hidden would be hard to discover.

They could rebuild the still. There was no way to recover spilled whiskey.

Grandpa Lee and Jodell pried open the first barrel and started to fill the glass jars in cardboard boxes on one of the sleds. Once they got started, and by using a hand pump, the process moved quickly and there was minimal spillage. Within an hour, the barrels were empty and the jars were stacked back in their boxes and on the sleds, ready to haul.

The mules stood patiently while the sleds were loaded and hitched back up to their harness, and while Jodell re-covered the cellar. Satisfied the area was secure, Grandpa Lee motioned for Jodell to put the lanterns out and they started off back down the side of the mountain.

The descent was much easier than the climb, even with the heavy load they now moved. The mules moved easily down the mountainside, the sleds bumping across the rough trail, but the jars sat securely in their boxes, packed tightly with straw and old newspaper. Even the wide saddlebags on the animals were filled with quart jars. A hundred gallons of the finest home brew made for a very full load.

They stopped several hundred yards above the car, waiting beside a rock outcropping that jutted out of the side of the mountain, giving them natural cover. Jodell made his way silently along the rest of the trail to where the car was parked. All seemed okay there.

Jodell stepped out into the clearing, slipped open the door, and slid in. Slowly, with no headlights, he drove the car farther up the dirt road to a small turnaround. By the time he got the car pointed back down the dirt road, Grandpa Lee had emerged from the other side of the clearing with the three mules trailing him.

Jodell left the engine running and got out to help Grandpa with the load. He opened the trunk and they loaded the jars off the sled and into the wooden boxes that were already in the car. It only took about ten minutes to finish the load-up, but both men knew this was one of the most dangerous times in the run. Revenuers could easily surprise them. So could cutthroats intent on stealing what they had worked so hard to create.

The Ford had been riding high in the rear when he had left the barn back home. Now she was practically level, thanks to the heavy-duty truck springs under the rear end.

"You got the mules now, Papa?"

"I reckon so."

"Then I'll be going, I guess. This is gonna be a long one."

"Boy, you be careful now. Don't try no more crazy stuff. Things have been heatin' up lately."

"I will, I will. I just hate these long runs. Even on a dark night like tonight."

"I know. I don't like 'em either, but the money is good and old man Smith is one of my oldest customers."

"Don't worry. I'll get it there."

"I'm not worried. But you keep a good eye on your mirror."

"Don't worry. Them revenuers ain't gonna catch me unless they got one of them jet planes."

Jodell watched Grandpa Lee and his beloved mules in his rearview mirror as he eased away down the logging road. The darkness finally swallowed them up. He was a half mile away from them before he turned on his headlights.

As he reached the steepest grade down the last hundred yards to the main road, he brought the car to a stop and pulled the shifter back down into first gear. He eased off on the clutch and let the heavily loaded car use the torque of the engine to ease down to the highway. The springs squeaked in protest as the car bounced over the ruts on the steep incline before it made the pavement.

When he hit the highway, he punched down on the accelerator and raced away, back past his grandfather's house and on out the highway, eastward, toward the Carolina line some forty miles away across the mountains. He cruised along, running eighty miles an hour when the road allowed.

Although the load had the car feeling balky, he still marveled at how well she handled the turns and hills. The narrow curves came upon him quickly at those speeds, but a quick tap on the brakes would drop the nose of the car downward, and he would drift smoothly through the curve. Then he would start working to set the car up for the next one.

After all, he knew where every twist and dip was on this stretch of road. He had made these runs many times. The miles unrolled quickly beneath him until he finally approached the Highway 11 junction. That was where he would make a turn and then a short run down the main U.S. highway before another jag for the state line.

Before he hardly had time to see it, he ran up on the butt end of a much slower car, an old sedan poking along well under the speed limit. Jodell waited patiently, looking for some spot in the shallow hills were he could see far enough ahead to ease around it. But as luck would have it, he found none, and sure enough, the old car turned south on Highway 11, directly in his way.

"Damn!" Jodell muttered, mostly under his breath. He continued to try to find clearance to pass, but now the traffic coming to meet them and heading toward the Tri-Cities of Bristol, Kingsport, and Johnson City was almost continuous.

When he finally found the opportunity and got past the old car, the clock on the dash showed he was a good ten minutes behind where he had wanted to be by then. He quickly ran his speed back up to eighty, then watched the illuminated area ahead for the turn-off that would take him over the mountains and into North Carolina.

When it finally jumped up into his headlights, he got on the brakes hard and squealed the tires as he made the cut. Then there was nothing ahead of him but the black of the mountains, the houses and brightly lit filling stations and roadside eating places left behind on the big highway. And there was hardly a light to be seen anywhere now. That was exactly the way he liked it.

Jodell could have taken a newer road that left Highway 11 a half dozen miles farther along. It was a better road, a quicker route, but there was also more traffic. He preferred the tight-spiraling mountain road he was on. Sure, it was slower going, but it was isolated. And he felt more comfortable there, too.

Sure enough, the road immediately got steeper and the turns tighter as Jodell wound higher and higher up into the Smokies. Several times he had to drop the car down into low gear as the blacktop seemed to climb directly for the stars. Sometimes the curves were so sharp that the switchbacks seemed to lie almost on top of each other. Even the Ford's powerful engine strained and groaned under the heavy load she was pulling tonight.

Finally he rounded a curve and the road flattened. He had topped the mountain. For a moment he could see the darkened valley spread out before him, its few lights sprinkled there as if cast there by some mighty hand. No matter how often he saw such high vistas in these mountains, they still took his breath away.

He dropped the car down into low gear again and began the slow descent down the other side. The big motor whined and raced as the heavy car rolled downward through the steep turns. Jodell rode lightly on the brakes, worried they might overheat under the burden in the trunk. He wanted the transmission to do most of the work as they defied gravity.

He knew that with no guardrails on the roadsides and with his car several hundred pounds overweight, he had to be extracareful. If the brakes failed or he got out of control in the sharp bends, he could be over the edge before he knew it. And the drop was farther to the bottom than he wanted to think about.

This wasn't Jodell's first time to make this particular run. But even that experience didn't diminish the danger of this route over the mountains. The very features that made it attractive for the run also made it dangerous as bottled lightning. The mountainside was littered with the wreckage of cars that had failed to negotiate the spiral turns. And Jodell knew few of those unfortunates had been as overloaded as he and the Ford were this night.

Finally he reached bottom, the roadway straightened noticeably, and the rises and falls were not nearly so dramatic as the last twenty miles had been. He quickly got back to speed. But the clock now said eleven-thirty.

"Gettin' late, old girl," he told his mount. "We gotta move, make up some time."

He'd hoped to be unloaded and on his way home by twelve-thirty, but even now, he was still a half hour from his destination. And that was assuming he didn't get stuck behind another slowpoke in a stretch of road that prohibited a pass.

It promised to be a late night after all.

There was one other thing to dread. Augustus Smith would always insist that the delivery driver share a drink or two of the merchandise with him before they got down to the serious business of exchanging cash. That was partly because he wanted the driver to sample the product to guarantee it was okay for his customers to drink. Sometimes the 'shine was literal rotgut, poison, blindness-inducing, all because its makers worked fast and sloppily. Sometimes it was simply awful-tasting. Smith didn't want to buy a load without both himself and the driver partaking of a good taste of it.

The thing was, though, that the better the quality of the liquor, the more he wanted to sample, and the longer the inevitable tall tale he would tell would be. Since Jodell knew this batch to be top-notch, it looked as if this trip had the potential of taking all night.

Finally, at an unmarked crossroads, Jodell slowed almost to a stop to make a hard right onto a rough, packed-clay road. It was only a short run, directly toward the foot of yet another towering mountain. The next turnoff was marked only by a stack of sun-bleached limestone rocks. It was an old gravel road that ran along the skirt of the mountain, then down a sharp ridgeline that overlooked the valley from which he had just climbed.

"I don't know how all these folks ever find old Augustus," Jodell mumbled. "They must be powerful thirsty to hunt him down all the way up here."

The old roadbed had been used for generations, first by wagons, then automobiles. It cut deeply into the side of the mountain, with tall cedars, firs, and pines forming a thick awning overhead. It finally dropped down into a wide hollow, the water in a swift-flowing creek running parallel to the roadway flashing white and frothy. Jodell's headlights periodically caught the bright brown glow of tobacco plants and tall, brown cornstalks in the fields on the side of the road opposite the creek.

Then he turned at a small, shaky bridge across the creek and raced up a narrow lane, passing a dark, isolated farmhouse or two along the way. Finally the road narrowed sharply and crossed another rickety old bridge where the creek took a sharp turn to the left. A stone gate framed the entrance to a driveway just past the bridge.

Through the gate and past a clump of towering oaks, an old plantation house rested majestically on a slight rise, as if surveying its realm below. In his headlights, though, Jodell could see that the house showed all the signs of years of neglect. Paint peeled from the tall columns in front and weeds grew up through rotten boards in the steps and porch. But from the top of the rise where it rested, the house held a commanding view of the hollow and its approaches.

A dim, yellow light burned on the old house's front porch. Otherwise, the place was dark. Jodell knew from Augustus Smith's stories that the house had been in his family since it was first built in the 1830s. The family fortune had been made in timber, corn and tobacco, and, even way back then, whiskey. The government had successfully ended the whiskey business during Prohibition, the tobacco allotments had been sold over the years to pay the taxes and maintenance on the place, and the timber had long since been harvested, so times were not nearly so good for this latest generation of Smiths.

Without the money Augustus got from bootlegging, the farm and the house would have gone back to the land years before. It was easy to see that the rest of the farm had long since been claimed by weeds and honeysuckle.

Jodell pulled slowly over the rough remnants of what remained of the brick-paved circular front drive and stopped in front of the main steps. There, in the flash of his headlights, sat Augustus Smith, waiting for him on the sweeping front porch.

He shut off the engine and climbed out of the car. In the darkness, he could see Smith return his friendly wave.

"Howdy. I was commencin' to worry about you, young fellow."

Jodell could now see the shotgun, leaning against one of the columns and within easy reach from Smith's rocking chair.

"Evenin', Mr. Smith," Jodell answered as he carefully negotiated the dilapidated steps.

"Ever'thing okay on the run over?" The old man finally rose from the chair, walked to meet Jodell with his hand outstretched. "And how's your grandpa and grandma and them?"

"They're fine. Just fine. So was the run, but I got stuck behind a couple of slow cars."

He took the offered hand and shook it vigorously. Smith had a surprisingly strong grip for a man his age.

"Any sign of law?"

"No, sir, but Grandpa says the G-men have been thick as fleas on a hound dog's belly the last few days over on our side of the mountains."

"Never let your guard down, boy. Get careless and they'll have you hog-tied before you can run to ground. And they say some of them boys got a mean streak and don't wait for no judge before they do some punishin' of their own."

"Yes, sir. I'm careful."

The two men turned and walked off the porch, back toward the car. Jodell noticed that Smith picked up his shotgun on the way. He figured the old man probably slept with the thing. He carefully propped the gun up against the side of the car as they went to work.

"Here, boy. Let me give you a hand with that stuff."

"Thanks." Jodell had the trunk open and handed him the first box full of jars. "Watch it. They're heavy."

"Now, son, you know I been hauling these old jars around since before you were a gleam in your daddy's eye."

They quickly stacked the boxes on the porch. Smith kept looking warily over his shoulder as they worked, back toward the oaks and toward the deep darkness at the back of the house.

Finally, when they had all the boxes on the porch, Smith disappeared into the house, then returned with a two-wheeled hay cart. They loaded it up with as many boxes as it would hold and wheeled the first load right through the house and out onto the back porch. It took three more trips to cart all the whiskey through to the back.

"You want me to help you put it into the cellar?" Jodell asked.

"Naw, I can manage it from here. I'll haul it down tomorrow in the daylight. I've done worked up a thirst. Why don't we just sit down and rest a bit? I know it was a long haul gettin' over here and we need to have us a taste or two of this before you head on back."

Smith slipped one of the quart jars out of the box, shook it, and held it up to the dim porch lightbulb. He smiled, apparently liking what he saw. Then he motioned for Jodell to follow him through the house, leading him to what was once the front parlor. He waved Jodell to a ragged parlor chair badly in need of reupholstering, and sat down himself on a battle-scarred old sofa.

Jodell knew the routine well. He smiled as he settled into the chair. He knew he would be lucky to get out with only having to down two or three drinks. But he knew there was no gracious way out of it. He accepted the offered glass and sipped politely at the clear liquid.

"Well, Mr. Smith. What do you think of the brew?"

"Son, it's mighty fine. Mighty fine, as always," he said, smacking his lips in obvious approval. To confirm his opinion, Smith turned up the glass and took another healthy drink. "I mean, real fine."

"Grandpa knows his business for sure."

"Son, let me tell you something. You make sure you learn your granddaddy's secrets, 'cause he makes the best corn liquor I ever tasted. And believe me. I sample a pretty good variety, and his is the very best."

"I been learning all I can, but cars are what I'm good at. Not whiskey, I'm afraid."

"Be a shame if your granddaddy's recipe died with him. It is a dying art. People in these parts have been making whiskey for nearly two hundred years, you know. Whiskey built this house, but look at it now. My daddy never learned the business from his daddy, so I couldn't learn it from him. Now I'm left to bootleg it, and that's all I know how to do."

"I'd still rather drive the whisky than make it."

"Drive for somebody else and you'll wind up in jail. Your granddaddy don't take no chances and he knows what he's doing. But don't let the tradition die in your family like it did in mine. You can be sure your father was learning the business when he was called away for the war. He was just gettin' to the point where he could make a batch almost as good as your grandpa. When I see you drive up in that old Ford, it reminds me of him. You look so much like him, and your grandpa says you can drive nearly as good as he could too."

"What do you mean 'nearly?' Folks back home say I'm the best they've ever seen."

Of course, he couldn't tell Smith about his recent thoughts about leaving the business. He wouldn't understand any more than Grandpa would.

"Maybe you are. You take after your daddy more than somewhat. Now here. Let's enjoy another snort of y'all's good work."

Smith was already refilling Jodell's glass without even asking for approval.

"Thanks, Mr. Smith. But this is gonna be my last one. I need to get on the road before it gets much later. And I need all my wits about me."

"Sit there, relax, enjoy, son. You can always go home when you can't go nowhere else."

"Okay, but only one more."

Jodell settled a little deeper into the chair. He was tired. It had been a rigorous several days.

"Let me tell you a little story about my great-great-granddaddy and how the damn Yankees put him out of the whiskey business. See, it happened like this . . ."

An hour and a third glass of the smooth liquor later, Augustus Smith finally wound his story around to its end. When he spotted the opening, Jodell jumped to his feet, said his good-byes, and walked out onto the porch before Smith could launch another tale. He took a long, deep swallow of the cool mountain air, hoping it would erase some of the fuzz in his head.

The clock on the Ford's dash screamed "1:35" Lord, he should have been home and in bed by now. Grandpa would be wondering if something had happened. But finally he was pointed home.

This time he took the direct route since there was no need to use the deserted winding road. With no traffic this late, it would cut close to half an hour off the trip as he allowed the Ford to gobble up asphalt much faster.

He felt better once he had crossed the state line, back into Tennessee. Home ground. No sign of any law all night. Maybe all the talk had been just that. Talk. He relaxed and let the car drive itself. He was half asleep when he buzzed past a barely visible lane running off the highway toward an old home site. Although he knew it was there, he didn't bother to look in the direction of a ramshackle old country church that sat back off the roadway in the triangle formed by the lane intersecting with the main highway. The churchyard was full of towering oaks. Rough wooden tables had been built underneath the trees and their shade for regular gospel singings with dinner on the ground.

It was so dark beneath the trees this night that even if he had turned to look, Jodell would never have seen the blue sedan hiding there.

The dark car eased out of the churchyard, its headlights still dead until he was on the highway and rolling, and Jodell's taillights had disappeared over the next rise. Now that its driver could see what was ahead of him, the sedan quickly came up to speed.

Jodell was clipping along at near eighty miles per hour when he caught the first glimpse of the car's lights behind him. He had seen no other traffic in the past twenty minutes.

"Uh-oh," he said to the Ford. "This time of night, that's either another whiskey runner or the law. And since he probably pulled out of that old churchyard back yonder, I suspect I know which one it is."

He pushed his foot a little deeper into the throttle. There was that familiar, comforting surge of power as the engine answered his demand.

Ahead of him, he knew, lay a series of tight turns as the road dropped down a short ridge and then rose quickly onto a wide, flat, open stretch which ran on for a several miles. The car behind him was clearly closing fast, but there were no police lights yet. The turns coming up were certainly going to slow him down.

He was already hard into the brakes as he swung into a sharp right turn, then twisted back to a quick left skew. The tires squealed and screeched in protest and he finally had to slow to little more than twenty-five miles per hour. Again the heavy whiskey-hauling springs in the rear made navigating these wound-up curves a real adventure. The trailing car was better set up for the turns, like a good race car on a tight course, and it was quickly gaining ground.

When he was able, Jodell kicked down hard on the gas pedal until the three deuces kicked in. But the dark sedan stayed close, less than five hundred yards back. Jodell steered gently through a series of familiar curves, but the other car kept up, not losing an inch. He apparently knew this road, too.

Then Jodell did a quick mapping from memory of

the road ahead. There was going to be trouble. This stretch of highway ended in a T intersection when it hooked up with U.S. Highway 11. There was going to be no way that he could put enough distance between himself and the sedan before he hit the intersection.

"And you know what else, Miss Delilah? If I was the law, that old tee is exactly where I'd have me a buddy waitin' for an old boy like me."

If that was the case, he would be trapped, no place to go. He would have to try to make a move and fast, before he steered right into a big old ugly trap.

He could imagine the revenue agent back there, smiling in the glow of his dash lights. Their trap would work perfectly. He would know that the car that had roared past him as he sat there in the churchyard was a moonshine car. Who else would be out, daring these winding roads at two in the morning? The high-riding springs in the rear end looked mighty suspicious, too. And every lawman in ten counties would, by now, be looking for the black Ford that had eluded them several times lately.

Jodell concentrated on the road ahead. Hit the ditch here and he would have no chance at all. Keep the Ford on the road and as far ahead of the sedan as he could, and maybe something would come to him. Some idea. Some escape route.

Thank goodness the repairs they had done after the race wreck seemed to be holding. The car was handling as well as it had in the first forty-nine laps of the fifty-lap race on Sunday.

He threw the car through corner after corner, almost willing it to maintain traction. But no matter what tricks he tried, the sedan stayed where it was. No closer. No farther back.

"He's got company waiting up ahead," Jodell said. "Else he'd be trying to force the issue and not layin' back like that."

It was time for drastic action. Another series of tight turns was coming up as the road cut a winding swath through a patchwork of fields and pastures. And the T intersection and the likely ambush were no more than three miles dead ahead. The Ford roared into one of the turns, gravel rapping at the underbody, and Jodell gave the wheel a hard pull to the left to push her through the corner.

A field of some kind stretched out from the very edge of the roadway with no sign of ditch or fence.

Jodell kept the front wheels straight as he entered the next turn. The car seemed to fight him for a moment, to question his decision to not turn with the roadway, but, as always, she ultimately obeyed, left the blacktop, and flew directly into the field.

Jodell fought his own first instinct and kept his foot squarely on the gas pedal, ignoring the brake. Thankfully, he had remembered correctly and picked the right place to go cross-country. The field seemed to be covered with hay or grass of some kind, with no deeply plowed furrows. But all the same, the car's front end shimmied violently as she rolled and pitched across uneven ground like a boat on rough seas. Jodell fought to keep his hands on the wildly lurching wheel.

Now, in his headlights, he could see a line of small saplings at the far end of the field. There was probably a road of some kind there. Farmers used such lanes to sled in their fertilizer and guano behind mules or tractors. If there was one there, it was still several hundred yards away, across dusty, pitching ground.

And then there was something else. Just in time to keep from diving into it nose-first, Jodell spotted a small creek that cut the field in half. There was muddy water in the branch, its sides were several feet high, and it was a formidable obstacle for him to have to deal with if he wanted to get to the other side of the field.

He braked to a stop. Maybe he could get a running go and try to jump it. No, it looked too far across for something as heavy as the Ford to hop like a steeplechase horse.

But then, strictly by luck, he saw in his lights what looked like a cut-through, and a place where someone had piled rocks in the stream bed to allow a tractor or hay wagon to be able to ford the creek. He didn't hesitate. He didn't dare look back, but he could almost feel the blue sedan's headlights creeping up on him. He drove the Ford right through the branch, splashing muddy water all over the windshield, the rear glass, and through the open window all over himself. The rear tires spun in the mud, but somehow found enough traction to pull out the other side. For once, the car's weight had come in handy.

Once on the other side, he ventured a glance backward. Sure enough, he could see that the pursuing car had apparently slid to a stop at the edge of the field, no doubt wondering what kind of whiskey-running fool would take off across such unknown territory. But even as he watched, Jodell could see that the lawman was through wondering and was already pulling into the field, giving chase again. The wheels raised a dense fog of dust that merged with what Jodell had already stirred up.

The Ford's rear end fishtailed when Jodell stomped the accelerator, the tires spewing dirt and rock behind. The dust he kicked up behind him was thick, solid, seemingly impenetrable. It was so thick he even lost sight of the sedan's headlights in the cloud for a moment.

No matter. He needed to concentrate on what lay ahead, watch for rocks and junk in his way. Maybe another creek or ditch. Suddenly the car plunged through the line of trees and bushes and he found himself in the narrow, ill-defined lane that ran there. As he turned in the direction where he figured Highway 11 lay, he dared one more look backward, across the field. He could just barely see the sedan's lights, dim and yellowed, almost lost in the dust cloud.

"How can that old boy see where he's going?" Jodell asked himself out loud. "If he's not careful, he's gonna—"

And suddenly the headlights dipped wildly, seemed to point drastically downward, then almost straight up again, into the night sky. And they had obviously stopped advancing across the field toward Jodell.

"Lord, Delilah! The dumb so-and-so ran into the creek!"

He let the engine idle and listened. He could hear the lawman's car, its engine racing, wheels whining pitifully as he tried to get it out of the branch. And then Jodell could clearly hear the string of epithets and screams of frustration, wafting across the field with the dust, as the cop vented his rage.

Jodell slowly drove on then, carefully steering around the deeper ruts and mud holes in the lane, until it dumped him out onto the main highway a half mile up from the T intersection.

"Well, baby, we won again."

He stomped the accelerator, hoping the symphony of the straight pipes would drift back to the field where the lawman was stuck. For a moment Jodell Lee allowed himself to feel true, deep joy. He was almost as elated as he might have been if he had beaten the Johnson man from North Carolina to the checkered flag the previous Sunday.

Almost.

Jodell could see, even from the turnoff, that something was wrong back at his grandfather's house. Three in the morning and lights were on everywhere in the house. That was too early for anybody to be up and around, even Grandpa Lee, and the old man would never turn on lights in any room he wasn't actually in at the time.

Then, when he pulled to a stop in the yard, he could see several strange cars parked around the porch and along the drive. And there, among them, was a black-and-white county sheriff's patrol car.

Oh, Lord! he thought. Surely that damned old Fed revenuer didn't take his little detour so seriously that he called for the sheriff to come intercept me! It wasn't my fault he was dumb enough to follow me across that old field. Shoot, they couldn't prove anything anyway. Or could they?

Just to be safe, Jodell pulled the whiskey car into the barn as quietly as he could, cutting the engine as he coasted past the blazing lights of the house. He could see several folks standing in groups inside, in the parlor and on the porch, apparently talking with each other, and one of them was the sheriff in his tan uniform and black boots.

Why were so many people there if the sheriff simply wanted to ask him where he had been so late on this dark night?

Without turning on any lights, Jodell closed the barn door behind him, fastened the hasp, and clicked the padlock shut. They rarely locked the barn shop. It wasn't usually necessary out here in the country. Burglaries were seldom heard of. The occasional tramp or Gypsy knew better than to steal from the folks there. But if the sheriff wanted to take a closer look at the Ford, he would at least have to go get a warrant, wouldn't he? Jodell didn't want to make it too easy for him.

But as he walked through the inky darkness back toward the house, he could see a familiar figure, there in the dim light of the porch. Joe Banker. Sitting there in one of the old rocking chairs, his head down in his hands, swaying gently back and forth.

"Joe, what's up?"

He dreaded the answer as soon as he asked the question. Something was awfully wrong here, and he was slowly realizing it had nothing to do with the revenuer back there in the creek.

"Jodell! We didn't have any way of getting in touch

with you. We figured you were still out on a run. It's . . .
I'm afraid it's Grandpa."

Joe's voice shook as he stood and came to meet
Jodell at the top of the steps. He stopped there to lean
against one of the roof supports as if the trip from the
rocker had worn him out. Jodell could hear the people
inside, their quiet voices drifting out the parlor window, whispering like they were trying to keep from
waking someone.

"What's going on?"

"Grandpa didn't come back from the still tonight.
Grandma first figured maybe y'all must've had some
kind of trouble getting the load hauled down from the
hollow. Then she got to thinking maybe the Feds
might have jumped you. She'd heard some shots early
but figured somebody would have come and told her
by then if they had shot y'all or if they had carried
you off to jail. But by midnight or so, she really started
to get worried, then one of the mules showed up by
itself. Grandpa wouldn't have ever let one of them
critters go unless something was bad wrong.

"She walked down to the highway and flagged
down somebody to come get me. I took the dogs and
a lantern and went up the mountain, backtracking
toward the still hollow, looking for him. I figured he
might have fallen and broke a leg or got on a snake
or something."

Joe stopped then and slid slowly down the length
of the support to sit wearily on the top step. He had
beggar lice all over his pants legs and blackberry briar
scratches on his arms. Even in the sliver of light that
spilled out from inside the house, Jodell could see how
pale his cousin's face was.

"What happened, Joe?"

"He was leading the mules down the mountain on

the back trail. It looks like he just sat down, leaned against that old oak tree, and went to sleep. Sheriff figures he must have had a heart attack. I don't know if Grandpa ever knew what hit him. Probably just thought he was tired and needed to stop and rest. The other mules were standing there, waiting for him to holler 'giddyap,' I guess."

Jodell sat heavily on the steps beside Joe. The entire night had suddenly turned dreamlike, as if he were watching it all through a filmy curtain, hearing the sounds above a muffled roar, as if he were underwater. He half expected to wake up any minute with everything perfectly normal, Grandpa calling him to come on and get to work and Grandma threatening to throw the grits and eggs out to the dogs.

But even then, as tired and as much in shock as he was, he instinctively knew that everything had suddenly turned around. That nothing would ever be the same again.

He had been so young when his father had left for the war that he hardly remembered him. Then the man had simply not come back home. Same with his mother. No one so close to him had ever died before. And Grandpa had been the only father he had ever actually had. Now he was gone.

Jodell Lee's life had just taken a big left-hand turn and he was having trouble keeping it in the groove.

It was two days later, after the funeral, before Jodell finally said out loud what he had been thinking since the morning after his grandfather's passing. He and Joe were walking slowly back down the hill from the old cemetery behind Caney Creek Church, acknowledging the kind comments of the others who had been gathered around the graveside. When they were out of earshot of anyone else, Jodell spilled what had been on his mind.

"I've been doing a lot of thinking about what we're going to do, Joe. Grandma and me. We don't make enough money off that old dirt farm to keep us going. Shoot, that place never has grown much more than weeds and saw briers. Without the whiskey money, we're gonna have a tough time of it."

"Can't you make the whiskey yourself, Jodell? You helped Grandpa enough out at that still."

"Naw. Not even close. He had just started sharing some of his secrets with me lately. I could probably make some brew all right, but it wouldn't be nearly as good as Grandpa's. And without that quality, it'll be hard to compete with the others. And things are changing anyhow. Two more counties downstate just voted to go wet, and there'll surely be more to follow. They're wanting the taxes on legal liquor. If the product ain't the best, folks will just drive down there and buy the legal stuff. Or the bootleggers will haul it back up here and sell it instead of what we make. It's cheaper for them in the long run."

Joe had stopped walking and was kicking at clods of dirt with the toes of his Sunday shoes. He reminded Jodell of an eight-year-old, forced to be somewhere he didn't want to be, dressed in his church best.

"Well, Mr. Jodell Bob Lee. If I know you, you've done begun to think of a way out of this mess. Ain't nothing nor nobody gonna beat you, I don't suspect."

Jodell could only grin at him.

"I've not had anything but time to think since Grandpa got killed. And I think I might have an idea or two. But I need your help on both of them."

"Well, I'm a mighty busy man . . ."

"Hear me out. First, I think I can pick up some

work with some of the other 'shiners. They know I can drive and that I will get their stuff to the bootleggers without spilling it all over the road. I just need you to help me keep the whiskey car running. Man's got to have the equipment to do the job, and that old Ford is the best car a runner could hope to drive."

"Shoot, Cuz, that ain't no problem a'tall, long as you get out of the habit of straddling ditches like you done the other night."

"Not by choice, I tell you. The other idea's a little tougher, though."

The two men had stopped beneath the shade of a huge water oak in the yard of the church. Other mourners had paused in clumps to talk about how beautiful old Robert Lee's funeral had been, how profound the preacher's sermon was. Jodell waited until a couple of them had wandered on by before he went on.

"Joe, what would you think about getting serious about racing?"

Joe looked hard at his cousin. "Whatta you mean, 'serious'?"

"Look, I know I can win some of these races. Finish in the money on some more. I would've won the last one if that guy hadn't of moved up the track and run into me. And I can make more in winning one race than I can make in three or four whiskey runs. Besides, I don't have to risk going to jail for a year or two. Shoot, I can split the money with you and Bubba and still be doing as well or better, once we get rolling. And besides, if we start to run some of those tracks down in the Carolinas, we can race three or four times a week."

Jodell's voice had gotten higher, more excited, his words coming faster and faster as he went along. Joe was making motions, urging him to calm down. A fellow shouldn't look so excited so soon after he had just buried his grandfather.

"Maybe so. Maybe so. There's no doubt we could get the car so she could win, and I know you can drive as good as anybody this side of the Cumberland Plateau. But what am I gonna tell my daddy when he wonders where I've run off to instead of being home to help him haul hay and cure tobacco?"

"You manage to come up with plenty of lies to tell him already. I don't expect you'd have trouble making up a few more. Joe, just think about it. That's all I'm asking you to do right now."

"Being gone so much sure would cut into my love life . . ." Joe was saying, but he was smiling as he spoke. There was enough of a sparkle in his eyes to let Jodell know he may have planted a seed that was already beginning to sprout.

Jodell had suspected already that the idea would be attractive to Joe Banker. He loved the crowds and excitement at the tracks. And especially the women.

Just then, Jodell caught sight of someone walking their way. Someone in a long, dark dress, and with beautiful blond hair.

Catherine Holt. He had meant to speak to her already, to thank her for coming to the funeral, for bringing over the coconut cake to the house for the wake.

He left Joe standing there in the shade grinning and went to meet her, to accept her sincere, sympathetic hug. Then they walked hand in hand all the way down to the side of the road where her parents' car was parked.

For a little while then, Jodell forgot all about tragic death and Grandma, whiskey running and car racing.

THE RACE CAR

The Ford was still covered in the dust and dried mud it had brought back from the field two days before. The front end had been knocked so badly out of alignment that he had been hesitant to drive it to his grandfather's funeral. He and Grandma were forced to hitch a ride with some of the kinfolk.

"I don't know that I would have tried to turn her into a swamp buggy." Joe Banker sucked on a soda pop as he surveyed the car with squinted eyes.

"It was either that or make like an airplane and try to fly her over the creek. I don't know what that revenuer had under the hood, but he was moving. Never had one catch up on me that quick and stay with me like that."

Jodell was sitting on the hard-packed floor of the

barn, leaning against the workbench and downing his own bottle of fizzy pop. Neither of them felt much like working this night for some reason. The funeral that afternoon had drained them and they had wandered on back to their homes after Jodell had said good-bye to Catherine. But somehow, instinctively, they had come back here to the barn shop as soon as the sun had fallen.

"Looks like they're gettin' serious about trying to catch you terrible old lawbreakers. Those cop cars usually can't even come close enough to you to get a sniff of exhaust smoke."

"I'm not sure what he had, but I don't want to run into him again. Somebody the other night said they might be part of that new federal task force. They'd heard they'd only been around here for a few weeks, staking out the highways between here and the other side of the mountains. Said they caught Cooter Chastain and they've still got him locked up over in Asheville. Just another sign whiskey-makin' may be over and done with for the Lee family."

Joe leaned over and studied the works underneath the Ford's front end. "Looks like an alignment and some soap suds should put her back in pretty good shape. Unless you tried to climb a tree with her and didn't bother to tell me about it."

Jodell only smiled wearily. "That ought to be all she needs. Maybe we can do that tomorrow night. I don't think I've got the energy this very minute."

"Me either." Joe took another mighty swig, then paused, belched, and stood there, as if there was something else he wanted to say but didn't exactly know how. He finally shrugged his shoulders and blurted it right out. "You know what you were talking about today at the church? About doing some racing? How serious were you, Cuz?"

Jodell didn't hesitate. "Serious as I could be. I don't see no other way."

"Well, I heard they're going to have another event in a few weeks out at Meyer's place. You wanna try to run out there again?"

"I'd love to. But right now I got to worry about tearing up the Ford like we did last time. It was way too much work, plus it cost me almost twenty dollars to fix her. This car is the only way I've got to make a living for Grandma and me for the time being. I can't afford to tear it up racing and not be able to do any whiskey runs. I talked to a couple of 'shiners already that came by to pay their respects. I can find the work, but I got to have the Ford."

Joe Banker had a sly grin on his face. "Well, Jodell, you ain't the only one around here that's been doing some thinking. I've been wondering why we don't fly in and build ourselves a real race car."

"Well, sure. If we can build one out of pine trees and honeysuckle vines. That's all I got an abundance of right now. I sure don't have the money to go buy a car." Jodell turned up the last of the soft drink and tossed the bottle into the garbage drum. When he looked up, Joe was giving him an odd, contemptible look.

"I'll be a son of a gun! Is that Jodell Lee sittin' over there in the floor, lettin' the situation get the best of him?" Joe walked over, bent down, and put his face two inches from Jodell's. "Is that my cousin, Jodell Lee, admittin' that he's done been beat already? Whipped from the get-go? Lapped before he even gets off the starting line?"

Jodell stood suddenly, his eyes flashing, and tapped

his cousin on his chest with a closed fist.

"Hell, no! I ain't beat! I'm just . . . I'm just . . . trying to plot my next pass, that's all," he yelled, but his eyes looked downward then. He refused to admit defeat, even when he felt it so strongly.

"Well, try this on for size. What about that old jalopy over yonder?"

Joe was pointing backward, over his shoulder, toward the carcass of the '38 Ford sitting in the back corner of the shop. The old junker's straight flathead-eight engine still hung from the crossbeam on a chain above the carcass of the car, dangling like a slaughtered hog ready for the gutting.

"That piece of junk? She hasn't run in years. Not since before my dad left for the war."

"Well, Cuz, many's the night I've rested over here while you and Bubba worked, and while I watched you two sweat and groan, I leaned up against this old buggy. She may not be too far gone. I can almost certainly fix the motor so she'll run. And if you and our lug-headed buddy can set up the drive train, we might could make her move. The frame and body don't look like they're in bad shape at all. Tires are dry-rotted for sure, but we can pick some of them up cheap at the junkyard."

Jodell was scratching his chin, actually considering the possibilities.

"I suppose we could set the drive train back in place, but I don't know about that motor. I think it got pretty hot more than a time or two. You know how easy it is to crack one of those things."

"Nothing ventured, nothing gained. Let me have a go at it. If it's cracked, I'll find it out soon enough."

Jodell followed his cousin over to where the old jalopy sat, hiding in the shadows. It had been there so long, he had almost forgotten it even existed. Grandpa had told him his father had always had plans to fix it up as an alternate whiskey car, but he had never gotten to it before he had gone away. So there it had remained for all those years, gathering dust.

Jodell took one hand and wiped away the grime from a fender. The paint looked bright enough beneath the powder. He patted her roof and felt the solidity of her. And for some reason, his fingers seemed to tingle when he touched her.

Then something powerful suddenly welled up hot inside him. His father's car! How perfect would it be if he could take this old jalopy, fix her up, and continue his racing career behind her wheel, her engine out there in front of him, pulling him along to victory?

Maybe he and Joe were crazy to even think they could make the old hunk of junk competitive on a race track. Or that they had enough money between them to put into her motor what she needed to fly with the wind once more. Maybe, out of grief and desperation, they were only kidding themselves.

But the alternative was to admit that they were already beaten, that the field had passed them by.

And Jodell Bob Lee would never, ever, do that.

GEOMETRY

In his half-sleep dreamworld, he thought the noise was his grandfather shooting at him again. But then Grandma's voice on the front porch below his window was enough to rouse him from his dreams.

"What you bangin' on my door so early for, Little Joe? You boys ain't going to church this early." Little Joe. That was what his grandmother would always call him, no matter his age.

"No, Granny." It was Joe Banker's voice. "Me and Jodell, we got some work we gotta get done this mornin'. We'll be at preaching next Sunday, you can be sure."

"Well, baby, I don't know about working on the Lord's day. Not unless you got an ox in the ditch, the Bible says."

"Yes'm. That's exactly it. We got an ox in the ditch."

But despite her reservations, she wouldn't let them go anywhere until she had fixed them a paper sack filled with fried pork sausage nestled inside tall biscuits, and others that were buttered and filled with her homemade blackberry preserves.

They were in the barn before Jodell could ask what the all-fired hurry was. He hadn't expected Joe until after nine o'clock, long after Grandma had gone on to church.

"You wanna tell me why you showed up at the crack of dawn?" he asked.

"Might have known you'd be sleepin' in after your big date with Miss Catherine last night. By the way. When's the wedding?"

If they were not so busy getting the '38 Ford hooked to the whiskey car, he might have sailed a wrench in Joe's general direction.

"Just tell me what the hurry is in us getting out to the track. We can't race until noon or so and it ain't even seven yet."

"I was talking to some of the boys down at the pool hall, and just before I beat their butts in a little eight ball, they told me that if we got out to the track before nine, then we could practice the car until ten-thirty."

"Are you sure, Joe?" Jodell coveted the thought of practice time. It would be invaluable in getting ready to race the new car.

"That's what they said. And even if it ain't so, we can spend some time working on the car anyway."

It wasn't like Joe to be early to anything, or to want to spend any more effort or time on any pursuit than he absolutely had to. This racing thing had taken hold of his cousin with a much tighter grip than Jodell could have ever hoped. He had taken special pride in getting the old jalopy's motor reworked and tuned like a whiskey runner. He had it running remarkably well. He'd passed up much of his pool-hall and dating time to do it. He had only failed to show up to work a few times, and now here he was, arriving with the morning sun and ready to go.

An hour and a half later, they where pulling into the track with the old sedan in tow. The old car didn't necessarily look pretty. Some of the other early arrivals gave it odd looks as they pulled into a slot in the roped-in garage area.

But looks aside, the car had performed decently on their test runs down several mountain highways the last couple of days. Jodell, Joe, and Bubba Baxter had put in countless hours getting the car back in shape, to the point where it would at least run and seemed to track a straight line.

Bubba was already at track, waiting for them. He made an expert catch of one of the biscuits Joe threw his way, then helped them unhitch the tow bar from the race car and unload and set up the tools. Jodell wandered down to where one of the track officials stood, who looked like the promoter's cousin, to find out if and when they could get out onto the track. He headed back to the car at a good trot, grinning broadly.

"For once, your pool-hall scuttlebutt was right, Joe. We can practice if we can get out there in the next few minutes."

"Hate to tell you 'I told you so,' but . . .'"

"Where's Bubba?"

"Off to find himself something to eat. Where else?"

"What about the sack of biscuits?"

"Gone. He went through them like Sherman through Georgia."

"Lord. Catherine and the twins are bringing a picnic lunch with them. Couldn't he wait?"

"They won't be here for at least another hour. Poor thing would be wasted away to nothing by then."

Ten minutes later, Jodell guided the car out onto the dirt track along with several other cars for the start of the practice session. He had no idea how the rebuilt car would actually run or handle on the circular track. They had worked feverishly, when they could, their labor sandwiched between several whiskey runs for Jodell, Joe's work on his father's farm, and Bubba's job at the mill.

It had taken the most of their time getting the engine back into its mounts under the jalopy's hood, and then getting a roll bar welded inside the cab. There had been little time to devote to setting up the car's suspension or to do any tricks to coax more speed from her. Jodell knew he needed this track time to see what she could do. And maybe they would have a chance to make some adjustments before the first heat race.

There were only a half dozen or so other cars practicing. That gave him plenty of room to run flat out, to try some maneuvers in the corners, to get a feel for the car in different places on the circuit. After three or four laps of feeling the car out, he started running noticeably faster laps. It didn't take him long to sense the best way to set the car up going into the turns. As he made the transition from the straightaways, the car had to be set precisely as it started the sweep into each corner. By letting the car drift just so, he could get onto the gas faster coming up out of the center of the corner and get a good bite with the tires coming down the backstretch.

If he stayed on the gas too hard going into the corner, then she wanted to continue to swing out wider and then would spin in the center of the turn. This would force him to get completely out of the gas until he could gather the wheels back up underneath him. That letup in the throttle could cost half a second or more in the lap time.

The only drawback to the line he was finding around the track was that it would only work if he was the leader, ahead of the traffic. Otherwise, he wouldn't be able to dictate his own line. A car in front or beside him usually would set the line. This caused many of the inexperienced drivers to either back off entering the corner or try to force the car through the turn. Jodell knew already that on dirt, if a driver forced his car to do anything it didn't want to do, it could easily head for the rail and off the track and maybe collect another car or two while en route.

As Jodell lapped the track, he could see Joe and Bubba standing along the backstretch rail. In one hand Joe held an old stopwatch he still had left from his days on the high school track team. Bubba beside him carried what appeared to be a hot dog. They were supposed to time every other lap while keeping track of the line Jodell took each time through the corners. His times would depend on where he caught the other traffic on the track as he reeled off hot lap after hot lap.

Jodell quickly learned something else as he negotiated the track. He could run much faster or decidedly slower, depending on how the car attacked its line around the speedway.

"Thank you, Mrs. Cummings," he suddenly said, out loud, laughing.

He had never, in his wildest imagination, thought he might ever find a use for all the boring theories and problems his old geometry teacher had forced him to absorb. But now he realized he was actually applying the basic mathematical rules for arcs which had been learned so begrudgingly.

The turns on the race course could, in theory, be broken down into a series of arcs. How a driver attacked each arc as he set up the car going into the corner determined how well and at what speed he could come off that corner. This was ultimately the fastest way around the racetrack.

After about thirty good laps around the track, Jodell pulled out of the first turn and steered up beside the rail. Joe and Bubba came running from where they had been watching along the backstretch.

"What you two monkeys think?" Jodell yelled over the roar of the motor. "It felt pretty good out there."

"The last couple of laps looked real fast. Or at least in comparison to the other cars you were out there with," Joe answered. He held up the watch to show the time for the last lap.

Jodell turned the ignition key off, unstrapped the seat belt, and climbed from the car.

"She felt pretty good. The giddyap of the motor off the corner was okay, nothing spectacular, but at least she seemed to want to stay under me. The 'shine car had almost too much power for the dirt. Just the touch of the throttle in the turn and you would break the tires loose in the corner. At least with this motor you really have to get into it before it breaks loose."

"I still need to work on that old motor. I can find you some more power, I think. Looks to me like the key to this track is going to be the line you take going into the corner. You won't outpower anybody with your car, but you can get in the throttle sooner without breaking the back end loose."

"Mrs. Cummings!"

"Huh?"

Joe and Bubba both gave him blank looks, but they understood what he was talking about when he explained the rule of arcs. They had both suffered at Sarah Belle Cummings's chalk-dusted hand, too.

"Next thing, you're gonna try to tell us you learned how to pass another car by diagramming sentences!" Joe laughed.

"You never know. Why don't you keep timing some of the other cars and let's see if we can figure out which are the ones to beat. Bubba and me have a few more things to do to get the car ready."

Bubba hopped up on the fender and held on to the window frame as Jodell cranked up and eased the race car back toward their slot in the pits. Bubba was underneath the car and Jodell had his head buried under the hood when they heard familiar voices. Catherine, Betty, and Susan had arrived with their picnic baskets.

Jodell was almost embarrassed for Catherine to see him. He was hot, sweating, and covered in grease and dirt. But she didn't seem to mind. She stood shyly and waved with her gloved hand. As she stood there in her cotton Sunday dress, Jodell thought she was the prettiest girl he'd ever seen.

Bubba was his usual embarrassing self with the girls. Jodell thought for a second that he was going to actually shake hands with Susan Thompson, but then she walked right past his outstretched arm and gave him a smack on a grease-streaked cheek. He turned brilliantly red and they all had a good laugh at his expense.

Susan went to work, helping Bubba shoe-polish on the number "34" on the car's doors. Betty wandered off to where Joe was still timing the other cars.

"I'm glad you came," Jodell said sincerely as he tried to wipe away some of the dirt on his face with a rag. Catherine stood farther from him than he would have liked, with her light blue dress and all his dirt probably having something to do with it.

"You know I wouldn't miss it for anything in the world. The car looks good."

This was the first time Catherine had seen her. She had known what was taking so much of Jodell's time and why it was so important. Her encouragement had meant a great deal to him. Some girls might have been jealous. Not Catherine. She had done nothing but bolster his resolve to finish the car in time to race this Sunday, even when it meant they had not been able to see each other as much as they both had wanted. She was glad to finally see what he had accomplished.

"Thanks. I just hope she can go round and round real fast."

"You'll do great, Jodell. You know why? Because you refuse to lose. You are the most determined man I have ever seen."

The smile she gave him then made him feel funny inside. He wanted to do nothing else but kiss her, but with the dirt covering him, he knew he shouldn't.

And that was exactly what he did.

The car seemed to buck beneath him as he slowly circled the track waiting for the start of his heat race. That was a good sign. She seemed to want to be unleashed, to be allowed to run. He checked the seat belt one last time as he kept an eye on the starter with his set of multicolored flags close at hand.

The green one. That was the one he wanted to see.

The cars bunched up tightly heading into the third turn, ready for a glimpse of the green flag. As they rumbled out of the fourth turn and each of them saw the green flag waving, the roar of their engines drowned out all the other sounds on the mountaintop. If there had been a thunderbolt from heaven, it would have been lost in the din from the cars as they raced off toward the first turn. Jodell found himself fourth in line, boxed in by a junker car on the outside, while the driver in front of him was struggling to keep his vehicle straight all the way through the corner.

He tried to keep a safe distance behind because it was clear the guy wasn't long for the track. Sure enough, on the second lap, the guy slid dangerously high, taking the car to his right along with him toward the short outside rail. Jodell didn't hesitate. He shot down to the inside of the two slipping and sliding cars and moved quickly past before they did something dumb and careened sideways back into his path.

Jodell worked the accelerator trying to maintain his momentum through the corners, tugging at the wheel as he worked to find his best line despite the dust and traffic all around him. Now he found himself only inches from the rear bumper of the second-place number 37 car, but the driver seemed to be taking up the entire track, purposely not allowing him to get past. Jodell gave him a gentle tap in the rear to let him know he was there, and faster, but the driver stayed directly in front of him, no matter where he went.

Then Jodell offered him a stronger bump and he could see the rear end sway precariously, the car on the verge of spinning out. The driver hung tough, though, not giving any quarter at all.

"I'd do the same thing," Jodell admitted to himself. "If I was that slow anyway."

There were only six laps to go, so it was hard to be patient, but finally the Chevy just ahead of Jodell slipped badly going into the first turn. The driver instinctively got out of the throttle to try to gather it back in, to get control before someone drove past him. Jodell was so close, trying to drive deeper into the corner, that he had no time to avoid giving the guy a hard nudge in the rear when he slowed so suddenly. It was a good, solid bump, and with the Chevy on the verge of out-of-control already, it spun sideways, up the track, out of his way. Jodell was finally able to punch his way past.

Fine for Jodell, but the two cars running side by side behind them had little place to go. The driver on the inside steered low and managed to follow behind Jodell, missing the spinning car completely.

The car on the outside, however, had no room to duck through anywhere. He swung as wide as he could, careening up the track, but he still clipped the rear corner of the Chevy, knocking it completely broadside to the rest of the field. Several other cars following closely joined the melee with a crash of colliding sheet metal.

Jodell could see the grandstand crowd, on its feet, cheering the action, but he didn't take time to watch the rearview mirror. He had another car to catch, and the yellow flag would probably be coming out by the time he got back around to the flag stand.

When he took the caution, Jodell finally had a chance to breathe. He looked to see if he could find Joe and the Thompson twins, who were on their feet with the rest of the spectators, screaming and waving him on. Over in the scorers' box he caught a glimpse of Catherine, her head down as she dutifully marked off another lap for him. It made him feel wonderful, somehow, to think of her keeping track of him that way, sharing his racing the way she was doing.

Dust and oil smoke rose from the pile of wrecked cars as they began to untangle and pull away. Despite the size of the wreck, all the cars were able to drive away, mostly with only some body damage. But as Jodell circled and could see the tail end of the field ahead, there was some obvious bumping and nudging still going on, some fists shaken out windows at each other. Obviously some of the drivers were unhappy with the way the race had gone so far and the order they had been placed in for the restart. The flag man held the start for another lap, maybe to see if another trip around would allow tempers to cool a bit.

Jodell anticipated the restart correctly, and that gave him a good jump up on the lead car as the two of them headed back into the first turn. With a fender on his inside, he was able to drive his line right on through the corner, then kept it into the second turn, even though the two cars touched viciously several times.

Jodell stepped hard on the gas, accelerating a half second earlier as they came off the corner. That was all he needed to pull in front of the other car and take the lead down the backstretch. He pushed the Ford harder and managed to put a couple of car lengths between them down the front stretch. Then, hunched over the wheel, he aimed the car exactly where he needed it to go, holding on to the lead the remaining three laps despite the other car looming in his rear-view mirror.

He was so intent on his driving, on holding the lead, that he hardly felt a thing when he sailed beneath the checkered flag. He pulled to a stop in front of the grandstand where a photographer waited, nonchalantly hopped out the window the way he had seen the Carolina drivers do, and tossed a wave to the cheering crowd.

That was when it finally hit him. A tingle spread all over his body, as if he had stuck his hand in an electric socket. It was like nothing he had ever felt before. He could see the twins and Joe, jumping up and down in the stands, Catherine waving from the scorers' box, and even Bubba, still down there in his spot along the rail in the first turn, doing some kind of buck dance in the dust.

The flag man came down and unfurled the checkered flag behind him while the photographer snapped a picture. Then, with his very first victory duly recorded, he was directed back to the garage with the rest of them. It was only a heat race victory, maybe, but it was his first trip as a winner beneath that magical checkered flag.

He hardly remembered driving back behind the ropes. Bubba was there, still dancing, covered all over in chalky dust.

"You won! Jodell, you won! You know what? You won!"

"Aw, it was only a heat race. We were in the right place at the right time." But when he had crawled from the car, Bubba grabbed him and they danced together, ignoring the strange looks and big grins of the people who were standing around nearby. The big man's excitement was contagious. "You're right, Bub! We won! We won!"

They finally settled down and Jodell retrieved a cold drink from the cooler. They had plenty of work to do to get ready for the feature race, but Bubba couldn't stop talking.

"That was some driving, Jodell. Shoot, that was something."

"I pretty much had it made after those cars spun out. I hate that I tapped that guy and spun him out, but he shouldn't have let up on the throttle so quick when he lost it in the turn. I couldn't help but pop him in the butt."

"I know. I saw it all. It's a wonder he didn't take

you out with him. But you won, Jodell! You won the danged race!"

"We need Joe to help us get ready. Where's he at?"

"He said he wanted to sit up in the stands so he could see better."

"See what better? The race or Betty Thompson?" Bubba appeared to actually be thinking about an answer to Jodell's question. "He better get his butt down here and quick. And he better have kept the stopwatch like I asked him to."

Jodell dived under the hood to take out the air cleaner while Bubba dropped beneath the car to stick another wedge into the right-side springs to tighten up the car in the corners. Jodell could still hear Bubba beneath the car, laughing, chanting over and over: "We won! By gosh, we won!"

He got the air cleaner off and balanced it on the fender, then came out from under the hood to grab another batch of rags and some cleaning solvent. Something dark, like a quick thundercloud, suddenly came at him from his left side. Before he could even duck, he took a sharp blow to his jaw that spun him around and backed him up a couple of steps. Whatever or whoever had hit him was standing there now, screaming obscenities and spitting in the dust.

"What the . . . ?"

Jodell shook his head and turned back to come face-to-face with what was apparently another one of the drivers. And the man was hot as hell, so mad he was foaming at the mouth. Jodell figured it had to be the guy who had been piloting the 37, the one he had bumped and spun out. And he obviously didn't understand the reason that Jodell smacked him was 'cause he let completely off the gas.

Jodell squared up slowly, looked the man in the eye,

and watched patiently for the next punch. He didn't have to wait long. A long, looping wind-up preceded the next swing, and that gave Jodell ample time to make a move of his own. He deftly sidestepped the incoming roundhouse punch, then gathered his weight underneath him and threw a powerful right that connected solidly with the other driver's left temple. When the man staggered sideways from the blow and bent forward at the waist to regain his balance, Jodell followed with a sharp uppercut squarely on the · jaw. The driver dropped like a sack of cordwood.

The entire fight took less than ten seconds. Bubba hardly had time to come scrambling from beneath the car. Wide-eyed, he took in the groaning, crumpled form of the 37's driver lying there, writhing in the dust, Jodell standing there massaging the knuckles on his right hand, and the onrush of people running over to take in whatever fight might remain. Bubba stood there, a good-sized crescent wrench in his right hand, feet spread wide, ready for anything that might come until he could ascertain what was actually happening.

By the time some of the track officials had hurried up, they found Jodell with his head back under the hood, getting the motor cleaned up. Bubba and a couple of onlookers were trying to help the woozy driver get back to his feet.

Joe was stepping across the rope into the garage when he saw everyone running. It had to be a fight, but he was doing all he could to keep straight in his head the times he had clocked. He didn't really have time to watch a couple of good old boys tangle. Sometimes it seemed to him that people only came to the races to see wrecks and fights. Only when he realized that the crowd was gathering around his car did he take off in a trot to see what was going on. He could see Bubba Baxter towering over everyone else.

"Hey, Bubba! Who you punching out now?" he yelled.

"Wadn't me. This driver here got his nose out of joint 'cause he got in Jodell's way and got his little tail bumped." Bubba pointed toward the rumpled driver, staggering through the gathered crowd back toward his own car, rubbing the side of his head with one hand and his bloody chin with the other. "He slipped up and hit Jodell when he wasn't looking. I guess that must've made old Jodell mad or something, 'cause he kicked the feller's butt."

"Well, I'll be, Jodell Bob! You punched out that big old bad race-car-drivin' feller? My, my! A whiskey man and a fighter! And now a winning race car driver to boot! Can I have your autograph, Mr. Jodell Bob Lee? Huh? Can I?"

"Why don't you just shut up and tell me what times you got?" Jodell's muffled words came from under the hood.

"Well, you are still my hero, Mr. Lee." Joe winked at Bubba. "Now, if you can put away your boxing gloves long enough, we need to go over these lap times."

Jodell pulled himself out from beneath the hood. "What we got?"

"It looks like the fast cars in the feature are going to be the five car, the forty-seven, and the fifty-eight. There are a couple of others that are fast, but not nearly as fast as those three."

"How about the thirty-four car? How do we stack up against the rest of them?"

"With a clear track, you could run about as quick as anybody. The five car seemed to get through the traffic a little better. He was awful smooth all the way around the track."

"What kind of line was he running?"

"Right down on the bottom in the center of the corner, then he would drift out high as he came out of his slide heading down the straight stretch."

"Hmmm. I was trying to cut the corner in more of an arc as I entered and exited the turn. I'll have to try that line in the feature and see how it feels. That's interesting."

Jodell was absentmindedly rubbing the goose egg on his jaw as he talked and all the time he was absorbing what Joe was telling him.

"Won't hurt to give it a try and see what you think. We know your line is a fast way around the track already. You won the race, you know. With the way we've got the car set up, his way might be slower for us. You never know until you give it a try."

Jodell nodded. He was already imagining how each line might work, how the car would feel as he steered through the corners.

The voice on the public address system gave the call for fifteen minutes to the starting line. The Ford was ready with only a few minutes to spare. They had found the wire screen over the front end, which protected the radiator from rocks, was loose and needed tightening up. Joe made his way back to the grandstand while Bubba stood by the car and helped Jodell get buckled in. Then he took a rag from his overalls pocket and cleaned the windshield one last time.

Sitting there, waiting for the command to start the engine, Jodell Lee felt strangely relaxed. His heart was pumping, his senses seemed to be turned up to maximum sensitivity, but he was amazingly calm, despite all the activity swirling around him. The crush of people still surrounding the cars, the surging, packed grandstand, the wind-whipped banners, the dust, the noise, the gyrating crowd lining the fence . . . all of it should have been near overwhelming. But the only calm place in all this storm of activity was right there where he sat, behind the wheel of the race car he, Joe, and Bubba had built with their own hands. It was like a comfortable, safe place of refuge for Jodell Lee. More than ever before, he knew that this was where he belonged, that this was what he was born to do.

He couldn't wait to crank the engine once more, to feel its powerful throb, and to drive it away to lead the others home.

J odell Lee sat with his arm resting on the lip of the window as the assembled cars moved off the line behind the pace car. He was lined up on the outside of the first row of çars because of his first-place finish in the heat race, with the three heat winners drawing straws for exact starting position. The rest of the field stretched out by twos behind them, their slots based on their own finishing positions in the heats.

Jodell watched the flag man even more closely than usual. As the driver sitting on the outside pole, he had to be careful not to get too far in the gas before the driver beside him as they paced the field for the start. The track officials had preached to him and the driver on the inside over and over how crucial it was not to jump the start or there could be chaos.

But sure enough, the 6 car to Jodell's inside stomped the gas and took off before the green flag could be seen, much less unfurled. That gave him a three-car-length lead coming out of the fourth turn when the start was actually given. The car in line behind the 6 saw what was happening and hit his own throttle early, passing Jodell easily while he was still trying to come up to speed.

The flag man apparently decided to ignore the jumped start and simply let them race on. There was nothing Jodell could do but try to catch up.

As they came roaring out of the second turn, he was able to pull back down in line behind the front two cars. The 6 and the 21 car led the field, while the 16 car pressed Jodell hard from behind, occasionally tapping his bumper to remind him there was someone there who wanted to go on by. He had to drive as much with his mirror as he did out the windshield as he worked to get better acquainted with how his own car was handling.

Pushing hard into the third turn, Jodell tried to drive deeper into the corner and open up some distance on the car behind him. He needed to get him off his butt. He sensed at once that he had made a tactical mistake. As he let off on the throttle through the throat of the turn, he had to climb on the brakes much harder than he had expected to keep from losing control. That caused the car to push upward, the centrifugal force causing the front end to try to head for the outside of the track. And that opened up the bottom line for the car that had been directly behind him.

The driver back there was alert, saw the sliver of daylight, and pounced like a wildcat on Jodell's mistake. He moved in beneath the Ford halfway through the turn and easily powered past him as they exited turn four onto the front stretch. Jodell cursed under his breath as he struggled mightily to get the car back under complete control. He stepped back in the gas, forcing the rear to power-slide back around, allowing him to gather the car back up. His impatience had cost him a hard-won spot on the track, but thankfully, the old Buick was the only one fast or alert enough to get past him.

The laps seemed to be winding down as if in fast motion, like one of the old silent films at the theater in town. Jodell remained mired in fourth place, behind the 16 car, but still ahead of the others. At least the front four cars had managed to break away from the rest of the drivers, but the front car was in serious danger of leaving him and the others so far behind they would never be able to catch up.

Jodell sensed that right now might be his last chance to get to the front because they were quickly catching up to a covey of slower cars that were marking the back of the field. The leader was already having some trouble getting past five or six slow cars that were fanned out all over the track. This gave Jodell and the other two cars an opportunity to bunch up on his back bumper.

Directly in front of the leader, two cars where running side by side for position in their own private little battle, racing hard trying to avoid finishing dead last. Jodell could see that the two slower cars were so close, another coat of paint on one of them would have them touching. Then, suddenly, they bumped fenders hard down the backstretch, then rapped each other again once, twice, a third time as they approached the third turn. The last time they crunched together, they didn't part. Their front bumpers were clearly hung up. Now the outside car began to slide sideways, on the verge of out-of-control. The car on the inside broke loose, bringing the other car's bumper with him, and headed toward the fence himself. The two sliding cars managed to block most of the track.

There was no place for the cars behind them to go. They scattered in all directions, throwing up a dense cloud of dirt and smoke that obscured the whole mess, from the crowd as well as from each other. The leader steered low to avoid the last place he had seen the two slower cars but guessed wrong where they were by then. He plowed hard into the passenger-side door of the car that was skidding lower on the track. To the outside, four more cars got tangled and slid against the low outside rail before they came to an abrupt halt there amid a shower of kicked-up dirt. The 16, directly in front of Jodell, jammed on the binders as he tried to slow enough to find a safe route through the free-for-all ahead.

Jodell smacked the 16's rear as he, too, tried to steer through the dust cloud. The 16 clipped slightly the front end of one of the wrecked cars as it skidded away from him toward the infield. Jodell swerved at the last instant, barely missing the same car the 16 had touched.

Even then, he could see that the impact with the car in front of him had crumpled the left front fender back and upward. He could only hope it had not bent the sheet metal back into the tire. He watched for any sign of smoke as he worked his way on through the mess. As he passed Bubba in the first turn, he motioned toward the injured fender, but Bubba was on the wrong side to get a good look at it. He could only shrug.

So far, the tire seemed to be holding air okay. Jodell

could only hope it wouldn't rupture when they got back to speed. That would be a real mess!

The pace car picked up the field the next time around and Jodell could finally catch his breath and take in the magnitude of the wreck. There where at least a half dozen cars entwined against the inside and outside rails. There was a gap hardly wider than one of the cars through which Jodell and the others who were left running could navigate.

The pace car slowed to a crawl around the track while the wreckers and some of the crews scrambled to clear the mess off the track. Several of the cars looked to be relatively undamaged, merely wedged into each other. Once the wreckers pulled one of the cars out of the way, three of the others were able to drive away, still able to race some more. The other three had to be snaked off the track, their days done.

Apparently no one had been hurt. The old funeral-home ambulance remained parked outside the fourth turn, its driver lounging shirtless on the hood.

Jodell considered his options as he circled slowly, using his hand to scoop in some cool air on his face. His own car was strong on the inside of the track, but the 16 was having success covering the inside line, too. The driver of the 16 would either have to make a mistake and allow Jodell to slip by on the inside or Jodell would be forced to take the hard way around him, trying to pass on the outside. He doubted he had enough power from his engine to successfully make a high pass on the outside. The motor Joe Banker had put together so quickly over the last couple of weeks was running beautifully, for certain. But it simply would not be able to outpower the old Buick on the outside.

Sitting there in the scoring stand sipping a soft

drink, Catherine Holt tapped her pencil nervously on her clipboard. Her heart was still running away from her. She loved seeing Jodell running near the front, but the slam-bang wreck had almost made her jump off the stand and run out there to check on him. But then she had seen him emerge at the other end, apparently okay, and she had concentrated on the lap numbers on her scoring sheet.

Down near the first-turn rail, Bubba Baxter was beside himself. He had had a good view of the wreck until the dust had swallowed the whole thing up. The last he had seen of the Ford was when Jodell drove into the cloud, and he had held his breath until he saw him spit out on the other side, apparently unscathed. But now he was worried about the damaged fender and whether it was touching the tire. He strained to see, but it was on the side opposite him. He could only cross his fingers and hope it would make it.

Up in the stands, with a twin on each side, Joe had the same worries. He also knew the engine was not powerful enough for Jodell to get around the other car on the high side. The inside was the only way to get past him, and he doubted the other driver would ever allow that to happen.

Finally, the track cleared, the pace car pulled into the infield as the cars began to bunch up tightly for the restart. Jodell tightened his grip on the wheel until his knuckles were white. He eased up closer until he was tight on the back bumper of the 16 car.

With more raw power, the 16 got a sizable jump on the start. Jodell fell three or four car lengths behind before he could work up through the gears. He tried to tighten back up on the 16 by driving his preferred line through the turns. Thank goodness they had a clear track ahead of them. That would give Jodell a clean shot at passing him if he could catch up and see even the slightest glimmering of an opening inside of him. Otherwise, the best he could do would be second. The thought of it made him even more determined to find a way around the guy.

There was one more problem. There were only seven laps left in which to make his move. He used the good handling of his Ford to pull up close exiting turn two. He was even able to give the 16 a couple of gentle taps in the rear, merely to make sure the driver knew he was lurking back there.

He made his first pass attempt in the third turn, swinging low as they dived downward going in, but the 16 chopped downward on the track, expertly cutting him off. Again Jodell had to jump hard on the brake pedal to avoid running into the guy's rear end.

The lead car was "shadow-driving." Jodell had heard the term in the pits. Any move Jodell made, the 16 driver was going to make the exact same move directly in front of him, effectively blocking him from any hopes of a pass. But Jodell thought he had a way to use that to his advantage.

He raced the Buick hard down the front stretch, tapping bumpers with him several times as they tried to set their own individual lines entering the corner. Jodell couldn't help but notice that the crowd in the grandstands was on its feet, the mass of people a shimmering wave of motion as they cheered the two of them on. With a slight twist of the steering wheel, he suddenly swung the car wide, clearly showing the Buick driver he was finally going to attempt the pass on the high side of the track. The 16 went with him, as expected, making sure he blocked the move to that side. Jodell could see the driver's eyes in his rearview mirror, watching him, so he pounded his steering wheel with his fists, as if furious that the pass had not worked.

As they came down the backstretch, Jodell gave the 16 another couple of bumps in the rear end. There were the eyes in the mirror again, wider this time. He had the old boy's attention for sure.

Once more he swung higher as they entered turn three, clearly trying to take the outside lane again. But this time, as the 16 eased up to block him, Jodell suddenly changed his arc through the corner, swinging sharply downward toward the low side of the track. The Buick driver had bought the fake completely!

Jodell rammed hard on the gas pedal as they exited onto the front stretch and, amazingly, swept past the Buick to take the lead. It had worked!

But almost immediately, before he had a chance to exult in his move, he felt a sharp tap on his own right rear fender near the bumper. The driver he had passed was trying to spin him out, to make him break loose enough so that he could come back around him and retake the lead.

Jodell had to admire the guy. He despised giving up the lead as much as Jodell would have.

He felt the Ford wobble underneath him from the lick as he fought the wheel to keep her headed straight. He never eased up on the gas, though. That would have given the other driver all the quarter he needed to sweep right on past him again.

By the time they entered the next turn, Jodell had surged ahead by a full car length. The lead was all his. Now all he had to do was keep it.

The last few laps seemed to last a year and a day. Since he could now run through the turns the way he wanted, Jodell managed to widen his lead to several car lengths as the laps unwound. He was so intent on aiming the car correctly that he completely forgot to look at the chalkboard on the inside rail where the laps were being counted down ever so slowly.

The white flag was a beautiful, pleasant surprise when he roared beneath it. Final lap. Almost home with the victory!

He checked his mirror one more time. There he was. The 16 car had not run away and hidden. He had suddenly pulled back to within a couple of car lengths, so close Jodell could see the determination on the driver's face through his own dust.

It was getting interesting up ahead, too. A couple of slow, lapped cars filled up the track in front of him. He had to be careful passing them. They were all that stood between him and the victory.

If one of them blocked him, even the tiniest bit, then the 16 would have all the opening he needed. He tickled the gas pedal exactly the right amount coming off the second turn. That gave him an extra twenty feet of lead over the trailing car.

The first of the lapped cars moved over obediently to the left and allowed him to sweep on by on the outside without slowing at all. No problem. He still had the lead he needed.

The second car, though, apparently didn't see him coming. Or didn't realize the leaders would run up on him so suddenly. The slower car held its line into the next corner as if he were all alone on the track, out for a nice Sunday drive.

Jodell had no choice. He had to go higher than he wanted to, scrubbing off some of the miles per hour he desperately needed as he slowed to stay on the track. The Buick had time to take a better line. That was all he needed. It gave him a chance to close the

16 up until he could put his own fender alongside Jodell's left rear quarter panel.

With his greater momentum, the 16 next moved up directly even with Jodell as they raced off the last turn side by side, dead even, headed for where the checkered flag was already hanging from the flag man's hand. Jodell did the only thing he could do. He kept the gas pedal on the floor and hoped the rear tires would hold traction all the way. He touched the steering wheel, nudging it a smidgen to the left. The move pinched the 16 down to the inside.

Just as they cleared the corner for the final dash to the line, the Buick, in his hurry to get ahead, cut the corner slightly too short. His rear tires broke loose from the dirt ever so slightly. But that was enough to bang hard into the left side of the Ford.

The impact jerked the wheel wildly from Jodell's hand. He grabbed it back, wrestling it back and forth, trying to keep the car in a straight line, her nose headed for the checkered flag.

They bumped hard again as the Buick driver tried his best to keep his own car under control. Jodell didn't remember closing his eyes, but he also didn't see the flag wave or the cars flash past the finish line.

But he did feel the strong jolt when the cars came together hard once more, close to where the finish line should have been. With this collision, the bumpers locked together in a tight embrace and the two cars went spinning off together in a wild dance, waltzing toward the track's infield, spinning in a crazy fandango.

Jodell struggled with the wheel to regain control, but he knew immediately he was merely along for the ride this time. The two cars that had locked horns for the last few laps were now hopelessly conjoined and were going wherever they pleased. The wild, bucking, twisting ride finally ended with the cars coming to a dusty stop almost in the first turn, amid the grass and wildflowers and dandelions that covered the infield.

Jodell had somehow had the forethought to keep the clutch kicked in throughout the roller-coaster trip, so the engine was still grumbling. He pulled the car back down into gear, rocked back and forth to free her from the grip the Buick had on her, and slowly rolled away from the clinch with the other car.

Only as he circled the track and the pace car driver waved him to the victory lane did he finally realize that he had actually won the race. Somehow, he had managed to put a fender out front at the finish line.

It was his race. He had won it!

The crowd was still cheering so loudly that he could hear them clearly, even over the Ford's engine. It was for him. It was a beautiful sound. He waved back to them as he took his victory lap. Surely they could see the grin on his face.

As he passed Bubba Baxter, the big man hopped the rail and climbed onto the running board. He held on tightly and rode all the way around on the cool-down lap, pumping his fist in the air the entire tour.

"We won! We won!" he screamed over and over. Jodell read his lips.

"We won, Bub!" Jodell screamed, but he knew Bubba couldn't actually hear him either, not over the drumbeat of the engine and the shrieking of the crowd.

He wheeled up to the start-finish line and stopped, ready now to be draped in the checkered flag for the photographers. Bubba reached through the window and slapped him on the shoulder. Joe came running at a gallop and hopped the low fence in stride, then pounded the hood while he screeched out an ear-piercing yell. Catherine was standing there, too, tears rolling down each cheek, clapping her hands.

He waved for her to make her way through the throng that had quickly gathered there, trying to be as close to the winner as they could get. She came directly to his window, dived through without any thoughts of modesty, and gave him a quick kiss on the mouth.

Finally Jodell unbuckled himself and struggled to get out of the car through the open window. The crowd wouldn't stop screaming. The race's wild and woolly finish had been one they would talk about for a while, and none of them wanted it to be over.

Then the driver of the 16 came walking up, his helmet in his hand. Several men stood back, sure there were about to be blows exchanged. Instead, the driver offered Jodell his hand.

"Helluva race, driver. You drove one helluva race," he said sincerely, shook hands, then pounded him on the back. Those close enough to hear cheered and screamed some more to show their appreciation of the driver's sportsmanship.

With one arm still around Catherine, Jodell hugged Joe and Bubba with his free one.

"Cuz, you drove the wheels off that thing!" Joe yelled, nodding toward the Ford.

Sure enough, the tire beneath the crumpled fender was flat as it could be, a big gash worn out of its sidewall. The sheet metal had finally rubbed its way through the rubber. Another half lap and the Ford would never have finished the race.

This time it was Jodell Lee who let go the resounding whoop. And then he tried to kiss everybody he could reach. Catherine, Joe, Bubba, the Thompson girls, a reporter from the newspaper, some spectators who happened to be standing there.

"Man! This winning is contagious!" he howled. "And I want me some more of it!"

GRANDMA'S BLESSING

When the newspaper came out the next Thursday, the front page featured a photo of Catherine Holt's full-body dive into Jodell's car window. Beneath the picture, the caption read: "Local boy Bob Lee wins feature race at the new county speedway, gets congratulation kiss from his girlfriend, Catherine Holt of Rocky Hill."

Jodell was at the kitchen table working on one of Grandma's fabulous breakfasts when he spotted the newspaper photo staring back up at him. He quickly read the caption, then tried to fold over the paper, to hide it from Grandma as she scrambled up a skillet of eggs on the old wood stove behind him.

But somehow, he suspected she had seen it already. She had been noticeably quiet since he had come downstairs. He would wait for her to speak.

"You eatin' without saying grace?" she asked irritably.

He quickly set down his fork, bowed his head, and mumbled: "Lord, bless this food I am about to . . . that I am receiving . . . to the nourishment . . . amen."

Then she was silent again, the eggs hissing quietly.

"What was it again that you and Joe had to do last Sunday that you missed church?" she suddenly asked without turning from the stove.

"We had to do some things with the car. Then I had a date with Catherine Holt. We had a picnic."

Jodell took a big bite of biscuit and sausage and chewed vigorously. He had not actually lied to her. Nor had he told her the absolute truth either.

"Well. That Catherine is from a very nice family. I know her momma from Missionary Union."

It was silent in the kitchen then, with only the scraping of her big wooden spoon on the skillet bottom. Jodell chewed some more, taking his time, giving her a chance to reveal how much she might know already before he stepped into something so deep he couldn't climb out.

Grandma threw him no rope.

"She is nice, Grandma. I like her a lot."

"Uh-huh."

"Yes, ma'am. I like her a lot."

She suddenly turned from the stove and flipped over the newspaper on the table. It almost landed in his near-empty plate.

"Must have been a real nice picnic. Even made the newspaper."

Caught! Nothing to do but come clean.

"Well, Grandma, the truth is that me, Joe, and Bubba have been doing a little car racing over at that track at the old Meyer place. We've just been having a little fun. That's all."

"That's all?" Grandma asked, looking down at him through squinted eyes. "Where did that car come from you're out trying to demolish?"

"It's that old Ford sedan of Daddy's. The one that's been out there in the barn for years with the chickens roosting in it. Me and Bubba and Joe fixed it up. Joe mostly."

"Your daddy's old car?" Grandma picked up the newspaper and studied the picture carefully.

"Yes'm."

He could see her lip quivering, a tear start a journey from her eye down her cheek. The realization that it was her son's car that the boys were racing had swiped away some of her anger. But the look on her face made Jodell feel awful. She finally gave him another hard look and tried to force some anger into her words.

"Don't you know you could get hurt doing something like this? You're all I got now, Jodell. I depend on you."

"I know, Grandma, but the whiskey runs are dangerous, too. And they won't send me to jail for a year or two if I get caught racing."

She whirled around, back to the stove, stirring the eggs before they stuck and contemplating his logic.

"But, Jodell, we need the money. We can't get along without it."

"Money? I won fifty dollars for winning that race Sunday. There was one a month ago over in Carolina that paid a hundred to the winner. Third place even got forty dollars in that one. That's a far cry more than I make on the whiskey runs, and it's completely legal."

Silence again. She turned and dumped the eggs on his plate, next to what was left of the grits, sausage, and biscuit.

"I don't like it," was all she said, and then she spun around on her heels and went on out to the parlor to see to some mending.

He finished his breakfast alone and then got busy on chores that had been waiting too long already.

That night Jodell sat alone in one of the rockers on the porch, cooling down from the day's work. He was also missing his grandfather greatly. This was the spot where they had had their better talks, where the old man would tell him tales of past whiskey runners or of things Jodell's daddy had done. It was about the only time Papa Lee ever became talkative.

It was a beautiful part of the day. The last of the sunlight was coating the mountain, turning the whole world red, with everything ablaze with the brilliance.

Jodell was taking a big sip of sweet ice tea when he heard the screen door behind him creak open hesitantly. Grandma emerged slowly from the house, carrying a cup of coffee, and then sat beside him in the other rocker.

"Beautiful sunset tonight, Grandma."

She didn't answer, but merely kept rocking, sipping her coffee, watching a couple of rabbits playing in the grass at the far end of the drive.

" 'Red sky at night, sailor's delight.' Means it'll be fair tomorrow so I can get the greens planted in the garden."

She now appeared to be studying something on the top of the mountain, maybe the old lightning-snag tree that had pointed toward the North Star for as long as he could remember. Grandma seemed to have only just now discovered it, though, giving it her full attention.

"It sure did cool down once it got dark. No bugs out. Real nice evening," he tried again.

Grandma rocked gently. She studied a hawk now, circling in the last of the thermals that rose up from the valley. Finally, she deliberately set the cup down on the porch banister and turned to face her grandson.

"I might have been a little hard on you this morning, Jodell," she said carefully, as if she had been practicing her words all day. "It was always your granddaddy that did the harsh talking when it was needed. I guess I ain't too practiced at it."

"Aw, I'm sorry, Grandma. We shouldn't have lied to you like that. We just didn't want you to worry."

"I'm still not sure I want you hanging out at some old racetrack. Especially when you're supposed to be in the Lord's house. I suppose they got all types of folks out there."

"Certainly no worse than what I'm around when I'm running whiskey. Or that I'll be bunking down with if I ever go to jail."

She was quiet again. He had stopped that argument cold.

"Yeah, the whiskey business," she finally said with a deep, resigned sigh. It was the first time he had ever heard her even so much as acknowledge the existence of the family's primary source of income. "I guess I've turned a blind eye to it all these years. I was brought up in it myself, Grandpa Matthews and all his brothers, my uncles, Claude and them. And I guess I've been resolved to that being our salvation, with you taking over where your granddaddy left off."

"I'm still going to have to drive some runs. I can't

count on winning every race, I don't guess."

The dying sun's rays gave the old woman's cheeks a bright crimson glow. She seemed to be looking for something again, off out there in the distance, toward the mountains and the first star that had appeared in the night sky. She suddenly turned toward Jodell once again.

"You look so much like your father now. I see it more and more every day. I suppose you are bound and determined to do this racing thing. I ain't surprised. I know I can't hold you back. Your daddy liked to go fast, too. Much faster than life around these parts would ever allow."

He almost told her about the thoughts he had been having lately. About how it would be to venture beyond this side of the mountains. The same mountains that sometimes revealed to him so much beauty. And that sometimes seemed to hem him in so completely that he felt he might suffocate.

"I can't help the way I feel, Grandma," was all he said, though. She knew him well enough. She had him pegged.

"I know. I've been praying hard ever since your granddaddy died, Jodell. Asking the Lord to show us the way." She pursed her lips and narrowed her eyes. "Now I'm startin' to wonder if this racing thing ain't maybe the Lord answering my prayers."

Jodell's face lit up with no help from the fading sun. "Maybe it is! It may well be!"

"Then I guess I better get started prayin' that if that's what He wants, He better keep y'all safe and help you win out there, hadn't I?"

Jodell slid from the rocker and reached to wrap her up in a tight hug. He didn't let go until the crickets had already started singing.

It was strange territory to all three of them, as foreign as the moon or Mars might have been. Oh, there were still pine trees and the same houses and the folks looked the same, but the mountains were in the wrong direction. That seemed to keep them off-balance for a day or so.

Jodell had been the closest to this new territory, making runs to within fifty miles or so of their first stop. That had been at night, though, and everything looked different now. And neither Joe nor Bubba had ever been this far from home before. Now Jodell thought he knew how Christopher Columbus or those other explorers must have felt. And those guys didn't have to worry about stuck fuel floats or tires going flat or some good old boy plowing into the back of you at eighty miles per hour.

It had been several weeks since the big win in the race at the track out on the old Meyer farm. They had used the time to work on the old Ford, get it souped up as much as they could, fine-tune the suspension to try to make her handle even better.

Now they were off. They had heard of dirt-track races on Thursday, Friday, and Saturday nights in small towns in North Carolina, more than a hundred twenty miles away. They left early Wednesday, probably with as much food and supplies as Columbus would have packed for the Atlantic crossing.

"Ain't hardly room for us in there, is there?" Bubba asked as he tried to squeeze into the backseat of Grandpa Lee's Ford sedan.

"Not with all them sacks of groceries you bringing," Joe answered. "We might near need a truck for Bubba's grub alone."

"I just hope we got enough power to make it up the mountain pulling the race car, Bubba, and Bubba's stockpile." Jodell grinned.

The tracks they were headed for ranged from the northwestern part of the state down to Hickory, the first two in towns so small Jodell couldn't even find them on his Shell Oil road map. They had to stop in Blowing Rock and Banner Elk and other crossroads towns to ask directions, the race car in tow always leading to curious onlookers and plenty of questions. The Saturday evening race was to be run at the speedway outside of Hickory.

They found the competition to be spotty at the out-of-the-way tracks, some very good cars and drivers, then some others who were in danger of killing themselves and anybody who got in their way. They managed to place fourth in the first race and would have done better except for a huge hump in the track in turn one that caused the Ford to bottom out each time through. Jodell had been afraid he would do serious damage, so he had eased into that turn each time, going only fast enough to finish in the money. They finished second at the Friday race, with a very good race car piloted by an obviously experienced driver edging Jodell out in the last lap.

The good news was that those two finishes won them enough money to cover their expenses for the trip, regardless of what they did at the Hickory race. That is, assuming they didn't do serious damage to the race car. There was several hundred dollars up for grabs there. Although disappointed they had not won either of the first two North Carolina races, they knew that any decent finish on Saturday night would send them home ahead, in the black on their first excursion. Racing would be paying its way from the start.

The men slept in the two cars each night, parked at various roadside picnic areas. Bubba had gone through most of the food they had packed by the time they had crossed the Smokies, so meals mostly consisted of Vienna sausages, tins of sardines, soda crackers, and hoop cheese purchased from various little country stores along the way. Jodell had already promised that if they earned enough money, they would stop at a barbecue place they knew on the way back and have a victory feast.

"I can taste it already," Bubba said, gazing wistfully into the distance.

"Heck, Jodell, old Bubba will run out there and push you around the track to victory himself if he figures there's an inside-sliced pork sandwich in his future."

Bubba didn't even argue. He simply closed his eyes and dreamed of the smoky barbecue.

They were at the entrance to the Hickory track by eight o'clock on Saturday morning. They quickly learned the drivers' gate wouldn't open until ten, so they had to wait outside in the grassy parking area.

"Y'all from Tennessee, huh?" the gangly-legged gate guard offered.

"How'd you know?" Joe asked. " 'Cause we showed up so early and eager?"

"Naw, 'cause I seen your license plates."

Bubba Baxter poked Joe in the back of the head, enjoying him being the butt of a joke for once.

"I reckon we got plenty to do in the meantime," Jodell said, suddenly serious. The other two groaned. Joe had already spotted a shady spot of grass at the far end of the lot that would be perfect for a nap, and Bubba had caught a whiff of something being fried somewhere close by and was homing in already. "Let's go over this car from top to bottom and make sure it's right after last night."

Jodell wanted to be able to run as soon as they got inside so he could try out the track. The Hickory Speedway would be a new experience. It was a four-tenths-mile oval, with slight banking in the turns, a true racetrack, unlike the tiny bullrings and undulating pastures they had been running on so far.

Even from the lot, they could tell things were a bit more serious here. There were grandstands for several thousand spectators, a true pit area, and an honest-to-goodness press box.

They cleaned as much of the dirt from the previous two races as they could. A hose pipe would have helped, but they didn't have access to one. Joe and Jodell spent a good hour under the hood. They had sprayed the radiator and front grill the last time they had stopped for gas. Otherwise, they may have been afraid to even run the engine. Clumps of red mud had washed out onto the cracked cement at the station, and they'd had to carefully wash it away under the steely-eyed scrutiny of the station attendant.

By the time the gates to the track opened, they had been joined by a dozen or more other cars, rolling into the infield with them. They got busy setting the car up, Jodell shooting more grease to every part that needed any while Bubba hammered some wedges into the right-side springs to allow for the slightly higher banking than they were used to. Joe was occupied taking apart the carburetor to inspect it. Stopping for a breath, Jodell peeked from under the front end and saw someone familiar.

"Hey, Joe! Ain't that the Johnson feller pulling in over there?"

"Where?" Joe asked, following Jodell's gaze.

"Over yonder, next to that blue Buick."

"Yeah, that's him, all right. Surprised you recognized him without seeing the back of his head crossing the finish line ahead of you. What's his name? Junior, right?"

"It's Junior. How can I forget that name? I can't wait to get even."

"Well, they'll be a bunch more you'll have to beat, too. You've heard all the talk about the local bunch around here."

"What talk?"

"Some kid I was talking to outside the gate. He said there was some smooth driver from not far from here in Hickory. Tough as nails, but a clean driver. Said he didn't have to bang and knock to win."

"I don't think I've seen a clean driver yet. They all

seem like they want to shove me off the track."

"The kid said this guy will race you hard, but he'll still give you plenty of room. He believes in taking care of his equipment."

"He mention the guy's name?" Jodell asked curiously.

"Jarrett, I think it was. Ned Jarrett."

"Huh!" Jodell grunted. He went back to his grease gun, vowing to look for this Jarrett fellow once he was out there.

They had already gotten to know many of the drivers and the characters who followed them. There was a sizable cadre of drivers who went from track to track, any place they could get to if it paid any money at all. By necessity, it had become a close-knit fraternity, and Jodell, Joe, and Bubba already felt they were being accepted into it. Jodell had earned respect in every race he had run. Joe had given a few tips to drivers that had worked, and such information was always appreciated. And Bubba had been more than willing to pitch in with a wrench or tire tool if one of the others needed help.

These men were a wild bunch. They tended to race hard, drink harder, and then fight harder still. But before the night was over, they would be best buddies again, ready to share a beer or an extra part or a couple of dollars for some gas, all with the same drivers they had been perfectly willing to shove into the fence or to beat senseless only a few hours before. The group had seemed to have evolved into one big, crazy family.

Jodell finally crawled out from under the car, satisfied he had done all he could for the moment. The breeze felt good on his wet back as he stretched in the warm sun. He paused to push down hard on the right rear fender, checking the stiffness of the wedges they had added to the springs.

"This feels better, Joe. I wonder . . ." He looked under the hood, but his cousin was gone. "Bubba, where's Joe? He done cleaning the carburetor?"

"I think he went off somewheres looking for a couple of jets and a float. He didn't like the looks of the ones in there now."

"Where's he gonna find parts out here?"

"He said he'd see if he could borrow them from somebody."

"Who in the world would carry an extra set of jets and floats?"

"Lot of the guys have them, Jodell. Joe said that red car over yonder has the better part of a whole engine in parts in the trunk. All Ford parts, too." Bubba wiped his hands with the rag from his rear pocket.

"I'm glad to see folks are so willing to help somebody that fully intends to show 'em his dust when we get out there on the track." Jodell squinted at the sun. "Speaking of which, it can't be more than half an hour before we get to practice. I hope he doesn't stand around and shoot the breeze too long."

Jodell was anxious to get onto the first real racetrack he had ever seen, much less driven on. He was strapped in and ready when the practice session was finally announced. Joe had returned with the carburetor parts, but they had not had time to put them in before the practice laps. Maybe they could get it done before qualifying.

When Jodell rolled up, there were three or four cars already sitting on the roadway that led out of the pits. He squirmed in his seat as much as the safety belt would allow and tapped impatiently on the steering wheel as he waited for the official standing at the end of the pit lane to wave him out on the track. Finally the flag man on his stand looked closely at his watch, then waved the green flag to start the practice session.

For Jodell, this was a new experience. The Hickory track hosted several sportsman-division races every year, and the professionalism of the personnel at the track was something he had not yet seen. They were more accustomed to running on makeshift tracks cut out of somebody's farm field, with officials who were more likely the promoter's cousin than a true racing judge. His heart thumped hard now and he was thrilled to actually be running on a real live racetrack.

But he was apprehensive, too. What if he didn't have the ability, or the car, to run out here with these drivers on this track? What if he was only fit to dodge cow pies and revenuers and eat small-track dust?

Well, he was about to find out. Hickory Speedway was about as serious as it got at this level of racing.

The feel of the car was definitely different as he drove down into the first turn. The slight bank of the turn allowed him to roll through the corner without sliding the car as much as he was used to. It also made it easier to get into the throttle without spinning the rear tires. He raced up the backstretch and then set the car smartly into the third turn. The Ford again got a much better bite in the corner than he had ever experienced, almost as if the car were glued to the track as it slid through the corner.

Jodell made several more easy laps before he began to try to drive hotter. In the infield, Joe and Bubba stood by the railing, timing each lap with the stop-watch. They could tell that with every passing lap the car was circling faster and faster. And even from there, they could see the broad grin on Jodell's face as he whisked past them.

After a dozen or so laps, he pulled the car off into the infield and rolled to a stop beside his crew.

"How were the times?" he yelled as he climbed from the car.

"Okay. Well, better than okay. A few more laps and you'd be in danger of breaking the sound barrier!" Joe kept looking from the watch to Jodell's face.

"This track is not like anything I've ever driven on. Maybe kinda like some of the better curves on some of them mountain roads. But out here they got one of those curves every few hundred feet! I can really control the car better through them. It's gonna take a little getting used to before I can figure out the best way around them."

"Watch some of those local boys. You can bet they'll know the fast way around. Specially Johnson. He's run a lot around here if I remember right."

"I haven't seen him come out yet. Maybe I can follow him around for a couple of laps."

"Just watch what everybody else is doing. Their line into the corner, how hard they drive into it, where they get in the gas coming out," Joe advised. "Bubba can watch, too. I talk better than I watch. I'm gonna visit with some of the others and see who they think is fast."

Jodell didn't answer. He climbed back into the car to go out again and make some more laps. By now there were a dozen or more cars practicing. He fell in behind three of them and tried to stay close, but not so close that he couldn't tell how they were driving into and out of the corners.

He could see that most of them braked early, then allowed the car to drift through the corner before getting gently back into the throttle through the corner and hard coming out the other side. After a few laps, he had adjusted his driving line to match theirs and didn't have any trouble at all in keeping up with them. He used the balance of the practice session to set his lines around the track and memorize how the car felt in each part. He now felt confident that he could at least match any of the top ten fastest cars he had seen so far. He could only hope none of them were sandbagging, not showing all they could do. And that there wasn't another car out there in the pits, with a driver who knew already that he was fast enough that he didn't need to practice.

The three of them leaned against the car, swigging the last of their sodas, and compared notes. Joe studied his clipboard and gave a report between swallows of cola.

"Old Junior was the fastest by about a tenth of a second. I didn't time anybody else that could keep up with him on a clear track. He'd slow down in the traffic and someone could run with him, but give him a clear track and he was gone. The five and the twenty-seven were plenty fast as well, and I think they are local drivers, too. The forty-eight, the sixty-two, the twelve, and the forty-two were next, all running about the same times as you were. Y'all were running about a tenth behind old Junior."

"He's got this track down pat. He is so smooth in the corners. He gets the car in just the right power slide and then slides right on through. I don't see how he stays in the throttle as long and as hard as he does."

"He ain't scared. That's why he does so good," Bubba offered matter-of-factly. The other two could only nod in agreement.

"That's true, but it's more than that," Jodell agreed. "He's got a touch on the throttle like I've never seen. I don't see any way we can beat that one."

Bubba Baxter slapped the roof of the Ford hard, puffed his chest up, and began to angrily shake his finger at the other two men.

"Hell, y'all wanna just pack up and head for the Cove right now?" he said, his voice immediately in full rant. Joe and Jodell looked at him as if he had lost his mind from the heat. "That guy ain't no tougher than you are, Jodell. You just have to drive smarter. Looks to me like he pushes his equipment way too hard. He keeps that up for a hundred laps and he'll break something or climb the fence. Just you wait and see." Bubba took a big draft of soda, burped, and then finished what he meant to say. "Y'all talking like we ain't got no chance. And looky here. I'll have none of it. I'm convinced we got the best driver out here and the best car on the track, and if y'all don't think so, if you're out here to run for second, then we'll chain this old Ford to the other one and snake it right on back home and go back to dirt farming and 'shine hauling and twine pulling."

Joe and Jodell's mouths fell open. When Bubba Baxter finally spoke his mind on something, he was usually correct. This was no exception.

"You're right, Bub," Jodell eventually said, embarrassed he had allowed his own confidence to slip. "We are going to win this danged thing. Then we'll collect our first-place money, hook up, and be halfway home before some of them even finish the race."

Joe smiled. "Old Bubba gets a mite testy when he ain't eat for a few minutes."

"Let's just see if we can qualify somewhere close to the front so I won't have to pass 'em all to get up to the lead. I'm used to heat races. This qualifying is something new to me."

"Aw, you just got to run as hard as you can and keep it straight coming out of the corners for one lap. If you don't get into a big old broad slide or break it loose when you get back in the gas, you'll be fine." Joe carefully consulted the chart of lap times on the clipboard. "I'd guess a twenty-four- or twenty-five-second lap will be good enough to run with the leaders."

"Let me try something," Bubba suddenly said as he disappeared beneath the front end and began working on the steering linkage. It took him half an hour to finish to his satisfaction whatever it was that he was doing. The final practice was about to start when he finally crawled out from under the front end, bathed in sweat, grease, and dirt.

"What did you do? This thing's not gonna come apart on me, is it?" Jodell asked.

"Naw! Like Joe says, I watch better than I talk. I seen some of them other boys adjusting on theirs. I couldn't figure out what they were doing at first, but then I got to thinking."

"Somebody call the newspapers! Baxter's thinking!" Joe shouted. Bubba ignored him.

"Like I said, I got to thinking, and I figured that if I put a little natural turn in the wheel to the left with a couple of shims, then it will make the car easier to turn and keep under control in these corners."

"Really think it'll work?" Jodell asked him. He couldn't remember ever asking Bubba what he thought of something, but somehow, he figured the big man was on to something here.

"We'll find out in this practice. All I did was toed the car in a hair to the left. You'll need to hold her a smidgen to the right down the straights, then let it flow freer into the corner as you turn into it. I can put it back before the race if you don't like it."

"That sounds logical to me. I'll give it a try."

Bubba beamed. Joe started off toward the fence with the clipboard in hand and the stopwatch dangling from his neck on an extralong shoestring. Engines fired all around him in the infield as he walked to the fence, the field coming noisily alive. The first cars were hitting the track as he propped a foot up on the inside rail and got ready.

Jodell climbed in the car and fired it up while Bubba stood with his head under the hood, listening to the sound of the engine. One of his giant hands rested on the top of the hood, and then, finally satisfied with what he was hearing, he gave Jodell a thumbs-up and slammed the lid. He secured it tightly in place with a piece of baling wire and waved him off toward the track.

Jodell did one slow lap around, feeling out the changes Bubba had made to the front end. He could tell no difference at all at slow speed. On the second lap, he rolled gently out of the second turn and kicked in the throttle as the car leaped ahead, galloping up the backstretch. He feathered the gas and turned in to the corner. The car turned naturally, as if guided by some big, unseen hand, making it easier to hold the power slide in the corner. The difference was subtle, but Jodell could tell that the change definitely helped free the car up as it slid through the modest banking of the turn.

After another couple of hard laps, he pulled in behind the fence where Joe and Bubba stood. He cut the engine off as he rolled to a stop. Joe trotted over and gave him the times in a shout, working to be heard over the roar of the other cars still circling the track. The grin on his and Bubba's faces told Jodell all he needed to know.

"You were almost five tenths of a second faster than the best time you did before."

"Great! How does that stack up to the others?"

"Right up there with the top five or six."

Jodell winked and flashed him an "okay" sign, cranked the engine again, and pulled back out on the track. He wanted to run the car hard, to simulate how it would be with competition all around him.

By gosh, he thought, we can actually win this thing!

Finally, satisfied, ready, Jodell watched for the entrance to the infield and prepared to pull in and wait for his opportunity to qualify. But behind him, two cars raced hard side by side down the backstretch all the way into the corner. Locked in their own private duel, neither driver was willing to show weakness, to lift his foot from the accelerator, even with their engines groaning, their tires squalling in the turn.

Jodell never saw them coming as he slowed for the pit entrance. Still, he was okay until the car on the inside made a slight bobble as he tried to hold his line. The car's rear end broke loose, sliding upward, banging hard into the other racer on the high side. The impact shoved him back down the track, his tail dragging him almost sideways, and he slammed hard into Jodell's right rear.

Jodell felt the car suddenly jump out from under him, as if being pushed along by a tidal wave. It jerked sharply to the left as the other car clipped his rear. That shot him downward, toward the inside guardrail fifty feet before the pit entrance. He couldn't do anything about it, it happened so suddenly. Next thing he knew, he had tagged the rail hard with the left front, then bounced back and hit it again, broadside on the driver's side, and then slid along, metal grinding, all the way to the pit entrance.

Both the other cars slid wildly up the track and whacked the outside rail with a thunk that brought the already considerable crowd to its feet with a roar. Even in practice, such a wreck would get their attention.

It took Jodell a moment to catch his breath and realize what had happened. He pushed in the clutch and refired the stalled engine. Thankfully, it obediently cranked right up. He pushed the shifter into first gear and tried to pull away.

There was an awful screeching from both the right rear and the left front of the car. The front end seemed to shudder in agony as he limped back to the pits.

Bubba Baxter was scattering the crowd of bystanders in all directions as he ran through the mob to where Jodell had pulled the Ford to a blue-smoke stop.

"She's hurt," he moaned as he screeched to a halt and kneeled down beside the car, surveying the damage closely.

Jodell climbed out the window and walked around the car, making his own inspection. His stomach turned. The left front fender and bumper were caved in, rubbing badly on the tire and its rim. The right rear fender was pushed in against the tire and wheel as well. The driver's side of the car had sheet-metal damage, but that wouldn't affect how she would run.

He could tell at once that the left front was the worst. And Jodell was even more concerned about what they might not be able to see, the front end and radiator.

"You see what happened, Bub? I'm trying to pit and the next thing I know, somebody's knocked me seven ways from Sunday."

"Them other two guys run all over you, Jodell. That's what happened. They just flat out run plumb, tee-totally, all over you!"

"We gotta see how bad she's hurt. We've got to qualify in less than an hour."

Joe came tearing up then, his face white, panting for breath.

"Jodell, you all right? All I saw was dust and tire smoke, but I could see you were in the middle of it."

"Couple of cars clipped me from the rear and I wound up kissing the fence." The three of them stood there, as if surveying the remnants of an explosion, wondering if they could ever put all the pieces back together again. Jodell finally spoke. "Well, boys, can we fix her?"

It was Bubba who opened his mouth first, already stepping to the rear of the car to begin tugging on the wrinkled sheet metal.

"Damn right we can! We ain't gonna stare her back into shape. Jodell, grab that sledgehammer and bring it back here to me."

Jodell fetched the sledge as ordered while Joe reached for the hood to try to get a look at the front suspension. He had to knock some of the damaged sheet metal aside with a hammer to get it loose, unlatched, and raised so he could peer inside. Meanwhile, Bubba began banging viciously on the twisted metal of the rear fender, his blows reverberating across the track. A whole section of spectators stood and cheered the fervor with which he had attacked the mess.

The three of them worked desperately over the next

hour to try to get the car in some shape for qualifying. Fortunately, most of the problem was the fenders that had been smashed in against the tires. There was also a badly bent front bumper. Thankfully, the radiator was still intact. That was a miracle, considering the heavy damage on the car's left front corner. Something could have easily been shoved back into it, and that would have ended the racing trip once and for all. Even if they could have found a spare, there was not enough time to change a radiator and do all the other repairs that were necessary.

With considerable effort, Jodell and Bubba managed to get the rear fender off the tire. It appeared to be none the worse for the rubbing it had taken moving from the wreck to the pit. Jodell crawled beneath the car and inspected the rear-end housing to see if it might have been bent or had been pushed out of place. It looked okay. He could tell for certain when he tried to move the car.

Meanwhile, Bubba took his sledge and went to work helping Joe on the front end.

"Bubba, we'll never get this piece of bumper off without a cutting torch," Joe said sadly. "There's no way you can get it bent out of the way."

Bubba gave it another couple of mighty blows with the sledge, almost moving the car sideways as he struck, but it didn't appear to budge. Finally the big man dropped the hammer and wiped the sweat off his face with his shirttail.

"All right then. I'll go and see what I can come up with."

And he was gone.

"How we looking back there, Jodell?" Joe hollered.

"It looks okay. Everything is still good and straight. Just body damage. How are you coming up there?"

"Okay, if we can get this bumper cut away. If Bubba can round us up a torch, we can maybe get it off. Even then, we'll have to change this flat tire and realign the front end."

"I'll get the spare out of the trunk," Jodell said as he rolled from beneath the car. He knocked the dirt off the seat of his coveralls.

Somehow, he knew Bubba would come through. He had to.

At the far end of the pits, the massive form of Bubba Baxter was circling through the maze of cars, trying to spy a torch somewhere. He was on the last row, intently gazing up and down the aisle between the cars, when he literally bumped hard into a tall, lanky kid, sending the boy sprawling backward into the dust and dirt.

"Oops. Sorry," Bubba mumbled, helping him up.

"Naw, it was my fault for wool-gathering," the young kid replied, slapping the dust off his jeans. "You in some kind of a hurry, big man. Need some help with something?"

"Well, yeah. We was in that wreck out there in practice and I'm trying to find a torch so we can cut part of the bumper away. Know anybody who's got one?"

"Should be. Where did I see that one while ago? It was on a roll cart with the gas cylinders."

"Well, thanks! I'll look some more," Bubba said, and turned to go off searching.

"Here, let's look over this way. Follow me."

The lanky kid took charge of the quest just like that, leading the way in search of the torch. It took him only minutes to find it, explain to its owner why they needed it, and start wheeling it off toward where the Ford lay wounded.

"Out of the way! I got the torch and I don't want to set either one of you afire if I can help it!" Bubba yelled, wheeling up like a fire truck to the rescue, just in the nick of time.

Joe and Jodell stood back and watched him and the kid set up the torch and go to work. Bubba was so massive, and the kid, while lanky, looked almost skinny standing there next to him.

"Who's your buddy there, big 'un?" Joe asked.

"Oh, sorry. This is ... uh ... uh ..." Bubba paused for a moment. "Shoot, you been so good to find me a torch and I ain't even asked your name."

"I'm Richard. My brother, Chief, and my first cousin, Dale, are crewing my daddy's car, and I'm their number one gofer today, or so it seems anyway. I seen y'all needed a little help and it might be me one day that needed the help."

Jodell rummaged through their two large toolboxes in the trunk of the Ford 'shine car until he found their pair of safety goggles. He tossed them to Bubba.

"Tell you what," Richard said. "I'll hold the end of the bumper with these big old pliers while you cut, 'cause it's gonna get a mite hot directly. Be careful and don't cut anything extra while you're at it. My brother, Chief, got a little crazy with a torch one time and nearly cut one of Daddy's cars in two!"

"This is our only race car, so I'll be careful."

Bubba lit the torch, the flame hissing out the end of the nozzle, then cracking and popping as he turned it down to a nice blue flame. Once he got it adjusted, he began to burn away at the bumper, sparks scattering as he cut. Meanwhile, Richard pulled hard on the large pliers, prying the metal away as the torch ate through. He dropped the hot piece of metal to the ground as it finally came loose, and the torch gave one last pop as Bubba cut off the gas.

"I can't tell you how much we appreciate your help, Richard," Jodell said sincerely, offering the kid his hand and introducing himself.

"No problem. Y'all would've done the same for us, Bob."

"You better believe it. Where y'all from?"

"We came up here from Level Cross. It's right outside of Randleman. My uncle Julie has a garage there."

"That's over by Greensboro, ain't it?"

"We like to say Greensboro is right near Level Cross. Where you cats from?"

"Up around Bristol and Kingsport. Way back up in the hills."

"Y'all race much over here?" Richard asked. "I don't remember seeing you before."

"First time into Carolina. We've mostly raced around home. But the money y'all pay over here beats running the 'shine for certain."

"Yeah, Daddy used to do a lot of drag racing on the street for money, but he decided he could win a lot more running in as many stock car races as he can squeeze in."

"Y'all must race all the time."

"Every chance we get. That's the only way to make any money at it."

"You don't say," Jodell answered as the thought of really racing for money sank in.

"Hey, I need to go back over and help Daddy with old number forty-two. Since it's getting close to race time, he'll be looking for me."

"Thanks for the help, Richard. Hope I can return

you the favor one day," Jodell said, offering his hand to shake.

"You race around these parts enough and I'm sure you will."

"Let me tell you again how much we appreciate your help."

"Don't mention it. I better get back over yonder and find Chief. I got to make sure the car is ready. We're about to start qualifying, it looks like."

"Well, good luck to you and your daddy. Pleased to meet you, Richard. I didn't catch your last name."

"Petty. Richard Petty. Likewise," he drawled, then walked off into the crowd, pushing the torch ahead of him.

The three of them were still working frantically as the first car rolled out for its qualifying lap. Jodell wanted desperately to be watching, to see what the other cars could do, but instead, he and Bubba had crawled under the front end, trying to get the wheels back into some type of alignment.

The other cars trying to qualify continued to roll off the line one by one. He could hear their engines roaring as they pulled out, then growing a bit quieter as they toured the far side of the track, then howling again as the drivers pushed their mounts hard to get to the finish line as quickly as possible.

Jodell knew they only had a few more minutes to get into line or miss their chance.

"You got it tightened back up yet?" Joe asked nervously from his perch under the hood of the car.

"Almost," Jodell answered. "Move it this way just a hair, Bubba, so I can tighten this bolt. How much time we got, Joe?"

"No more than five minutes. We gotta get it now or we'll never make it out to the line."

Jodell fumbled with the bolt. The wrench slipped off once again, dropping squarely on his forehead and nose. He didn't take the time to rub the welt it left there or to check for blood. He reset the wrench and twisted one more time.

Their first race on the big track, against the best drivers, and here they were, stuck with the hood up in the pits.

Grandma, he thought, *I hope you've been praying hard. We sure need the help right about now.*

"FINISH FIRST BUT FIRST FINISH"

Got it! That's perfect. Now tighten everything else down."

Jodell had to scream the words to be heard over the din of the engines on the track as he scrambled out from under the car and dusted himself off. He could only hope the front wheels were once again straight and true. Maybe saying so would make it so.

Joe hurried to get the hood closed and wired shut as Bubba wiggled his huge frame out from beneath the car. Jodell hit the starter button and the big motor roared.

Please, he thought, his fingers crossed. Please let the rest of her behave as well as that old motor.

He threw the car into reverse and gunned the engine. The tires spun, kicking up dust as he backed up. He jammed the gearshift into low and headed off toward the end of what was now a very short line of qualifying cars. He listened carefully for any scrapes or groans or squeaks that weren't supposed to be there. He rested his hands on the steering wheel lightly, feeling for any shimmy or wobble. The ground was so uneven it was hard to tell if the front end was aligned once more or not.

By the time he pulled into line, there was only one car left sitting there and another already out on the track. The track official who was handling the qualifying gave Jodell's car a quick once-over, then motioned for him to ease up into place as the other car pulled off the line with a puff of blue smoke and a shower of gravel.

Jodell tapped his fingers nervously as he waited his own turn. The other car zoomed past, starting its qualifying lap. Then, before he realized it was time, Jodell was being waved out onto the track. Now there was no time to be nervous. He could well have been back home, in his bed upstairs, dreaming about being in this very spot. It was, after all, a dream he had had a thousand times.

Jodell Lee grinned, gave the car a big drink of gas, popped the clutch, and spun out onto the track. All the while he was trying to remember every inch of the track he had traveled during the practice laps. Where should he be in every turn? How should he steer into the straights? How low? How high? How near the ragged edge?

He quickly had the car up to speed as he came around to take the green flag to start his qualifying run. He drove deep into the first turn, letting the car slide up until it caught the groove that had already been worn into the track during all the practice and qualifying. Hard on the brakes for an instant, Jodell allowed the car to drift before he got back into the gas and roared off down the backstretch.

He followed the same procedure through turns three and four, exactly as he had done in his previous tour of the track, then raced under the flag stand as the man vigorously waved the checkered flag.

That was it. The hay was in the barn. Jodell had driven his first qualifying lap on a real-to-life race track. And mercifully, it was over before he had even had time to think much about it. Instinct had gotten him through. That and a good car. He could only hope each had been enough to get him a good spot.

Jodell had concentrated so hard on driving smoothly throughout the run that he hadn't paid much attention to how the car had handled after the wreck. On the cool-down lap, he swung the car from side to side trying to get some feel for how things were meshing. She didn't seem to be handling too badly, though he could still feel the rear fender rubbing slightly when he cut sharply in the corners. That little problem they could easily take care of before the race started.

As he rolled into the pit area, Bubba stood and guided him in next to where their tools were spread. Jodell shut the engine off and climbed out through the open window.

"How'd she run, Jo-dee?"

"Like a cat with a big mean dog hot on its tail."

"Good and fast then?"

"Yep, she's still plenty fast. I think I got a pretty good lap in. Where's Joe?"

"He's still over checking on your time and seeing where we get to start," Bubba said as he unfastened the hood.

"Let's hope it's up front somewhere. With this

many cars running, it'll be nothing but a wrecking yard in the back of the pack."

"You looked about as fast as anybody out there to me. How'd the front end feel?" Bubba asked.

"Seems to be okay. We still got to get this back fender knocked off the tire a little more, though. We surely don't need to cut a tire down out there."

They were busy banging away again with the sledgehammer when Joe came walking up with his clipboard and stopwatch.

"You got a decent enough lap," he reported. "We start eleventh. That Johnson kid you ran against before got the pole, and the Petty kid's daddy is going off second. There's a couple more Grand National hotshots ahead of you . . . Lee Petty and some of them . . . out here trying to make some easy money."

"That's some pretty tough company. But five hundred dollars is a lot of money, too." Jodell grinned, licking his lips. Neither of the other men could keep from noticing the glint in his eyes. "If we could win it, we could probably buy us a big chunk of one of those Grand National cars and get serious about racing with all them boys."

"Tell you what. You keep the car on the track and right side up first. Then maybe we'll start running off and leaving Junior Johnson and them in our brand-new race car another time," Joe said. But he was grinning, too.

In the hour and a half left before the start of the race, the three of them furiously rechecked the alignment on the front end and then Joe went over the motor with a fine-toothed comb one last time. They even found the time to have a hot dog and a soda as they sat for a moment in the shade and talked with some of the other drivers and crew members.

A quick drivers' meeting was held just before the start of the event. An official with the track went over some of the rules for the race, including the procedure to follow during caution periods when the pace car would be pulling out to pick up the field when a yellow flag waved. He knew some of the drivers had never raced on a track that had a pace car. Then, as a final warning, he mentioned that there would be a dozen sheriff's deputies on the grounds in case any of the drivers let any on-track differences continue once they were off the track and in the infield area.

Then, finally, the call came to line the cars up. Jodell fired the engine and pulled through the infield area toward the starting line. Joe and Bubba took a shortcut, climbed the pit railing, and joined him at the line. Jodell shut the engine off, took a damp rag, and wiped the sweat from his forehead.

"Whew, I never thought we'd ever make it here after the way things have gone so far," Jodell said, squinting up into the blazing sun.

"I know what you mean," Joe agreed. He was leaning through the Ford's window, making sure Jodell's seat belts were tight and not twisted. "I thought she was headed straight for the wrecking yard after those cats got into you."

"I've seen some in the wrecking yard that looked better." It was Bubba's muffled voice coming from somewhere beneath the car. He had dived down there to take one more look at the hurried front-end work they had done.

"Well, Bubba, if I'm gonna tear one up, then I'm gonna at least do it bang-up."

"Drivers to your cars." The order came crackling over the PA system as if from on high, like the voice of God Himself. "Five minutes to the start."

The crowd cheered the command. They were ready for the action to begin.

"Well, boys, this looks like it."

Jodell gave his face one more good wipe with the cold rag, threw it in the floorboard, and took a hard grip on the wheel. Joe scurried off to the scoring stand while Bubba made certain for himself that Jodell was well strapped in.

The grandstands were packed with waving, screaming fans, primed to watch the race. The sun was starting to fall deeper into the afternoon sky, toward the mountains to the west. A gentle breeze blew in across the Piedmont, just enough wind to keep the day from becoming unbearably hot. It would also blow some of the dust away from the crowded grandstands.

"Gentlemen, start your engines!"

Jodell hit the starter button and the engine rumbled immediately, obediently. He gave Bubba an enthusiastic thumbs-up and dropped the car down into gear. The big man gave a good-luck slap on the side of the door and headed off to his usual position on the inside rail, where he could get the best view. And where he could also eat dust for the full hundred laps.

Jodell gently ran the engine up through the RPM ranges one more time, listening to the changes in pitch exactly as someone would while tuning a piano. The roar from the other cars was so loud he had to concentrate carefully to pick out the sound coming from his own motor. He eased the clutch in and felt it engage as the car rolled a couple of feet closer to the car in front of him.

He checked over the gauges in the car one last time, then saw the starter climb up the ladder to the flag stand. In front of the field of cars, the pace car slowly moved away. The last of a flock of beauty queens quickly exited the small wooden stage behind the flag stand before the field of cars could roll past and dust them good. A huge roar from the crowd almost drowned out the noise from the cars as the field moved away from a dead stop.

Jodell tugged on the steering wheel as the racers slowly circled the track, still trying to get some feel for the car after all the banging and beating they had been doing on her. The wheel felt good and tight and the car seemed to drive in a straight line. With a little luck, they may have actually gotten everything lined back up right. At this very moment, though, it was too late to do anything about it if they hadn't.

The first pace lap had Jodell's adrenaline pumping. He tightened his grip on the wheel until his knuckles ached. The grandstand flashed by as they entered into a second lap.

As they rumbled past the scoring stand, he allowed himself one brief thought of Catherine. He missed her. He had to admit that. There were some things he wanted to tell her when he got back. Things that had to do with him and her and their future together. Things he had been seriously thinking about between races on this trip.

And he was homesick, too. It would be good to get back across the mountains to familiar territory. But it would be even better if they had the winner's trophy and the prize money with them!

He forced himself to focus on the track and where he wanted to put the car each trip around. Thank goodness, as they rolled past the flag stand again, they got the one-lap-to-go sign.

He didn't think he could stand another slow lap. He was primed, pumped, and ready to finally race. The misfortunes of the day so far were now long forgotten, replaced by that insatiable, burning desire to win that smoldered so hotly inside Jodell Lee's gut.

The race cars came down the backstretch on their way to the start, then tightened up as the double line dutifully followed the pace car through turns three and four. Jodell pulled up tightly, almost kissing the rear bumper of the car in front of him. Then he went ahead and gave him a gentle nudge to let the driver know there was someone back there intent on getting past him quickly and any way that he could.

He could see the other driver's wide eyes in the rearview mirror. Jodell gave him a broad grin, a casual wave, and a wink.

As the lead cars came off the fourth turn, the flag man held the green banner high in the air. They gunned their throttles in anticipation, then sent their cars hurtling off under the waving flag, storming toward the first turn. The thunder of their engines was deafening. The sun flashed off their windshields and chrome like sharp lightning.

Jodell had bumped the car in front of him several more times as he watched out of the corner of his eye for the green flag. The driver had still hesitated, allowing the cars in front of him to pull away. Jodell finally went ahead and got into the throttle an instant before the other driver did and pushed him up and out of the way as he came off the fourth turn toward the start. He made it a three-car-wide tandem as they crossed the start line and then beat the other two cars to the racing groove as they headed into the first turn.

The starting flag had barely dropped and he had improved two positions already! He was in the top ten!

Jodell screamed with glee as he kept the car pinched down low on the racetrack, as it slid through turns one and two to the inside of the other drivers. He burped the gas as he started off the second turn and pulled easily into a spot ahead of the other two cars. Now they could taste his dust!

Heading into turn three now without a car on the outside, he was able to drive the Ford deeper into the corner, then let it drift up until it found the slight hump that ran all the way around the turn. The circular mound helped the car follow the groove. Jodell came off the fourth turn and pulled up tight on the back bumper of the next car that was in his way, blocking his route to the front. It took him another full lap to get past that car as he patiently waited for it to slide up the track enough to open up the inside groove to him. But once the opening was there, Jodell quickly seized the opportunity and pushed the Ford through it without hesitation.

"Finish first but first finish," Joe had told him more than once in the last couple of days. In other words, be patient. Sometimes it was a hard promise for him to keep, but Jodell knew it was a sound philosophy. There would be plenty more laps ahead in which he could get to the front. But if he should wreck on the first or second lap, then they would be halfway to Chandler Cove before the checkered flag flew for the winner.

Within the first dozen or so laps, the lead cars were already passing slower cars that brought up the end of the field. A young kid Jodell didn't know held the lead while Junior Johnson and Lee Petty battled it out for second place. The spectators had never settled back into their seats since the start. They obviously knew what to look for and cheered enthusiastically at the various battles being fought and won all around the track.

Suddenly, coming off the fourth turn, two cars rammed together hard. They seemed to embrace, then waltz each other up toward the outside rail. Locked together the whole way, they slammed into the rail hard and then bounced, spinning, back across the track toward the inside rail. A third car piled into the first two with a metallic crunch, followed closely a fourth whose driver couldn't manage to steer away. Like pins clobbered by a bowling ball, the cars were sent scattering everywhere, momentarily blocking the track. Another couple of cars joined the melee with the crunching of metal before it was done.

Bubba, covered in a fine powdery dust, stood as usual with one leg perched up on the inside rail. He could see the wreck unfold down toward the fourth turn. He peered through the dust, steam, and smoke to see the cars all go spinning in every direction.

Then an old Buick seemed to come out of nowhere, headed straight toward where he stood. Before he could react, the front end slammed into the inside guardrail right where he had been resting. He barely had time to jump back a step or two as the mangled race car smashed into the railing. Hot water from the ruptured radiator instantly spewed all over him as he scrambled to get out of the way. The big man danced and swatted as if he were being assaulted by a swarm of angry bees.

Joe, seated high up in the scoring stand, saw that the wreck thankfully was happening well behind Jodell and that he was able to safely pass the start-finish line as the caution flag dropped. He watched the cars as they collided with each other and into the guardrails, leaving steaming, spewing vehicles scattering and skidding everywhere.

Then he watched as one car, in what seemed like

slow motion, headed straight for where Bubba Baxter had propped himself along the inside rail. Joe couldn't help it. He had to laugh as he watched that mountain of a man trying to scramble out of the way as the radiator's hot water chased him away from the rail. Joe was laughing so hard he almost missed scoring Jodell's lap as the caution flag waved. The other scorers looked sideways at him, not sure what he found so funny about the massive melee that had claimed so many race cars out there on the track.

Jodell threaded his way through the wrecked cars after taking the caution flag, and slowed. He'd worked his way up to sixth place and now had a chance to close in on the leaders. Junior Johnson, with his lead foot and knock-you-out-of-the-way driving style, managed to pass or knock out of the way the young kid and assume the lead. Lee Petty still sat in third place. Another regular Grand National driver held down the fourth spot, with that Earnhardt kid sitting in fifth. In his mirror Jodell could see that a couple of upstarts like himself were lined up behind him, gunning to get past him.

The cleanup took a good five minutes, and that allowed Jodell a chance to catch his breath. But he also noticed for the first time that the heat in the car was staggering. As long as he had been driving hard, concentrating on getting past the others, he had been perfectly comfortable. Now he sat drenched in sweat, and only the goggles he wore kept it from trickling down into his eyes.

He relaxed the iron grip he'd held on the steering wheel since the green flag and took a moment to look around. The crowded infield, the packed grandstand, the ragged line of cars, all came into focus as if they had suddenly appeared out of a fog. So far, all he'd seen had been the green flag and all the cars that were lined up directly in front of him. In his mind all he could see were the cars that were riding stubbornly between him and the black and white checkered flag that waited for him at the end of the race.

When the green flag waved to restart the race on the eighteenth lap, all the peripheral activity faded once more into the background. Jodell became all business again, too. He hounded the cars directly in front of him, drifting high, diving low, giving them a sharp tap here, a firm push there.

Then he realized the only cars ahead of him were the lead three. He locked himself tightly on the young kid's bumper. Petty had gotten around the kid, too, and was having his own private battle with Johnson for the lead. Try as he might, though, Jodell could not find a way to get by and into third spot. The kid's car was simply too fast, too strong in the turns, and the kid was too good a driver to give up any more track positions than he had already. Lap after lap slid by beneath them, but it seemed everything Jodell tried came up lacking, short of bulldozing the kid out of the way going into the corner.

With his handling off just a tick still from the wreck, if he bulldozed the kid, he ran a good chance of wrecking himself. Even with a little more power than the kid seemed to have, it simply didn't appear that it was going to be enough. The kid would have to slip up or blow up. All he could do was hang close, hope the first two cars didn't pull away, and look for his chance to sneak around.

When the caution waved on the fiftieth lap because of another big pileup, the same four cars at the front of the field raced back to the line, with the rest of the drivers locked in their own races back in the pack.

Petty had managed to get by Junior Johnson, and Jodell was still dogging the kid, doing all he could to stay glued to his bumper, sliding with him through every corner.

Jodell was thankful for the latest caution laps. With another fifty circuits to go, he was beginning to get tired. This was the longest race they had run yet, and it was beginning to wear on him. That, the late nights of racing, and sleeping in the car for the last few nights had left him stiff and tired, plain tuckered out.

And the heat! Man, it was close inside the car! Jodell now wished he'd put the water bottle in the car as Joe had suggested. His arms felt as if they were weighted down with lead as they hung loosely on the steering wheel. The sweat stung his eyes. The air in the car seemed too hot and too heavy with the choking red dust to breathe into his lungs.

But as they got the one-lap-to-go signal, it all faded away once again as Jodell focused in tightly on finding a way around the kid who was blocking his charge to the front.

My, my, he is one tough customer to be so danged young, Jodell thought. That was when he caught a glimpse of the boy's name stenciled above his window, half covered in dirt, as they approached the flag stand one more time. Well, I'll be! No wonder he's so tough.

It was that Jarrett boy, Ned, that everyone had been talking about before the start of the race. And he was as good as advertised!

The cars rolled around the oval heading slowly into the first and second turn, then tightening up, bumper to bumper, going through three and four. Engines revved tighter and tighter as they awaited the first sight of the waving green flag signifying the restart.

Jodell got a decent jump and suddenly found himself up on the inside of Jarrett's car. Either the kid had missed a gear or the car's engine had hiccuped. Not that it mattered, it was the opening Jodell had been waiting for. He cleared Jarrett as he slid the car through the first turn. Coming out of two, he nestled his front bumper right up on the back of Junior Johnson's car. Johnson, in turn, had his bumper firmly planted inches from the rear of the number 42 car of Lee Petty.

But just as quickly as he had put the car behind him out of his mind to concentrate on the car ahead, he felt a solid punch from behind that almost sent him sliding. It was Jarrett and he wanted his spot back!

Jodell couldn't help it. He instinctively eased off on the accelerator with the bump in the butt, and before he knew what had happened, the kid had swept past him again to the inside as the cars flashed across the start-finish line.

"Damn," Jodell muttered under his breath. He knew he had let the jab from behind distract him enough to lose the hard-earned spot. "Never again," he vowed, and bent over the wheel, eyes squinted, teeth gritted, crunching on the dust in his mouth.

The two lead cars broke away from the rest of the field and resumed their private battle without missing a shot, Petty and Johnson battling furiously as the laps wound down. When the next caution slowed the field on the seventy-sixth lap, it was clear those drivers' tempers were getting as hot as the steamy, dust-filled air inside their cars. They continued to bump and nudge each other, even under the caution, shaking their fists wildly at each other.

Jodell stayed mired in fourth, even though he had

managed to swap positions twice with Jarrett over the last fifteen laps. Each time, one or the other of them had made the tiniest mistake and the other had quickly taken advantage of the bobble. Jodell was having to grudgingly admit to himself that this was still a learning experience, no matter how good he thought he was. He was amazed at how smooth a driver Ned Jarrett was on the slippery red clay surface. The only mistakes he made seemed to be when he would get himself chopped off by slower race traffic forcing him up high as he slid through the turns past them.

During this latest yellow flag, Jodell reached for what had been the wet rag that he had carelessly tossed to the floor. Now it was mostly dry from the heat of the engine through the floorboard and stiff with dirt. It was all he had, though. He draped it over the back of his neck and tried to wipe away the perspiration from his face that was now making it difficult to see even the track ahead of him. He also tried to stretch his cramping right leg and to relax his shoulder muscles that were tying themselves into knots.

As he kicked the gas pedal to the floor and felt the car surge out of the fourth turn to take the green on the seventy-eighth lap, all the discomfort departed. The fog in his brain cleared and he settled in to race to the end.

With their years of experience showing, Johnson and Petty got a good jump once again on the restart. The battle they were waging was almost certainly part of a continuing war between the two, skirmishes fought most Saturday nights or Sunday afternoons somewhere on similar battlegrounds.

Johnson showed no rust from some recent jail time up in Ohio, the result of his part in a moonshining episode. He seemed determined to make up for every race he had missed in the meantime. Petty, making one of his rare appearances off the Grand National circuit, was probably only interested in picking up the winning purse, but he drove as if he were going for the championship that very afternoon.

From his place in fourth spot, Jodell had a good view of what happened next. Petty put a fender alongside Johnson as they came up off the second corner. They bumped and rubbed all the way down the backstretch. Then he drove Johnson deep into the third turn, and as they slid out of the fourth turn, he had managed to put a nose out in front.

Johnson would have none of it. He turned down on Petty, trying to kill his momentum. Lee would have none of it. He held his line, causing the cars to smack together again hard. They swung through the first and second turns as if they were locked together at the door handles, then raced off down the back straightaway once again.

Johnson nosed his way back out in front, but Petty hit him hard in the rear in the next corner. That pushed Junior up high and allowed Petty to get back under him once more.

"Lord, this can't go on," Jodell muttered to himself. Something was obviously going to give, and soon. It would have been fun to be in the stands, watching from a safe distance. Jodell had to watch closely through the windshield of the car in front of him to see which direction to dive to get out of the way when the inevitable happened.

As they drove down into the start of the turn again, Johnson returned the shot in the rear, pushing Petty high and into a wide slide. Lee had been there before and knew what to do. He managed to hang on and race side by side down the front straight. The paint-swapping went on for two more complete laps around the track.

The crowd in the grandstand was screaming wildly at the ongoing battle for the lead. After all, this was what they had paid their dollar to come out to the racetrack to see. Hats were waving, arms were raised high, as every fan cheered for one driver or the other. There were no in-betweens.

The laps started winding down as the beating and banging conflict for the lead became even more frantic. With fifteen to go, Petty almost lost control of the old '36-model Chevy diving into the third turn. He crossed the car up to block the track, but Junior Johnson had apparently had enough. He stayed in the gas, plowing into Petty and bulldozing him out of the way.

But as the cars spun, Petty's Chevy clipped Johnson's rear end, turning both of them in to the outside rail. Jodell and Jarrett, racing hard for third and admittedly still watching the show in front of them, barely managed to avoid the spinning cars. They raced hard back to the start-finish line to take the caution flag with fourteen laps to go. As they circled back around the track, Jodell could see what was left of the two wrecked cars that had most recently been the race leaders. A tow truck had pulled up to haul Johnson's wrecked car away from the guardrail while Petty limped around to the pits with a crumpled rear fender and a flat tire.

Not far behind the slow-moving 42 car was Junior Johnson, running along behind Petty, stopping every few steps to angrily kick a heap of dirt at the mangled rear bumper of the Chevy, following all the way back to the pits. The crowd in the grandstand roared.

Now Ned Jarrett held the lead spot, with Jodell

tucked on his bumper as they waited for the track to be cleared. There were ten laps to go by the time they got the wrecked car and various pieces of both race cars picked up out of the way. The crowd was even wilder now. The combat between Jodell and Ned had been just as fierce as the seemingly continuous battle Petty and Johnson had been waging, and the run to the checkered flag promised to be an even wilder affair.

As the green flag fell with seven laps to go, the red clay track lay clear in front of them. During the caution, Jodell had reached out the window and used his sweat rag to try and clean a spot on the windshield so he could see what was in front of him, and especially the rear bumper of Jarrett's car. He took several deep breaths to set his concentration for the final seven-lap shoot-out. It might be the last chance he would have to breathe for a while!

The cars rumbled through the center of the third and fourth turns, the three cars still on the lead lap at the head of the field. They bunched up tightly as the flag man waved the green flag frantically at the onrushing cars. Ned Jarrett got a good jump. It took Jodell a full lap's worth of breakneck driving to run him down again.

Once there, though, Jodell stayed glued to Jarrett's rear bumper as they broad-slid through the corners, as he mirrored the lead car's every move. Jarrett's smooth driving style paid off handsomely as the two of them faced a clear track ahead. Jodell tried hard to get off the corner to the inside so he could beat the leader down into the next turn, but try as he might, he kept coming up a fender short each time. Jarrett had a knack for pinching him off just enough going into the corner to effectively kill any of his momentum coming out.

The jockeying continued, back and forth, as the drivers raced cleanly for the finish. Then, with two laps to go, Jodell finally managed to get the Ford's nose up under Jarrett coming off the second turn. He raced him hard down into the third turn, driving him as deep as he could into the arc of the turn. That forced Jarrett's broad-slide to carry him higher up into the turn and allowed Jodell to pull out in front by a fender.

Jarrett, however, was able to keep the RPMs up in the motor and powered back strongly to run side by side as they flashed under the flag stand in a tight tandem.

The crowd was on its feet, a writhing mass of humanity, cheering riotously as the two cars zoomed beneath the waving white flag in a dead heat.

Jodell drove the car as deeply into the first turn as he dared, trying to drive Jarrett high without making the contact that might eliminate both of them. Jarrett again proved he was not the meek kid he appeared to be. He anticipated Jodell's move and boldly cut his own car downward on the track, trying to force Jodell to back off the gas.

It worked. Jodell had to ease off for an instant to keep the two cars from colliding and taking them both out of the contest like Petty and Johnson.

Off the second corner, they raced side by side again down the short backstretch. This time Jodell concentrated on driving smoothly into and through the corner, knowing he couldn't afford to make a mistake as he came off the fourth turn. Jarrett stayed in the gas, trying to power-slide around him as they came up off the final corner.

Both cars straightened up coming out of their slide through the curve, each driver with his foot shoved hard to his respective floorboard. Jodell bobbled slightly, having to saw at the wheel with the minutely cockeyed front end skewing ever so slightly, and that allowed Jarrett to pull up almost even with him.

In the last desperate sprint to the finish line, Jodell could hardly see anything at all through the dust. It was as if it were only he and Ned Jarrett, all alone in the middle of a thick, red cloud, with no one else in the world to get in their way.

He could barely make out the flag man, furiously waving the checkered flag already. That was how close they were to the end. To his right, the Chevy was still in his peripheral vision. Everything else was a blur.

Jodell Lee had no choice in the matter. He was no longer a driver. He was simply a passenger, his foot nailed to the gas as the cars flashed by, side by side, to take the checkered flag in what had to be a photo finish.

There was no way he could tell who had won.

As they passed the flag stand, Jodell finally exhaled the deep breath he was certain he had been holding for the entire duration of the last two laps. Then, suddenly, he felt the car jerk slightly and then start bouncing wildly. It felt as if he had somehow steered into one of the rough, rutted logging roads that criss-crossed the mountains back home, or had pulled onto one of those furrowed fields to try to escape a pursuing federal man.

He wouldn't know until later that the radius rod had broken beneath the car and that he was riding on four stiff springs with nothing to hold them down.

The car bounced once, twice, then a third time, rolling like a boat on rough seas.

Jarrett saw the car beside him begin to bounce wildly, then start to swerve. He got out of the gas and jumped hard on the brakes.

The first turn came up fast. Much too fast. Jodell wrestled with the wheel, trying to make the car turn left.

And that was all it took.

The Ford swerved sickeningly, turned over, then started barrel-rolling wildly end over end through the first turn. Jarrett jerked his own steering wheel as Jodell's car flipped in front of him. He clipped the rear of the Ford as it sailed over the outside guardrail. The car rolled over another time or two before finally landing heavily on its top, the still-spinning tires pointed upward toward the blue sky.

Bubba watched wide-eyed as the car flipped out of the turn. Then, with a sick feeling in his stomach, he took off across the track as soon as the last race car had gone past. The dust hadn't even settled yet when Bubba reached the smoking, steaming wreckage of what was left of the Ford. He dropped to his knees and peered into the driver-side window. Jodell hung there, dangling upside down, still strapped snugly in his seat belt.

Bubba squeezed into the car through the compacted passenger-side window and unsnapped the web belt, grabbing Jodell and pulling him away from the jagged, hissing wreckage. Jodell was woozy, disoriented, so Bubba threw him over his shoulder like a sack of flour and ran with him to get as far away from the smoldering car as he could. A tongue of flickering flames already licked from under the hood and then quickly ran back toward the rear of the car. Bubba laid Jodell down in the red dust of the track just as the gas tank exploded with a smoky *whoomp*.

"Oh, man. What happened?" Jodell whispered as he groggily tried to sit up.

"You okay, Jo-dee?" The big man was sobbing. Tears rolled down each cheek.

"Huh? What?" Jodell's eyes seemed to be crossed as he tried to focus on Bubba's grimy face.

A curious crowd had quickly gathered around them. Joe Banker had run all the way from the scoring stand and he was out of breath when he stumbled into the throng.

"Is he okay?" Joe hollered. "Y'all step back here. Give him some air."

With some support, Jodell managed to finally get himself sitting upright. He peered out between all the legs that stood around him to locate what was left of the Ford, resting there on its roof, now being sprayed down with fire extinguishers, buckets of water, and shovels full of dirt by some of the assembled throng.

"Hey, Joe. Who won?"

"Huh?"

"Who won the race?"

"Well, to tell you the truth, I don't know. I was too busy gettin' over here to see if you was killed to stop and ask anybody."

"Aw, I'm okay. But who won?"

"You did!" one of the onlookers yelled.

"Yeah, you won, boy," someone else confirmed.

Someone else offered him a jar of ice water. He grinned and took a deep drink and then started to try to get to his feet. Only then did he realize how tired and sore and dizzy he was.

And that was when the promoter showed up with the track photographer and a bevy of beauty queens.

"Man, oh man! What a race! Whew! That was some driving!" the man crowed. "You can come drive my track any day of the week!"

Jodell could hardly hear him. The thunder of the cars still reverberated inside his brain.

The checkered flag was held high over Jodell's head as the beauty queens stood, smiling, on either side of him, doing their part to hold him upright. The promoter stuffed the five-hundred-dollar prize into Jodell's hand.

All the while the photographer was snapping away, his flashbulbs popping like brilliant white lightning, framing a picture that would forever occupy a prominent place on Jodell Lee's wall, wherever he might be living at the time.

There he would be, the moment captured forever, framed perfectly. The hard-earned checkered flag was unfurled above his head, his face wet and dirt-streaked, a trickle of blood from a cut running down his cheek, a beautiful, grinning girl on each side of him, a wad of money in his hand, and behind him, the only race car he had, flipped up on its roof like a foundered turtle, flames and smoke spewing from her.

But he had done it. He had won! Won at the big track, outdueling men who did this for a living in cars backed by real money. No matter how it had been finished, after the cherished checkered flag had waved, he had won himself a real race.

And that had been the moment when Jodell Bob Lee had acknowledged a strange new feeling deep in his gut. It was almost certainly a form of hunger. But it was a different kind of craving, a gnawing, burning sensation that would clearly be difficult to completely satisfy.

"Bubba? Joe? Let's get this mess cleaned up."

"But, Jodell, that thing's—" Joe started.

"We gotta get back home and get ready."

"Ready for what?"

"Ready to go do this all over again."

"Do what all over again?"

"Race! Win! This is only the first one. We gotta have some more of these checkered flags, boys! There ain't nothing like winning!"

He grinned broadly, but there was a wild look in Jodell Lee's eyes. A look so dead-set strong, so fiercely determined, that neither Joe nor Bubba questioned him further. They simply shrugged and winked at each other and ambled over to try to figure out how they could sweep up and tow away what was left of the mangled Ford race car.

After all, they still had to get back home to the other side of the mountains, and it was already getting late.

Racing action that's so authentic you'll
feel the hot rubber up your back!

Jodell Bob Lee goes for the green in

The Road to Daytona

Book Two in the
Rolling Thunder **Stock Car Racing**
Series!

"I took the dictionary and I found me the page where they defined the word 'second' and ripped it right out of the book. Far as I'm concerned there's no such word in the English language."
          —Jodell Bob Lee, stock car driver

J odell floored the Ford's accelerator. He felt the smooth power as the V8 engine responded to his emphatic command and as it obediently pulled the car easily down the front straight. The vehicle sang. He smiled to himself and enjoyed for a moment the throbbing of the steering wheel in his hands, the pulsing of the accelerator against his right foot, the feel of raw power that the car's body transmitted all the way into the deepest marrow of his bones.

Jodell eased off on the accelerator a bit going into turn one, once again allowing the car's momentum to carry it through the corner. He did the same for the next several laps, getting a feel for the track and its characteristics, as well as for how the new car felt beneath him. He had tried it out on the mountain roads back home, doing all he could to simulate the turns he knew to expect at Darlington in the sharp switchbacks and one-eighty curves, but there had been no way he could get the exact feel there. Not until he was actually out here, doing it for real.

He noticed that most of the other rookies were running much slower than he was, some of them actually avoiding the high banks completely, cautiously keeping their cars down on the apron of the track as they navigated the turns. Coming up off the second turn after his seventh or eighth trip around the track, Jodell knew he had reconnoitered all he needed to. He had assayed the track to his satisfaction and knew the only way to learn more was to test it at speed. And test his mount and himself at the same time.

He grinned broadly, tapped the dash, and talked to the car, the way he always did.

"Okay, sweet little Susie. Let's see what you can really do."

And with that, he let out a quick yelp, danced once more on the accelerator, and he was off as if he and the Ford had accidentally trod on dynamite.

Jodell jammed his foot down even more fervently on the accelerator as the car came up off the second turn. He had a clear track in front of him as he roared down the back stretch at over a hundred miles an hour. The air that rushed in his window was cooling on Jodell's face. It felt almost as good as the sheer sensation of speed, the surge of power, the rush of adrenaline.

Going as fast as he was by then, the third turn came at him very quickly, sooner than he had anticipated. He got out of the gas entering the corner, but it tightened up on him dramatically as he hit the middle of the turn. The car wobbled once, then twice. For an instant, Jodell thought he might be losing her, with the rear end about to slide up and toward the dreaded car-eating, driver-maiming rail. But he held on tenaciously, like a rider holding the reins through his horse's stumble, and was able to gather her back up as she rolled out of the fourth turn.

Then he pushed her hard again, the motor screaming as he flew down the front straight running much deeper into the corner than he had planned. Once again, the car wobbled slightly, but once more she claimed a firm grip on the asphalt, dug in, and he was able to power up off the turn, building momentum and speed for the straight-away.

The run down the back straight was lightning quick again. Jodell Lee drove as deeply as he dared into the narrow and tight third and fourth turns. Then, before he knew it, the rail in the center of the turns had rushed up at him and he had to jerk the wheel violently at the last instant to try to keep from smacking it hard.

The guard rails seemed to reach out, to be grabbing for him as he roared up into the center of the turns. For an instant, it felt as if they were trying to suck him toward their unforgiving metal clutches. But then the car's rear end caught traction just as the right rear fender kissed the rail slightly. Surprisingly, the car held her own perferred line, never scrubbing off any speed.

"Girl!" he said to the car. "That was unbelievable!"